JAN   2011

the

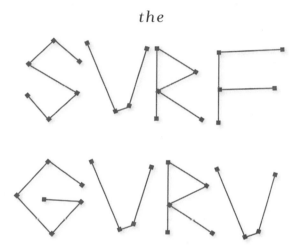

ALSO BY DOUG DORST

Alive in Necropolis

RIVERHEAD BOOKS   *a member of* Penguin Group (USA) Inc. New York 2010

the

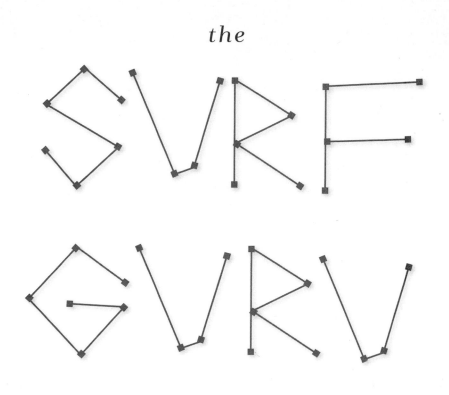

stories   **DOUG DORST**

RIVERHEAD BOOKS
Published by the Penguin Group
Penguin Group (USA) Inc., 375 Hudson Street, New York, New York 10014, USA ·
Penguin Group (Canada), 90 Eglinton Avenue East, Suite 700, Toronto, Ontario M4P 2Y3,
Canada (a division of Pearson Penguin Canada Inc.) · Penguin Books Ltd, 80 Strand,
London WC2R 0RL, England · Penguin Ireland, 25 St Stephen's Green, Dublin 2, Ireland
(a division of Penguin Books Ltd) · Penguin Group (Australia), 250 Camberwell Road,
Camberwell, Victoria 3124, Australia (a division of Pearson Australia Group Pty Ltd) ·
Penguin Books India Pvt Ltd, 11 Community Centre, Panchsheel Park, New Delhi–110 017,
India · Penguin Group (NZ), 67 Apollo Drive, Rosedale, North Shore 0632, New Zealand
(a division of Pearson New Zealand Ltd) · Penguin Books (South Africa) (Pty) Ltd,
24 Sturdee Avenue, Rosebank, Johannesburg 2196, South Africa

Penguin Books Ltd, Registered Offices: 80 Strand, London WC2R 0RL, England

Library of Congress Cataloging-in-Publication Data

Dorst, Doug.
The surf guru : stories / Doug Dorst.
p.   cm.
ISBN 978-1-59448-761-3
I. Title.
PS3604.O78S87   2010   2010008995
813'.6–dc22

Printed in the United States of America
1 3 5 7 9 10 8 6 4 2

Book design by Stephanie Huntwork

While the author has made every effort to provide accurate telephone numbers and
Internet addresses at the time of publication, neither the publisher nor the author assumes
any responsibility for errors, or for changes that occur after publication. Further, the publisher
does not have any control over and does not assume any responsibility for author or third-party
websites or their content.

The following stories have appeared, sometimes in different form,
in the following publications:

ZYZZYVA: "The Surf Guru"; StoryQuarterly: "Dinaburg's Cake";
CutBank: "La Fiesta de San Humberto el Menor"; Ploughshares: "Vikings";
The Sun: "Jumping Jacks"; Epoch: "Twelve Portraits of Dr. Gachet"; McSweeney's: "The Monkeys
Howl, the Hagfish Feast" (originally published as "A Long Bloodless Cut") and "The Candidate in
Bloom"; Five Points: "What Is Mine Will Know My Face" (originally published as "Black Roses");
Five Chapters: "Little Reptiles"; Gulf Coast: "Astronauts"; "Jumping Jacks" was anthologized in Po-
litically Inspired: Fiction for Our Time, edited by Stephen Elliott (MacAdam/Cage, 2003).

For my family

CONTENTS

The Surf Guru

~ ~ ~

Elements

The Surf Guru spends most of his time sitting expec-
tantly on the redwood deck of his dull-green, two-story
house atop the cliff at Padre Point, a favorite spot for surfers
in the know. He watches the surfers and looks out at the
ocean. He often sips Chianti as he watches and looks. Sometimes he nods off in the afternoon and only awakens late at
night, when the ocean breeze tickles his nose with smoke
from the bonfires below.

His business

He owns a company that makes top-notch equipment
for the well-prepared surfer as well as the casual beachgoer.

The name of the company is GOO-ROO, and it appears on surfboards, wetsuits, quick-release leashes, wax, baggy trunks, SPF-50+ waterproof sunblock, fashion eyewear, sport sandals, sneakers, sheepskin ComfyBoots, sarongs, rain gear, board racks, beach towels, fanny packs, umbrellas, neckties, EZ-rinse home hair-bleaching systems, shock- and pressure-resistant ISO-6425 chronographs, antibacterial towelettes, feature films, and dog food.

For years GOO-ROO has been at the forefront of beach technology. The Surf Guru innovates, quietly, as if he were dreaming, and then two MBAs, Chad and Olivia, bring his visions to the marketplace. Everyone who surfs at Padre Point wears GOO-ROO and rides GOO-ROO. Everyone except the red-haired boy.

Power

Some say the Surf Guru controls the tides.

The red-haired boy

At this very moment, sunset is approaching and the red-haired boy is surfing a three-foot swell. He rides a LoweRider board and wears a Pacific Skin wetsuit. Both of these items cost significantly less than their GOO-ROO equivalents.

The boy thinks his LoweRider board is more responsive than any GOO-ROO board he has ever tried. And unlike his old GOO-ROO wetsuit, the Pacific Skin model doesn't chafe him in the neck and crotch.

In the Surf Guru's eyes, the red-haired boy is not unlike someone who invites himself to dinner and then insults the cook.

Competition

When LoweRider products first came on the market, the Surf Guru asked Olivia to invite Mr. Lowe to the dull-green house for lunch. He wanted to meet his competition.

"That's impossible," Olivia said. "There is no Mr. Lowe. He is a marketing fiction."

The Surf Guru poured some Chianti into a GOO-ROO coffee mug. "So many fictions," he said, sighing.

The Surf Guru's wife, cinematically

He met his wife on the beach. He was surfing, trying out a board fitted with prototypes of the soon-to-be-famous GOO-ROO HydroRip fins. She was a sunburned art history and modern thought double-major looking for her car keys in the sand. He came out of the water and found her keys instantly, as if he could see things she couldn't. Six months later they were married.

After ten years she had had enough.

"You are so remote," she said.

"I am not remote."

"Then you are stoic."

"I am not stoic."

"You are no fun."

"The dog thinks I'm great fun."

"You are turgid," she said.

"That is an interesting word. The word *turgid* is itself quite turgid. It is very successful at being what it is."

"Unlike this marriage, which is not successful at being anything," she responded cinematically. She packed up all her things except for her GOO-ROO-branded apparel, which she cut into shreds with pinking shears and piled on the bed. She then took all the dog food in the house and dumped it on the front steps. These were symbolic actions, she said, and she hoped they would haunt him.

Stray dogs congregated in front of the house for weeks.

Drainage, Part I

He watches the surfers every day, admiring their fluid recklessness, their joy and struggle, their twinned senses of community and territoriality. He pretends not to notice when they glance up at him with furtive reverence.

Some of them are kids, trying to catch a few good waves before or after school. Some are in their twenties, hoping for a breath of freedom before they head off to their jobs drafting contracts or designing urban drainage systems or selling fitness accessories. Some are older than the Surf Guru himself; they are gray-haired and leather-skinned, and they just stay all day.

Sometimes he feels as if he is watching over a nursery school, where children play duck-duck-goose and learn essential social skills. Then those children grow up and return with their own children, passing on the legacy of the waves.

Credo

All the rivers run into the sea, yet the sea is not full; unto the place whence the rivers come, thither they return.

Hats

He wears many hats, not altogether metaphorically. His favorites are the fez, the miter, and the mortarboard, but he has many others, from all corners of the globe. When he feels giddy (often, but not always, from too much Chianti), he opts for a hat with a plume—the puckish Tyrolean, perhaps, or the stately shako. When the aches in his fused vertebrae tell him a storm is coming, he dons the biretta, the hat of wariness and watchfulness.

Drainage, Part II

Chad and Olivia bring him a financial report every Wednesday. The report tells him how much they've spent on manufacturing and promotions, how much has been bled out by his ex-wife and the attorneys, how much he's lost in the latest Wall Street panic, how much he's shrewdly invested in livestock farms and vacation properties he will never use. Included under the heading "Personal Consumption" is the money spent on Chianti, microwavable vegetarian entrees, and hats.

Each week he pretends to read the report carefully. When Chad and Olivia leave, he tells the dog, "It is essential that they believe I care deeply. This is how the world works."

Fetching, Part I

The dog is uncannily—perhaps miraculously—skilled at fetching.

They share a small but important ritual: The Surf Guru throws a tennis ball off the deck of the dull-green house into the ocean, and the dog scampers away and returns with the ball in under three minutes. Every time. Over and over. "Faster than you can boil an egg," he once boasted to his wife. "Boil your own goddamned eggs," she replied.

Neap tide

The red-haired boy, frustrated by the calm surf, slaps the water with an open palm, demanding one good set before he calls it a day. Moments later, as the sun nicks the horizon, a head-high wave rises from nowhere. He positions himself expertly, catches it. He drives down the line into a heavy roundhouse cutback, then glides through a string of graceful turns in the pocket.

The Surf Guru applauds, quietly, with his fingertips.

Fear (the largest eyes of all)

Sharks rarely venture into the bay. They prefer the darker, bruise-blue waters off the coast, where fear is easier to come by.

Bobby Cordero is molting

Three years ago: It is a cold, rainy morning, just past dawn, and Bobby Cordero, a regular, has Padre Point to himself. Even the Surf Guru is gone, convinced by Chad to make a rare promotional appearance at the GOO-ROO Aloha Cup at Waimea.

The wind is up and the waves are big. Bobby needs to clear his head, and this is the way to do it. He rides double overheads for an hour and feels his spirit rise up and dance a rumba with the sea. He is oblivious to his hangover, to the rent he can't pay, to all those accusations of squandered potential, to the green-eyed girl who won't return his calls. He is also oblivious to the fin rising and falling in the surf behind him.

Bobby catches a set wave, but drops into it too late. He manages to carve off the bottom into a floater, then elevator-drops and loses his balance; he pitches into the water and is driven face-first into the sand. There is a slash of pain in his ankle, then a wrenching tug. Then fire in his legs and side, a glimpse of thrashing gray and a flat black eye, a strange warmth bathing his body. A crushing blow to his chest that squeezes the air out of him, and with that a mysterious clarity: he remembers that he should yank on the shark's gill slits, a trick he learned from the *GOO-ROO Surfer's Survival Guide.* He grabs and yanks, loses hold, grabs and yanks again.

Then he finds himself on the beach inside a ring of wide-eyed, shrieking people, and he calmly, sleepily stares at the cuff still fastened around his ankle, at the rubber cord that trails from it, at the clean slice where the leash was bitten through.

In the hospital, they have to cut open his GOO-ROO wetsuit. They try to sew him up, but Bobby has lost too much blood, and he dies on the table amid rags of black neoprene. One doctor tells the local news it looked as if poor Bobby was molting.

The Surf Guru returns to Padre Point immediately and arranges a ceremony for Sunday afternoon. He spends thousands of dollars on flowers—hyacinths, lilacs, and mums. With a single phone call to the city council, he has the road that runs along the cliff closed for the day. Everyone comes. Some weep. Some vow revenge against all things selachian. Some throw flowers off the cliff. Some of the flowers fall into the water; some come to rest on the cliff side.

The Surf Guru watches the ceremony from his deck. He wears the Greek fisherman's cap, the hat of sorrow and solitude.

Survival of the fittest

The *GOO-ROO Surfer's Survival Guide*, priced at $16.95, is also available with the Surf Guru's autograph on the inside front cover for $19.95. Even though the autographed version has sold 750,000 units, only three purchasers have complained in writing that the autograph looks suspiciously like a dog's paw print.

The red-haired boy does not own the *Survival Guide*, but he knows that if a shark ever attacks him, he should yank on its gill slits. "It's intuitive," he says.

The Surf Guru, upon rising this morning

Surfers fill the bay. A hundred GOO-ROO boards twinkling. A hundred black wetsuits with *GOO-ROO* stamped in screaming green across the chest. It is an ordinary sight, but today he is taken aback. So many pieces of himself, spread across the water, carried by the waves like so much flotsam.

He eats a big breakfast. He worries that he has been losing weight.

(For a poodle, maybe)

The Surf Guru's wife once bought a cable-knit doggie sweater at a church craft fair, but the dog bit her when she tried to force its legs into the sleeves.

Later, he and the dog played fetch with the sweater until it fell apart. From inside the house, she watched them with mercury eyes.

Two voices, Room 613, the Empyrean Hotel & Casino, Reno

— We shouldn't do this.

— *I'm not his wife anymore. Legally or otherwise.*

— That is an excellent point. Still, it doesn't feel right; he trusts me.

— *You deny yourself. Everyone around him does.*

— I don't understand.

— *Is that really all you want? To be his lackey? That's your destiny? Your dharma? Your raison d'être?*

— Now that you mention it, I would like to play the saxophone professionally. I'd like to be the man who resuscitates bebop.

— *Then make it happen. Believe in yourself. Seize the day. Et cetera.*

— I'll need money.

— *Yes, you will. But you're resourceful. Of your several fine qualities, it is perhaps the finest.*

— I love you.

— *Shhh. Don't spoil everything.*

A fine vintage, Part I

The red-haired boy picks off a nice right and executes a quick barrel and a vertical snap. He swoops long, smooth lines across the wall of water.

The Surf Guru pours another glass of Chianti. Even though his back is knotted up and burning with pain, he puts on a beret, the hat of restrained contentment.

Closed out

The trophy case in the dull-green house is empty. In an effort to raise capital, all 473 of the Surf Guru's trophies were sold to a surf-themed pizza chain owned by an aging former star of Hollywood beach movies. They are now mounted on the walls of Shred-Boy Pizza franchises in twenty-six cities worldwide, including brand-new airport locations in Athens, Saskatoon, and Las Vegas.

Tombstoned

Olivia calls Chad in a panic. Next year's line of GOO-
ROO boards, the Poseidon Series, must be renamed. Lowe-
Rider, it seems, has just filed on all commercial uses of
"Poseidon."

"They found out," she says. "We must have a leak."

"Don't be silly," Chad says.

"I'm not being silly. I'm talking about *corporate
espionage.*"

"Sometimes coincidences are just coincidences," Chad
informs her. "You can't just go around believing everything
that appears to be true."

Olivia's heart pounds as she tries to think of a suitable
alternative. Neptune? Triton? Apollo? Vishnu? Tangaroa?
Quetzalcoatl? Ra? It's no use. All the gods have been trade-
marked.

Nothing

GOO-ROO dog food is a bomb. A white elephant. An
albatross. A millstone around the corporate neck. No matter
how bright the colors on the bag are, no matter how scrupu-
lously the ads are targeted, it's a money loser year in and
year out. Finally, Olivia confronts the Surf Guru, suggests
cutting production costs by using cereal fillers and fewer or-
ganic ingredients. The Surf Guru shakes his head—the dog
enjoys GOO-ROO dog food, will eat nothing but. Olivia is
instructed to change nothing.

The dog also likes Chianti. Even after a brimming bowl-ful, he still fetches with aplomb.

Fetching, Part II

The Surf Guru notices a girl in her early twenties walk-ing along the beach. He can tell even from this distance and in the failing light that she is beautiful. He decides that she has the features of a Byzantine Madonna. He does not care if he is imagining this.

She is returning from work. She wears a business suit and walks barefoot, carrying smart shoes in one hand. She needs the beach, he thinks, maybe more than she knows. He wonders about her name. It is certainly not Polly or Molly or Jill or Francine; it is exotic, like Nadia, or simple in its ele-gance, like Catherine. He quickly reminds himself that she, too, would ultimately find him turgid.

She stops and sits on the sand. She watches the red-haired boy surf. The boy launches into a snap-air floater, then drives off the bottom and carves improbable arcs all over the bowl.

The Surf Guru applauds, quietly, with his fingertips. As he watches the boy paddle back out to deep water, he tries to call up images of a long-ago self. He fails; his memory feels diffused, diffracted, dishonest.

He leans forward in his chair and pets the dog, asleep at his feet.

Musings from an orthopedic deck chair

If the Surf Guru felt like expressing himself verbally on the subject of feelings, he would say, "What I am currently feeling is a peculiar mix of longing and fear, of nostalgia and hope, of power and restraint, of shining and fading." His voice would tremble for an instant, but he would smooth it out, so as not to let you notice.

Sunset

The red-haired boy undoes his leash, tucks his board under one arm, and walks through shallow water toward the girl. He shows her his LoweRider board.

The Surf Guru imagines the boy telling her that the Lowe-Rider HyTyde fins shred, that they give him more control than he ever dreamed possible. With the boy's voice—an easy tenor, unroughened by time—echoing through his head, he closes his eyes and conjures up a design for a New & Improved GOO-ROO HydroRip Mark II fin.

Drainage, Part III

The numbers do not work out.

Olivia scans the reports one more time. The numbers still do not work out.

She pounds the desk. She looks up at Chad with wet, puffy eyes. "I don't understand," she says. "It's as if the money is disappearing."

"Yes," Chad says. "It's as if." He sips his martini, then traces his finger around the rim of the glass, coaxing forth a high, quavering tone. With much satisfaction, he recognizes the note as an F-sharp. He has been working on his ear.

A salt-rimmed glass

The girl takes pen and paper from her blazer pocket and writes down her phone number. She presses the scrap of paper into the red-haired boy's hand, and they hold the contact an instant longer than they need to.

The boy glances up at the dull-green house and notices the older man sitting high up on his deck, hands tented in front of his face. "See that guy?" he says, pointing. "Dude controls the tides."

She proposes that they head back into town together, maybe grab a margarita at Imelda's on the way. This boy, after all, has stories worth hearing.

The mother of invention

The Surf Guru closes the sketchbook in which he has calculated the specs of the new fins. He takes a swig of Chianti from the bottle.

As the sky darkens, he thinks about those kids—that Madonna in a blazer, that boy who surfs LoweRider—and he thanks them. He cannot describe what they have given him, but he knows he could never have received it from the GOO-ROO faithful, with their cash-register receipts and ninety-day warranties and worshipful online reviews.

Gulls squawk. Wind blows. Waves break. On a boardwalk in the distance, a glowing Ferris wheel spins.

He stands up and stretches his back. He walks stiffly into the house and looks through his collection of hats for something appropriate. He looks and looks.

Drainage, Part IV

Chad and Olivia arrive at the dull-green house to give him the bad news but find the deck chair empty. Olivia fears the worst; she knows his mind has been darkening. She searches the house, terrified of what she might find. Meanwhile, Chad fixes himself a martini, humming the lead line from Charlie Parker's "Now's the Time."

"*He's gone*," Olivia shouts from downstairs.

Also gone: the dog and the wide-brimmed petasos, the hat of nascent defiance.

Passage

Underlined in blue in his wine-stained paperback copy of *The Compleat Yeats*, left on the dinette:

Winter and summer till old age began
My circus animals were all on show

Payoff

Three weeks later, Olivia receives an envelope in her mail-box at home. It contains the designs for the new fins and a short note, hastily scrawled: *It's all yours now. Just don't change the dog food.* The postmark is smudged, unreadable.

A fine vintage, Part II

The girl waits as the boy gets his things together.

Dinaburg's Cake

~ ~ ~

The man at Kacy's door was smaller than she'd expected. His voice on the phone had been deep and rich and confident, full of the urgency of business. Now here he was, slightly built and barely up to her nose. Patches of sweat darkened his pink polo shirt under his arms and in a diamond shape over his chest. He thrust out his hand. "Joel Dinaburg," he said. "That's Dinaburg, as in *dynamo*. Father of the bride."

She invited him inside, where the air was cool and whispery. "I'm surprised you came alone," she said. "I usually get to meet the lucky girl." Their footsteps were silent on the thick hall carpet, which was the color of eggshells.

"My daughter doesn't think the cake is important," he said. "She told me she'd be happy with Pop-Tarts."

"That's cute," Kacy said, not meaning it.

"No, it isn't," he said. "There are guests at a wedding,

and they want cake. So dear old dad has to fly in and spend his weekend tasting cakes all over town." He patted his forehead dry with a handkerchief. "Thing is, I haven't found one that I'd feed to my dog. Or my neighbor's dog, the one that keeps crapping on my azaleas. You're my last hope."

"Good choice," Kacy said. "I'm the best around, and I don't mind saying so."

"I don't mind, either, as long as it's true," he said.

In the dining room, seated at the long mahogany table, he explained that the wedding would be there in Austin, not in New York, because his daughter and her fiancé were grad students at U.T. and wanted to keep their own distractions to a minimum. "These kids," he said, "they think the wedding's all about them." Kacy liked his accent. His hard consonants could hammer in nails.

They looked at her portfolio, a leather-bound book filled with photos of her finest work: wedding cakes rippling with seas of perfect buttercream waves; a trio of *croquembouche* pyramids atop a sprawling expanse of chocolate; an abstract, sharp-angled sculpture in hazelnut *dacquoise*; buildings, logos, and faces all reproduced with perfect, sugary accuracy. "Most people want something simple and traditional for weddings," she said, "and I'm happy to oblige, but when I'm allowed to be creative, I really shine." She played up her twang. *Oblahge. Ah really shahn.*

He pointed to a cake she'd made for the opening of a club at Second and Brazos—a replica of the building's interior, which was an unruly clash of I-beams, steel cables, and rebar. "Nice. That's *pastillage*, right? I never had much luck with *pastillage*."

"You know your stuff."

"I was a pastry chef once," he said. "Before I got into wealth management."

Kacy smiled—not her saleswoman's smile, but one that had risen out of her unsummoned. Here was someone who could appreciate her talent, unlike those Barbie-doll mothers and daughters who waved their Martha Stewart magazines in her face and demanded that she smother their cakes in poured fondant and gum-paste roses! She served him three samples: white genoise punched with amaretto and layered with strawberry cream, Kacy's Four Chocolate Delight, and spicy carrot cake. "The carrot cake is fresh," she said. "The others have been frozen. I run a small operation. I can't keep fresh samples of everything."

"Don't worry," he said. "I know what freezing tastes like. I can account for it."

Kacy settled into her chair and watched his little plum-shaped face as he ate. He chewed thoughtfully, silently, with his eyes closed. He tilted his head back and worked the taste over in his mouth, his eyelids fluttering in what she hoped was bliss. She sat with her hands in her lap, rubbing her knuckles, twisting her ring, and she waited for him to choose.

"Excellent," he said, finally. "All of them. But this one's the winner." He tapped a fork on the plate where the Four Chocolate Delight had been.

"It's my favorite, too."

"Would you be willing to work with me on the design? I have some ideas."

"Absolutely," she said. "You're the customer."

And they talked. They talked about the different shapes

they'd woven from spun sugar. They talked about roulades and pistachio nougatines. They talked about how so much depends on the quality of your butter. Before he left, he asked if he could see her kitchen. "Someday," he said, touching her arm, "I'm going to quit the money world and start a business like yours." She covered his hand with hers and held it there, just long enough to suggest *there is something passing between us.* And if she was mistaken, so what? She was a saleswoman. Nothing wrong with a little flirtation to grease the pan of commerce, so to speak. Forty-two years old, and she could still catch a man's eye when she chose.

She led Dinaburg into the kitchen, which was all polished white and gleaming silver. Three years before, when she'd decided to go into business for herself, it had been built as an addition to the house, connected to the family kitchen by a set of pocket doors she could close when she needed to work in peace. She had watched as the new kitchen took shape, watched as the raw floor was tiled with perfect white hexagons, as cabinets were installed and industrial refrigerators were fitted into nooks, as ovens and cooling racks were wheeled in, as the last dusty boot print of a contractor was mopped away. The business—Kacy's Kitchen—took off immediately. Some nights she'd stay up long after Roger and the kids had gone to bed, sitting at the small desk in the corner, planning her schedule and sketching designs until she drifted off to sleep, lost in the room's warm baritone hum.

"Hello," Dinaburg said, looking away from the sixty-pound mixer he'd been admiring. "Who's this pretty young lady?" Kacy's sixteen-year-old daughter was standing in the doorway, a ring of car keys swinging from one pudgy, quick-bitten finger. She was wearing her new hat, a white cloche with a silk sunflower on the front. She peered into the kitchen, as if she weren't allowed to cross the threshold. Which she wasn't, of course, because of the hair situation. One stray hair in a cake could ruin Kacy's reputation.

"Mr. Dinaburg," Kacy said, "meet my daughter, April."

"That's a beautiful hat," Dinaburg said.

April stared at her shoes, as if the compliment had come in a language she didn't know.

"What do you say, April?" Kacy prompted.

"My mom picked it out," April said.

"*Thank you* would be a more ladylike response," Kacy said.

April stuffed her hands into the pockets of her baggy jeans, which Kacy thought made her legs look like tree trunks. "I'm going out with Skillet," she said.

Skillet. Like some gap-toothed idiot popping out of a cornfield on *Hee Haw.* Dinaburg probably thought they were all a bunch of hicks. "His real name is William," Kacy explained. She turned to tell April to be home for dinner, but her daughter was gone. For a big, clumsy girl, she could disappear quickly.

"Pretty soon you'll be making a cake for her big day," Dinaburg said.

"Oh, we're not in any hurry," Kacy said, with the carefully cultivated lightness she used whenever she talked about April. Frankly, with each bride she saw while assembling her cakes on-site, with each pink-cheeked young woman suffering radiantly through jangly nerves and sprayed-stiff Jackie O. hair, she found herself less and less sure that April would ever get married. All she did was mope, mope, mope. Only sixteen, and already her ankles were disappearing in fat. And, of course, the hair. Good Lord, the hair. "No," Kacy said, "we don't want to push her."

After Dinaburg left for the airport, Kacy poured herself a glass of wine to celebrate. He'd told her he'd call as soon as he got the go-ahead from his wife. A January wedding at the Four Seasons. Five hundred guests, many of them wealthy and important: a software mogul from California; several congressmen; even Rudy Giuliani himself! It could be the break of a lifetime. She'd be called for jobs in New York, Washington, San Francisco. She'd have to hire employees. Down the road, if April matured a little and stopped with the hair strangeness, maybe they could even work together, mother and daughter.

She drank the wine in three large sips and allowed herself the luxury of stretching out on the couch and closing her eyes. The wine spread warmth inside her, and the central air purred and breathed cool air over her skin. Five minutes of peace. Then back to work: Marisol was coming to clean in the morning, and Kacy had to tidy up. She took the vacuum upstairs into April's bedroom. She opened the curtains, and golden afternoon sun lit the room. The pink walls were bare—no photos of friends, no posters of pop singers, no prints of horses, nothing. As if April were unwilling to let slip even the tiniest bit of information about who she was.

She pulled the bed away from the wall and looked behind the headboard. A layer of April's mouse-brown hair was spread over the baseboard molding and the carpet. *God-damnit.* She'd expected this, but that didn't make it less of a disappointment. She kicked the vacuum on and watched the hair disappear into the nozzle as the motor whined. She cleaned it all up—every strand, as far as she could tell—and pushed the bed back into place.

Kacy had discovered the hair behind the bed when April was eleven. She'd stared at it for minutes, trying to understand how it had gotten there. There was only one explanation, hard as it was to believe: her daughter would lie in bed and pull her hair out, over and over and over. The image sickened her. It was the kind of behavior you'd expect of a sick dog or a lab rat, not a healthy young girl. She'd cried, then, right there on April's bed. After a while she decided the best plan was to clean up the mess and keep mum. Her daughter wasn't a freak. Her daughter could work through problems on her own. And at least you couldn't see any bald spots.

Four years later, on the day of her mother's funeral, she noticed a patch of scalp in the center of April's head, just above the hairline, as obvious as a third eye. That night, she walked into the bathroom while April was brushing her teeth. She faced her daughter in the mirror, pointed to the bald spot, and said, "Do you want people to see this?" April stared at the reflection of the two of them while toothpaste foam leaked sadly from the corner of her mouth, until finally she squeezed her eyes shut and shook her head no. The next day, Kacy bought four hats and left them on April's bed. She could cover herself up until the hair grew back. It would be their secret, and they'd get through it together, the way Kacy and her own mother had when Kacy was seventeen and got pregnant in the bed of Tommy Odom's truck. She and Mother went to the doctor together, took care of business, and never spoke about it again.

April's hair grew back, but new bald patches had appeared on her head in cycles: at her temple; at her pate; in a ragged circle at the back of her head; then at the temple again, after the hair had grown back in. Kacy was reminded of cattle moving from pasture to pasture, grazing each space barren before moving on. And Roger? He'd never seemed to notice, and for her money, if he couldn't be bothered to pay attention to how his daughter looked, then he didn't deserve to be part of the solution.

It's a stage, Kacy reminded herself. *She'll grow out of it, and later, she'll be amazed that she ever did this to herself.* She went to close the curtains and paused at the window. A hummingbird darted between honeysuckle blossoms. Next door, Mr. Weeks, a bent and sun-scorched old man, was tending his tomatoes. Through the trees, a sliver of Town Lake sparkled in the sun. A world of whites and golds and greens where nothing was hopeless, where no cause was lost.

Kacy was sitting on the living room sofa with her sketchbook open on her lap when Roger arrived home with Kenny, their five-year-old. Before she could ask Kenny how his T-ball game had gone, the boy spotted Mooch, the family beagle, screeched joyfully, and chased the dog down the hallway. It was a typical entrance for Kenny; ever since he'd learned to walk, the dog had of necessity developed quick reflexes and a streak of paranoia. Kacy listened to them run up the stairs, to the dog's collar jingling and Kenny's little feet pounding. Roger sat next to her and kissed her hello with sweat-salty lips. His skin was flushed, and he was breathing heavily.

"I thought the idea was to tire *him* out," Kacy said.

"I did my best," he said. "I'm no superhero." He took off his Astros cap and ran his hand through his thinning, sweat-soaked hair. "He did well today. His swing is getting better. He actually hit the ball a few times."

"But," Kacy prompted. Kenny was a sweet kid, but there was usually a *but*.

"But he kept running to third base instead of first. I don't think he was confused. He just seemed to like running the wrong way."

"That's not so bad."

"Could be worse. The Poirier kid wet his pants in right field."

There was a thud from upstairs. "Please tell me he didn't hit his head," Kacy said. Little accidents were part of life with Kenny, a kid with so much love to give that he usually ran into things in his haste to give it.

Almost immediately, they heard him start running again. "He's fine," Roger said. "Remind me to check the wall, though."

"I made a sale today," she said. "A big one." She told him about Dinaburg and the lavish wedding.

"He's from New York?" Roger said. "Charge him double. He won't notice."

"I love it when you act ruthless," Kacy said. Of course, if he actually were ruthless, he'd have made partner last year. Instead he'd been told he'd remain *of counsel*, which translated to *Don't get your hopes up.* Since then the wrinkles around his eyes had deepened, and his cheeks had begun to sag into premature jowls. He had a disappointing tendency to let his setbacks eat him up. That was life, though: people disappoint you, so you'd better be able to take care of yourself.

Kenny came into the room with Mooch padding along behind him. The dog turned in circles before choosing a place on the rug to lie down. Kenny did the same, and they curled up together. "I hit the ball today," Kenny said.

"I heard," Kacy said. "Maybe you'll be a pro-leaguer someday."

"Big-leaguer," Roger said.

"You know what I meant."

Kenny smiled and closed his eyes, feigning sleep. He hugged Mooch tightly to himself, and the dog didn't resist.

"Where's April?" Roger asked.

"Out with William," she said.

"Skillet?"

"William. Call him William."

Watching Kenny, she remembered how different April had been, even at that age: shy, cautious to a fault, secretive, and prone to disappointments Kacy could see but not understand. Here was her brother, eleven years younger and completely unplanned, a high-spirited boy who loved his dog. She couldn't help but look at him and think, *Maybe this one will turn out normal.*

Kacy waited for Dinaburg's call. She'd perfected a new red-raspberry glaze, and she was eager to pitch it to him. He phoned the following Thursday night, while Kacy was frosting a cake shaped like the state capitol building for a reception at the Austin Historical Society. She sat at her desk and flipped open her sketchbook. "I've come up with some ideas I think you'll love," she told him. "This could be my best work ever."

"We've decided to go with someone else," Dinaburg said.

Her stomach plunged. "Pardon?"

"We're getting a cake in Manhattan and flying it in."

"Why?" she managed to ask. "You said you loved mine."

"Mrs. Burroughs, or Kacy—may I call you Kacy?—I enjoyed meeting you, and I thought your cakes were fantastic, really first-rate stuff."

"Then I don't understand."

"We found one that tastes better."

"The sample was frozen. I explained that. You said you wouldn't hold it against me." She felt herself gaining steam. She could push him, sell him. She could still win.

"You know what I think the difference is?" he said dreamily, more to himself than to her. "The water. There's something about New York City water. The way it makes things taste. It's magic."

"The water?"

"What I mean is, you're at a disadvantage. Your water just doesn't have that same pizzazz. I'll tell you a story: a friend of my father's was a bagel maker on the Lower East Side, and when he retired to Boca Raton, he opened a new shop, but he could never get them to taste—"

"Cakes aren't bagels. I don't *boil* my cakes. Most don't even have water in them."

"Trust me, it makes a difference. It's like my wife says—"

But Kacy had stopped listening. She murmured a good-bye, and she didn't wait for him to offer one in return. She put the half-frosted capitol building into one of the refrigerators and turned out the lights. She slid open the doors to the family kitchen, closed them behind her, and dropped three ice cubes into an iced-tea glass, which she filled halfway with scotch. She swirled the glass, watching as the ice cracked and spun.

In bed that night, Roger nudged her awake three or four times because she was grinding her teeth. The first time she apologized. The second time she said, "Deal with it." The last time she stayed awake long enough to watch him leave their room with a pillow under his arm.

On Monday morning, Kacy called the number on Dinaburg's business card. The phone was answered by a secretary with a haughty tone, who pecked at Kacy with questions (Was she a client? No? Had she been referred to Mr. Dinaburg?) before putting her through.

"I have an idea," Kacy told him. "I could use your water. You could ship it to me."

"I appreciate the offer, Kacy," he said. "I do. But it's a done deal. Signatures have been signed. Cash has been paid. I'm sorry."

After hanging up, Kacy flung open her desk drawer and took out a pack of Winstons that Marisol had left the last time she'd cleaned. She shook out a cigarette and rolled it in her fingers. She'd quit smoking three years before, so her taste buds could be in top shape. She considered lighting up, could almost feel the smoke caressing her lungs, but she tucked the cigarette back into the pack. She wasn't about to let a man like *Dinaburg-as-in-dynamo* drive her back to a habit she'd worked so hard to break.

April appeared in the family kitchen and began pawing through the fridge. Her hair was limp and greasy, and a patch of scalp glared out at Kacy, pink and naked in a morning sunbeam. Kacy considered throwing the pack of cigarettes at her daughter. "Here," she imagined saying, "try being self-destructive like a *normal* person." But she didn't throw the cigarettes, and she didn't say anything—proof, maybe, that she was not the worst mother in the world, after all.

A week later, Kacy called Dinaburg again. She reached the same secretary, who sniffed and put her on hold. After a few minutes with Neil Diamond crooning tinnily over the line, Dinaburg picked up. "I'm sorry to bother you, Joel," Kacy said, "but could you tell me where you're getting the cake? I need to know my competition."

"Sure," he said, as if nothing were wrong, as if he'd never raised her hopes and then crapped all over them. "We're getting it from Rona Silverman. You've heard of her, right? She's famous. A New York institution."

"Rona Silverman," Kacy repeated. The name was bitter on her tongue.

She drove to the library and found a profile on Rona Silverman in a magazine called *Bridal Elegance*. The full-page photo showed a birdlike, maroon-haired old woman inspecting a cake through gold pince-nez, surrounded by three shiny-toothed young men in starched chef's coats. The article gushed about Silverman's attention to detail, claiming that she spent afternoons picking flowers and bringing them to her kitchens for her assistants to study and re-create in painstakingly detailed gum-paste miniatures, which were then put in tiny boxes and filed away in refrigerators. Kacy quietly tore the article out of the magazine, folded it, and tucked it in her purse. Gum-paste flowers! A cheap gimmick. Dinaburg ought to know better.

On the way home, she stopped at a red light on Guadalupe, the sky blackening behind her as an early-summer storm rushed in toward downtown. She was watching a cluster of spike-haired kids slouch around a storefront when she saw April walking past them on the sidewalk. Yes, it was her daughter: the thick legs, the slump-shouldered trudge, a newish bald patch on the back of her head. And no hat. Good Lord. Kacy was about to honk the horn and call to her, but she stopped herself when Skillet—wearing a ridiculous pair of orange-plaid bell-bottoms—emerged from a café and flagged April down. They walked together, talking, and Skillet gave no sign that he noticed how mangy she looked. For once, Kacy found herself thankful that men refuse to see what they don't want to see.

The light turned green and Kacy drove, not wanting to interrupt them. After she'd gone a few blocks, though, thunder cracked and rain poured from the sky, beating insane drumrolls on the car and sheeting over the windshield. She turned off Guadalupe and doubled back to find her daughter, to get her home safe and dry. She made three circuits, rolling slowly along as she watched for April and Skillet through the passenger-side window, ignoring the honks behind her. But the two kids were gone, as if they'd melted away like spun sugar in the downpour.

One night, Kacy dreamed about Dinaburg. They were together in her kitchen, cooking by candlelight. A bottle of champagne appeared in his hands, he popped it open, and they each drank a glass. They used the rest of the bottle to make a champagne reduction. Dinaburg held her by the hips as she stirred the hot mixture on the stove. Then, suddenly, she was supine on the butcher-block island in the middle of the kitchen, and he was frosting her naked body with champagne buttercream. He started at her feet and worked his way up, over her legs and hips and breasts, and then covered her entire face, and then all she could see was a smooth sheet of yellow-white. When she felt him bite off her big toe and understood that she was made of cake, she found she didn't mind being eaten, not really. Not until she felt bites on both her feet at the same time and heard an old woman hack out a snicker. Then she knew Rona Silverman was there with him, in Kacy's own kitchen, and they were laughing together as they ate her up. She awoke in the bed alone.

Roger was in the kitchen, making coffee. The circles under his eyes were even darker than usual. "You're not going to have any teeth left," he told her. "You sounded like a goddamn blender last night." He snapped the lid onto his plastic travel mug and walked out the door with his shirt poking through his open zipper. She let him go.

Kacy returned home from a Texas Businesswomen's Club luncheon hosted by the governor's wife—for which she'd baked a raspberry gâteau with a sweet mascarpone icing that had seventy-five female executives moaning in caloric ecstasy (and made with a splash of good old Austin municipal water, thank you very much)—and she found a message on her business line from Dinaburg. "Calling to talk cake with you," he said. He left his home number. She immediately memorized it.

Her mind raced happily with the possible reasons his deal with Rona Silverman had fallen through. Had he come to his senses, remembered the sweet, smooth glide of the Four Chocolate Delight across his tongue? Or maybe Rona Silverman had died. Kacy imagined a photo of the old crone in her stupid pince-nez on the *New York Times* obituary page.

"Hello, Joel," she said when he picked up. "It's Kacy."

"Such a quick response," he said. "Ever the professional. How are you?"

She told him about the governor's mansion and about the gâteau. She told him how busy she'd been lately, spending ten hours a day in the kitchen just to fill orders and even more time experimenting with crème fraîche infusions and searching for even better-tasting butters and flours and vanillas and rums. She was, she said, doing the best work of her life. She stopped herself, realizing she should let him talk. She wanted to sound casual. She asked him how his azaleas were.

"Doing fine," he said. "The neighbor's dog dropped dead. The guy thinks I poisoned it, which, for the record, I didn't. But I called about business."

"I can do the wedding," Kacy said. "I've kept the date open, just in case."

"No, no, no, Kacy. Like I told you, we're already committed."

She was confused. She would have said something, but she was afraid she'd cry.

"I've had my own kitchen designed," he said. "I based it on yours. I'd like to fax you the plans. Could you take a look and tell me what you think?"

"Sure," she lied. "Happy to."

When the fax came in, Kacy studied the plans, making comments on the paper with a thick black felt-tip. She kept her notes brief. MAKE ISLAND WIDER. WHERE IS HOBART? LOCATION OF SINKS=DUMB. She faxed the plans back to him an hour later, then opened the best bottle of scotch in the house and toasted her brand-new vow never to call him again.

. . .

Time passed. It got hotter, and people complained about the humidity. Lawns browned under the sun. The free-tailed bats gave birth to their pups under the Congress Bridge, and every evening hundreds of tourists watched them blacken the sky as they flew in search of food.

Kenny went to day camp, which he loved, even though he was banned from arts and crafts after gleefully showering everyone in grout on Mosaic Ashtray Day. Roger lost a trial, got steamrolled in two settlement negotiations, and spent his nights buzzed on Lone Star, watching Astros games with Kenny snoozing on his lap. Kacy couldn't tell if Roger looked content or inert, and she was irritated by the possibility that it could be both.

April spent most of her time in her room or out with Skillet. She wore hats when she left the house, but Kacy doubted she kept them on. Her fears were confirmed one afternoon at the fitness club, when her friend Helen Swindon asked if April was ill; when Kacy said no, Helen tactlessly mentioned the name of a hairdresser who "worked miracles." That night, Kacy slipped a note under April's door: *It's OK if you don't like any of your hats, but you need to wear one. Do you want people to laugh at you? Let me know what you like, and I'll buy it. Please. I love you.* After that, April started wearing a navy wool watch cap she had bought on her own. It was ugly, Kacy thought, completely unladylike and far too warm for a Texas summer, but April wore it happily, and it was better than no hat at all.

For Kacy, it was a summer of work, work, work. Orders poured in for weddings and museum functions and book-release parties and golden anniversaries and retirement dinners. The local weekly honored Kacy's Kitchen with a Best of Austin award, finally. She didn't sleep much, and when she did, she usually woke up with a headache and a sore jaw. Even so, she worked right through the discomfort and fatigue, humming through her coffee-fueled days in high gear. She was never late with a job, never cut corners, made sure everything was perfect. It made all the difference between being the best and being nobody.

Summer ended. April and Kenny went back to school. The nights turned chilly, and the bats flew back to their caves in Mexico. And still Dinaburg did not call.

The day before the high school closed for Christmas break, Kacy got a call from Mr. Gomez, April's social studies teacher. He was worried about April, he said, because when he'd looked in on the class during their final exam, he'd seen her pulling out her own hair.

"Are you sure?" she asked. "That doesn't sound at all like April."

"I saw her. She stopped when she saw me looking."

"Well, better her own hair than someone else's."

"I'm serious, Mrs. Burroughs. It could be a sign of some, ah, psychological issues. And, ah, if something's wrong, I'd like to see her get, ah, help. She's a special girl—"

"We know that," Kacy said.

"—and I'm concerned for her."

"Your concern is appreciated, Mr. Gomez. I'll look into it."

"Is there anything you can, ah, tell me? I mean, how are things at home? If you don't mind my asking."

Kacy did mind. "Things at home," she said, "are just fine, thank you." Which they were, really. She and Roger were together, which was more than you could say for most families these days. And if Mr. Gomez was blaming her for working, he could go straight to hell, because the hair problem had started long before Kacy's Kitchen opened for business.

"I didn't mean—"

"I'm sure you didn't," Kacy said, and she hung up. Her chest tightened, and her heart speed-thumped, and she was afraid she might throw up. It was the same feeling she'd had a few weeks before, when she'd opened the oven door and found her butter cake had fallen and it was her fault, she'd overbeaten the egg whites probably, and there was nothing she could do but watch the cake sink farther into itself, ruined.

She took her glass of scotch into the bathroom, set it on the vanity, and locked the door behind her. She looked in the mirror and ran one hand over her jawline, seeing for the first time how her teeth grinding had bulked and hardened her jaw muscles. She caressed the nascent sags of skin under her eyes, trailed her nail along a crease across her forehead that she didn't remember being so deep. She lifted a hand up to her perfectly bobbed chestnut hair, took hold of a single strand, and yanked. It stung, although not as much as she'd expected. She held the hair up to the light. The root was white and oily-looking. Disgusting. She let go and watched the hair flutter into the sink. She plucked out another, and then another, and then a few more. Why on earth would April do this?

The house was still. Cool, contracting metal ticked somewhere inside the ventilation system. And aside from that, nothing. Silence. As if there were nothing else in the world, nothing beyond her standing alone in this bathroom with a spent drink and a sink littered with her hair. With a blast of water, she rinsed the hair away.

The front door banged open and Kenny unleashed his little-boy war whoop. She heard him chase Mooch down the hallway and up the stairs. She just couldn't take it, all the thumping and screeching, not today. "Kenny!" she shouted at the ceiling. "Goddamnit to hell, not now!" Above her, the footfalls stopped dead.

Kacy and Roger spent New Year's Eve at the Johnson Library at a black-tie benefit for leukemia research. They both drank heavily, and Roger draped himself all over the chesty girl who was serving champagne. After the obviously repulsed girl pried him off, Kacy told him he disgusted her, and they'd stopped speaking. When Kacy awoke the next morning, she could taste cigarettes and alcohol in her mouth, but she felt surprisingly clearheaded. She was alone in the bed; Roger was sleeping it off elsewhere in the house.

A new year. Clean slates, new hopes. She picked up the phone on her nightstand and called Dinaburg at home, humming as her fingers danced over the buttons.

He answered. "Kacy," he said. "Happy new year!"

"Happy new year to you, too. How's your kitchen?"

"Great," he said, "though I don't get to use it as much as I'd like. It's funny—I was just thinking that I'd like to talk shop with you. The other night I made a Prinz Tom torte that came out *aces*. My wife's sick of hearing about it. She sure loved eating it, though."

She asked him how the plans for the wedding were going.

"The groom hasn't run away to Mexico or anything. So I guess we're in good shape."

"You know, Joel," she purred, "you never told me about the cake you're getting. The Rona Silverman."

"We designed it together. Nine tiers, white and dark chocolate—El Rey and Scharffen Berger, of course—with chocolate-dipped strawberries on top and decorations that'll knock everyone's socks off. And it's going to taste *incredible*."

"The water."

"Like I said, it's magic."

"When does the plane get in? I could pick it up. I could assemble it for you, help with the decorations."

"No need. One of Rona's assistants flies in with the cake."

"Still," Kacy said, "I have to taste it. I mean, I'd like to. Or see it. Could I see it?"

"I don't see why not. Professional courtesy, right? It's coming in on Friday, the day before the wedding. Let me check the time. Hang on." Then, in the background, Kacy heard a woman's angry voice ask him what in hell he thought he was doing. The voice demanded that he hand over the phone.

"We have no need for your services," the voice said to Kacy. "My husband should have made that clear ages ago. And you've kept calling him—"

"I have not," Kacy said.

"Don't lie to me. You've been all over our caller ID. Know what I think? I think you're stalking our cake."

"That's ridiculous."

"It's *freakish*, is what it is. I promise you, if you come anywhere near us, I'll have you hauled off to jail. This is my only daughter's wedding, and it will not—repeat, *will not*—be fucked with. Not by you. Not by anyone."

What was her problem? Kacy wasn't going to do anything wrong. She just wanted to see this cake that everyone thought was the best goddamned cake ever in the whole wide world. She opened her date book to look at the days that she'd blocked out for the Dinaburg wedding. When she got to the right page, she saw that her notes had been obliterated by huge, childish, purple-crayon letters: KENNYS BIRDAY! I AM 6! She had forgotten. Good Lord, she *was* a freak.

That week Roger finally won a trial, and he and Kacy slept together. It was passionate and dramatic, celebratory and desperate, with lots of twisting and licking and shoving and clutching and sweat. When they rolled apart from each other, Kacy felt herself melting away with a warm, dreamy clarity she hadn't felt in ages.

They were awakened when Kenny's panicked cries tore the quiet of the dark house. Roger slung on a robe and went to help him. Through the half-open doorway, she saw them walk hand in hand toward the bathroom. She heard water running; heard Roger talking in a hushed, reassuring voice; saw him carry the towel-wrapped boy back to his room; heard clean sheets shaken open; and heard Kenny murmuring quietly, the sound of a child feeling safe and loved. A clot of emotion formed behind her eyes, filling her head with a dense, wet pressure. She'd been finding herself choked up a lot lately, suddenly and for no good reason—a happy ending in a sitcom, the taste of cinnamon, a rainbow in the mist at the car wash. She wasn't prone to swings like these, and she distrusted them, but this one seemed to make sense. Roger was a good man and a good father. Her eyes teared up, and in her vision the light from the hallway sent out fuzzy winking-crystal rays.

Kenny's light snapped out, and Roger came back into the room. He sat on the edge of the bed with his back to her. She admired his silhouetted shoulders. *Honest shoulders*, she thought.

"He shit the bed," Roger said.

"Was it a bad dream? What was he saying?"

"He said he had a scary dream about his mommy."

"Should I go in there and show him I'm all right?"

"He was scared *of* you, not *for* you."

She stared up at the ceiling. She was getting what she deserved; that was the worst part.

When Roger's breathing slowed into a rhythm of sleep, Kacy got out of bed and crept down the dark hallway to April's door. She turned the knob quietly. She wasn't intruding; she just wanted to watch her daughter sleep, watch her breathe, watch her wake up in the morning, watch as her fingers went to her head and started pulling.

She was inching open the door when it hit something solid. She pushed a little harder, but the object wouldn't give. She leaned her weight against the door, but she couldn't get any traction on the carpet in her slippers, so she kicked them off. Leaned again. Still nothing. She put her eye up to the narrow crack and saw what was stopping her: April had barricaded her bedroom door with her desk, the beautiful cherrywood writing desk that Kacy had spotted at an auction and bid on ferociously because it was just so *perfect* for her daughter. She sat down, beaten, with her back against the wall. The central heat clicked off, and somewhere downstairs the dog sneezed, and then everything was still.

The day before Kenny's party, Kacy drove all over town, picking up party favors and groceries and film, swearing that she'd make up for whatever she'd done wrong and give Kenny his best birthday ever. She was ruthlessly efficient in her shopping, and on the way home, since she'd gotten every-thing done in half the time she'd allotted, she took a quick drive out to the airport. She put on her sunglasses even though the day was cloudy, and she drove around the airport loop again and again, hoping she'd get lucky and spot the cake. She tailed a shuttle van from the Four Seasons, watched as passengers climbed on, but they were all corporate types with briefcases—nobody burdened with a nine-high stack of cake boxes. After ten or fifteen passes through the loop, a policewoman waved her down and asked if everything was all right. The officer's scrutiny burned through her. "I'm supposed to pick up a friend," Kacy managed, "but I guess he's not here."

"Can't keep driving through," the officer said. "Park and go inside, if you want."

She would not remember driving home. Inside the garage, she opened the trunk to find that the ice cream had melted and one carton had leaked, sending out skinny liquid-strawberry fingers that pointed every which way.

She made Kenny's birthday cake that evening—a perfect reproduction of his baseball glove in sweet, sweet yellow cake and milk-chocolate icing. She'd found the mitt in the garage, cradled inside Roger's larger mitt, each with the same smell of leather and grass and neat's-foot oil. She incorporated every detail into the cake's design: the checkerboard webbing, the smudgy grass stains on the fingertips, the violent slice down the middle of the palm from when Kenny had left it in the yard and Roger had hit it with the lawn mower.

The house was quiet; everyone had gone to bed. Often, when she baked, she'd enter an intense state of focus—a trance, even—and when she was done, she'd be surprised at how much had gone on without her. She looked at the clock. Dinaburg's cake must have arrived. It was there. In downtown Austin. At the Four Seasons. One-point-eight miles from where she was sitting in her white, white kitchen in Travis Heights. *I will not try to find the cake*, she told herself. *I will not go there. I will not call there.* She sat at her desk and shoveled fistfuls of Tootsie Rolls and lollipops into little paper loot bags for Kenny's friends. The air held the sweet, buttery smell of baking and the homey warmth still radiating from the ovens. This usually calmed her—the aroma, the heat— but now it just reminded her that she'd spent all night baking a childish yellow cake instead of the crowning work of her career, the cake that would win her customers in New York and London and Paris, the cake that would land her in the pages of *Bridal Elegance*. She picked up the phone and called the hotel. An eager-to-please young woman told her that the Dinaburg-Fleischner wedding would begin at five-thirty the next day. *There was no problem*, Kacy told herself. Kenny's party would end at six. She could do it all: make Kenny happy, talk to Dinaburg, see the cake in private before it got wheeled out to the reception. She could even bow out of the party a little early. Roger and Marisol could handle it.

Upstairs, she changed for bed and slid under the covers next to Roger. He was snoring lightly. She nudged him awake and told him she might have to leave Kenny's party as soon as it was over. Or maybe just a tiny little smidge early. He harrumphed and turned away. She lay still, letting her mind zoom from image to image: Dinaburg's cake, chilling inside the hotel walk-in. Kacy bursting into the reception and knocking the cake to the floor as five hundred snobby mouths drop in horror. Running into Rona Silverman herself at the wedding and calling her a gum-paste fraud. The cake in the walk-in again, only this time, Dinaburg standing with her, boasting, gloating.

Holding the image of him, she slid her hand down her bare stomach and touched herself. She could seduce him tomorrow, if she wanted to, right there in the walk-in. She could undo the trousers of his tux and coax him into hardness even as the cold air prickled their skin and made his scrotum shrink tight around his balls. Yes, she could take him there, could lay him down on a serving tray and take him, fuck him, own him, while his wife and his daughter and the guests and the rabbi and Rona Silverman all looked at their watches and wondered where the hell the father of the bride was.

The weather held, so they had the birthday party outside. Wearing a gold mylar birthday-boy crown, Kenny opened all of his presents, flinging shreds of brightly colored wrapping paper into the air faster than Kacy could collect them. The entire cake was wolfed down in no time—why had she bothered with all the details?—along with quart after quart of ice cream, and the backyard was humming with sugar-fueled little boys with buzz cuts and wide-open mouths that were short on front teeth. Mooch the beagle nosed around under the redwood picnic tables, lapping up bits of cake from the grass. Skillet was there, too. He'd appeared in their yard that morning like a stray, his dyed-black hair sticking up in unruly tufts. He wore a pair of blue service-station coveralls with a name patch that said WOODY. There was an angry silver spike through the skin beneath his lower lip, and

Kacy noticed he was trying to grow a mustache, without much success.

Marisol sat with her, watching the boys play. Kacy tried to sneak a glance at her watch, but Marisol saw her. "You do that all afternoon," Marisol said. "Why?"

"I have a wedding after this. I can't be late. I know that sounds awful, but I have other responsibilities. It's just a fact."

Marisol nodded. "I am a mother, too, Mrs. Burroughs."

"So you know how I feel."

"You go when you must go. I will take care of the things here." Marisol gathered up all the used paper plates and plastic utensils and carried the garbage bag up to the house.

April—wearing a dirt-smudged beer-logo bucket hat that Kacy guessed was Skillet's—was playing with the boys, letting them chase her, weaving and feinting with more agility than Kacy had thought her blocky frame would allow. When Kenny hurled himself at April's leg and clung while she ran, April laughed—a rich, honest, adult laugh that Kacy couldn't remember hearing before. Skillet was camped out on a chaise longue with a cup of fruit punch, watching April with a dazed, sleepy smile.

Roger, to whom she'd hardly spoken all afternoon, appeared on the patio and blew a four-fingered whistle that stopped the boys in their tracks. "Know what time it is, fellas?" he called out, lifting a huge papier-mâché baseball out of a cardboard box. "It's piñata time!" He held the ball over his head proudly, and the kids clustered around him as he walked across the grass to the sturdy live oak that grew in the yard. With a short length of rope, he hung the piñata from the tree's lowest limb.

Kacy seated herself at one of the picnic tables and surveyed the scene. She'd leave soon. Right after the piñata. "I think that's going to be too high for them," she called out.

"No, it's not," Roger said in a sugary, carefree tone that she knew was meant to rankle her. He looked up at the baseball, and then down at the little people jostling around him. "They can ride on my shoulders."

"Whatever you say," she said. She flicked a glob of brown icing off the table and sucked her nail clean.

Roger told Kenny to be polite and let his friends go first, so Kenny just danced in place and sized up the ball with eager eyes. April tied a blindfold on the first boy in line and then handed him a broomstick after Roger hoisted him up on his shoulders. Roger bobbed gently through an orbit around the ball, letting the kid get a few licks in, but never allowing him enough leverage to do more than rock the ball harmlessly. After a few more boys had their turns, Skillet took over piggyback duty, and Kacy was pleased to see that he was following Roger's lead, rigging the game so the birthday boy could strike the killing blow. When it was Kenny's turn, April lifted him onto her shoulders. She brought him close to the piñata and stood still, but Kenny missed the ball entirely, slashing wild verticals through the air.

Kacy looked at her watch. It was 4:52. *Hit it, Kenny. Why can't you hit it?*

"Level swing, Kenny," Roger coached. "Focus."

Kenny hit the ball dead-on. Nothing happened. Twice more, and still nothing happened.

"Hold on," Roger said. "I have an idea." He jogged over to Kenny's pile of presents and picked up the baseball bat he'd given to his son, a gleaming piece of lacquered ash. When he'd brought it home the week before, Kacy had tried to convince him that the bat was too big for Kenny, but he'd waved her off, tied a blue bow around it, and hidden it in their closet. Every time she'd looked at the bat since then she'd been more and more certain that it would break something of hers. It was just a question of when and what and how badly.

Roger slid off the bow and handed the bat to Kenny, who squealed when he felt the heft in his hands.

"I don't think that's smart, Roger," Kacy called, but at the same time she felt herself drifting, disconnecting, her attention captured by the faint but steady *chik chik chik* of the sprinklers next door watering Mr. Weeks's garden.

Roger turned to her with his hands on his hips. "It's fine," he said. "It's a baseball bat, for Christ's sake."

"My mother says you shouldn't take the Lord's name in vain," a redheaded boy said.

Roger turned to him. "Thank you, Peter," he said.

At that moment, Kenny swung so hard he lost his balance, and April lurched sideways to keep him from falling off her shoulders. Someone shouted, and Kenny swung again just as Roger turned back to look. The bat caught him squarely in the face. Kacy heard bone crunch. She guessed it was his nose. She'd watched it happen without really seeing it; she'd thought vaguely of shouting a warning, but her mouth felt heavy and slow and it had stayed closed.

April screamed, and Roger fell, his hands clutched to his

face. Kenny lifted his blindfold, saw his father bleeding, and burst into tears. Kacy ran to them and took charge. She ordered the boys—including the bawling Kenny—up to the house, where Marisol could watch them. She lifted Roger by the elbow, silently cursing him for getting hurt when the danger was so obvious, and now she'd have to waste hours waiting in a hard plastic chair outside the emergency room and she'd miss Dinaburg and the cake entirely. She had her car keys already in her hand when a better solution struck her. After all, Roger wouldn't be any worse off if she met him at the hospital later.

"Take your father to the hospital," she said to April. "I have work to do." When the stunned faces turned to her, she felt the warm, buzzy lightness that comes with decisions you can never unmake. Blood streamed through Roger's hands and speckled his sweatshirt and jeans. His eyes on Kacy were calm and lucid, which Kacy thought was remarkable, considering the pain he had to be in. "I warned you," she said. He shook his head slowly, said nothing, and hiked up the sloping lawn toward the garage, stopping halfway to pick up a crumpled party napkin off the grass and clamp it to his face. From inside the house, Kenny let loose a piercing, frightened wail that Kacy knew would be heard for blocks, and then the screen door slapped open, and Kenny ran outside and launched himself at Roger's leg, clinging, crying. Kacy watched as Roger knelt and spoke softly to him, wiping one bloody hand dry on his jeans before running it through the boy's hair.

Kacy looked at April, at her chunky legs and acne-pitted

cheeks and the little half-moon of scalp that interrupted her hairline, and she saw the only thing she could save. "Change of plans," she said. She took the key to the car off her ring and handed it to Skillet. "You drive him, William," she said. "April, you're coming with me in the minivan."

Skillet stood still, the car key resting in his open palm. The key was the same silver color as the piece of metal he'd seen fit to stick through his face. He looked stupefied. Kacy wondered if he was on something.

"We should be with Dad," April said in the van. "This is fucked. This is so *fucked.*"

"There's something I want you to see," Kacy said, "some people I want you to meet." She imagined the Dinaburg girl, a pale East Coast beauty, slim and beautiful in a Vera Wang dress, with a torrent of tight, dark, beautiful curls. "And let's clean up the language."

The tires squealed as Kacy turned onto South Congress, narrowly beating a red light. April, with the filthy bucket hat clenched in one hand, started running her other hand through her hair, front to back, front to back, front to back, in a perfect, metronomic rhythm. Her eyes were far away. "Don't worry, honey," Kacy said as they drove across the bridge. "Everything's going to be all right. You'll see."

They arrived at the Four Seasons at 5:21. Kacy left the van with a valet and hurried into the earth-toned lobby, pulling April along with her. Between two lemon trees in terra-cotta pots, a sign with *Dinaburg-Fleischner Wedding* in white plastic letters pointed guests to the east wing. They went downstairs, where Kacy knew they'd find the dressing rooms for the wedding parties. She heard Dinaburg's voice raised high with good cheer and, with a tug on April's arm, followed it to a half-open door. Dinaburg, wearing a white yarmulke, stood with his back to them, a glass of red wine in his hand. He looked good in his tuxedo, she thought; his shoulders sloped more than she liked, but his butt had a cute little curve to it—not like Roger's sheer-drop wall of an ass. She caught a glimpse of a long white dress in the far corner of the room. The bride was surrounded by people—one of whom, Kacy guessed, was Dinaburg's snarly bitch of a wife— but she could tell that the girl was a tiny thing, with porcelain skin and a button nose and thin wrists and the dark curls that Kacy had imagined.

She pulled her daughter close, about to whisper, *See the bride? Doesn't she look beautiful?* But when she turned to look at April's full-moon face up close, she stopped herself. She saw patches of hair missing from both of April's eyebrows. Some of her eyelashes were gone, too; what had once been soft fans now looked like insect wings torn apart by cruel little boys. Pinpoints of blood red dotted the rims of her eyes, which still held a vacant, checked-out look. She instantly regretted bringing April with her. Forcing her to admire Dinaburg's daughter would be awful, unforgivable. "Let's go," she said, leading April away from the door. "Let's go see the cake."

"Who were those people?" April asked.

"They're from New York," she said.

The kitchen staff said nothing when they walked through

the swinging doors. They all recognized her from previous weddings; they'd jumped at the orders she'd barked, kept a safe distance while she'd added the final decorations and circled the cake, searching for imperfections. "Where's the cake?" Kacy demanded. "I'm a special consultant to Mr. Dinaburg." One of the dishwashers pointed to the leftmost walk-in and turned back to his work. Kacy pulled the handle and opened the heavy silver door. They went in.

The cake sat tall on a serving cart. Mist swirled in on currents of humid kitchen air. She felt a strange mix of disappointment and glee. The cake was big, garish, loud, a monstrosity. Nine tiers of chocolate excess and opulence and self-indulgence. Strawberries crowded out by outrageous gnarls of gold-leaf spirals and clots of gum-paste tulip blossoms.

The cold snapped April out of her stupor. "OK, so it's really big," she said. "Can we go see Dad now?"

"Shush." Kacy studied the structure and detected a slight tilt in the third tier and a bulge crowning the sixth. April was right—there was no reason to stay. Dinaburg, she decided, was just a little man with too much money and no taste, and Rona Silverman—with her maroon hair and her tiny, tiny flowers and her magic New York water—was nothing special at all. But she had to be sure. She peeked back into the kitchen to see if anyone was watching. She had an easy path to a knife on a cutting board across the room, and calmly and confidently, she walked out to get it, plucking a clean white hand towel from a laundry box on the floor on her way back.

When April saw her approaching with the knife, she

crossed her arms over her chest and said, "Don't. Jesus, Mom, that's somebody's cake."

Kacy laid a hand on April's folded arms. "Come on," she said. "It'll be our secret." Under the gentle but insistent weight of Kacy's hand, April's arms returned to her sides, and as Kacy hunched over the lowest tier of the cake and pierced the dark chocolate surface, she heard her daughter's breath quicken and thought, *She likes this. She's having fun, too.*

She carefully ran the knife through the cake and excised a piece—a thin piece, but thick enough so she'd be able to get all the flavor—and she folded the towel around it loosely. She looked at the wounded cake. Silverman's assistant, if he was good enough, would be able to cover it up. She silently dared him to try.

"Let's go," she said. "Walk like you belong."

And April did. She walked quickly and confidently toward the service exit. Kacy watched her, struck by her daughter's poise and confidence. It dawned on her that April might have barricaded her bedroom door that night because she'd had Skillet in there with her. She was thrilled. Not that April was sleeping with him—if that loser got her pregnant, she'd kill him—but that April was capable of connecting with somebody, that Kacy hadn't ruined her, that April might not blame her for everything that was wrong in her young life.

They emerged from the building in a small parking lot, where a dozen young people in kitchen garb leaned against cars and smoked. They walked right past a tall, well-muscled young man in a chef's coat with SILVERMAN CATERING stitched over the breast. He was flirting with a waitress, steadying his tall chef's hat on her blonde head, and he didn't even glance at them. They jogged around the hotel on a flagstone walk-way, running in rhythm with each other, Kacy in her tennis shoes and April in her clompy black boots. As they waited for the valet to appear with the minivan, Kacy unfolded the towel. Daubs of chocolate icing stuck to the terry cloth. She held the cake out to April. An offering.

They ate with their fingers.

"What's the verdict?" Kacy asked her daughter, her depressed and mangy daughter whom she loved more than anything.

"It's good," April said, a chocolate-buttermilk crumb clinging wetly to her upper lip, "but not as good as yours," and that was all Kacy needed to hear.

La Fiesta de
San Humberto el Menor

~ ~ ~

It will be a hot day, perhaps the hottest in years. It is only nine o'clock, yet sweat soaks my clothes as I sit alone in the shade of my fruit stand. It has not rained in weeks. The air is as still as San Humberto's bones.

The great saint is buried in a vault beneath our cathedral, along with the remains of the hyenas that he collected on his travels across the water. Each morning since his death three hundred years ago, the church bells have rung at eight o'clock, sounding the beginning of the daily Mass in his honor. The bells woke me today. In my throbbing head it sounded as if they were calling out, *No fruit! No fruit! No fruit!*— admonishing me for another late night with the bottle, for another wasted morning. Once again I have disappointed my early customers, the people who like to eat fruit on the cathedral steps as they wait for Mass to begin. Now, with everyone filling the pews inside, the town is quiet except for the buzz of fat, dizzy flies as they circle and dive and swarm.

I pass several minutes admiring a sturdy beetle as it rolls a dung ball many times its size through the dirt. When I look up again, I see someone running toward me from the town square. Though my vision is blurred, I know it is my friend Vargas, the carpenter. Vargas is a fat man. He runs neither often nor well. When he reaches the stand, he leans on it to support himself. He holds his side and doubles over like a man stuck by a knife. I give him the glass of lemonade I have made for myself; he needs it more than I do.

"Manolo," he says through shallow breaths. "Come to the square. You will not believe what you see."

"Who will watch the stand?" I ask.

"Your fruit is safe. Everyone is at Mass."

We walk toward the square, shading our eyes from the sharp morning sun. "What news could be so important that it makes you run?" I ask.

"You would already know if you had not slept so late," he scolds. Vargas likes to think it is his job to teach me lessons. I have told him he is wasting his time. Lessons are burdens, and I do not need any more of those.

He turns to me. "It was another one of those nights, yes? You drink and you clean the gun?" He says this quietly, with concern.

"I did not touch the gun," I lie.

The square is at the exact center of the town, where our two alamedas cross; one runs north–south, the other east–west. In the southwest corner of the square is our town wishing well, shaped from rough-cut chunks of limestone. As we pass it, I mouth a prayer of contrition to the saint and drop in a coin, as is my custom. There is no splash, just the flat sound of the coin landing in the muck below.

Vargas leads me through the square to the mayor's office. A scroll hangs from the door on a braided purple cord. The parchment is thick and smooth, with bright purple and yellow borders, long black leather fringes attached to the corners, and elegant script that glitters as if it has been written in gold. I want to touch it to see what the gold feels like, but Vargas grabs my wrist. "You might smear it," he says.

"Is it the pronouncement for the Festival?" I ask.

He nods excitedly. This is strange. Usually the pronouncement comes in the form of a name scratched in charcoal on a torn scrap of paper that is nailed to the door.

"Why such a fancy scroll?" I ask. "It is only Ayala who will hang this year. No one special."

He grabs my elbow. "That is the news," he says, and he is shaking with excitement. "It will not be Ayala. We *have* someone special. Let me read for you." Vargas knows I broke my eyeglasses in the bar last week defending my daughter's honor, such as it is. "'Attention citizens! The infamous bandit El Gris has been captured in our town! Next Friday he will receive his punishment at the Festival of San Humberto, where the great saint's hyenas will run fast and hungry! Rejoice in your safety! Rejoice in our justice!'"

El Gris! My pulse races. It is a feeling of triumph, a feeling that everyone in town must be sharing this morning, all of us, together. El Gris is a ruthless murderer, robber, and thief, a man who shoots, then laughs, then shoots again. It is said that he has had his mane of gray hair since he was a teenager, that it turned gray overnight from the thrill of his first kill. El Gris was a plague on this land long before Lars Jarlssen ever came from across the water with all of his riches and built his house with its swimming pool and bought the village bar and turned its back rooms into a brothel and cursed us with his verminous pet spider monkey and doubled the price of tequila and stole my wife and children away from me.

"We have never had such a famous person to hang," Vargas says.

"This is San Humberto's doing," I say. "The saint is showing us His hand. Reminding us of His goodness."

"That is possible, I suppose."

"El Gris is too smart to be caught by any man."

"What if he wanted to be caught?" Vargas says. "What if he wanted to repent, and he turned himself in?"

I laugh and shake my head. "The heat makes you foolish," I say. "One can bathe a hyena, but one can never remove its stink." Vargas nods, and I tell him, "You see? I have lessons to teach, too."

On our walk back to my stand, I see two boys running away with their arms full of my guavas. They yell and laugh. It is too hot to chase them.

El Gris has nearly taken my life twice.

The first time was twenty years ago. I was young, I was muscular, I had hair, I had many friends. I was walking home from the bar—at the time, Vargas's grandfather owned it—

and we had been celebrating the engagement of Vargas's oldest sister. I walked through the square and turned onto the west road toward the one-room house Madalena and I had shared since we were married the year before. I heard someone clear his throat behind me. I turned and saw El Gris leaning against the wishing well, his long gray hair bright in the moonlight. "Good evening, friend," he said, in a voice that told me I was not his friend at all. I saw his right hand move for his gun, and my instinct took over. I leaped into an alley and ran, taking a snake's path through the west side of town, staying off the road. I hid behind the *pescadería*, behind a stack of crates, kneeling amid the old, stinking fish that had been left out for the dogs. I remained there for hours, trying not to breathe, watching the moon cross the sky. When I ran, I did not look back. At home I fell into Madalena's arms and told her my story. "You did the right thing," she said. "You have too much to live for." Then she bathed me and made love to me. I believe this was the night Ysela was conceived.

The second time was four years ago. El Gris robbed and killed six merchants in a rampage along the west road. His path ran right past my stand, but I was not tending it that day. Madalena had left with the children only days before, and I was at home, facedown on the cool floor, trembling, sick with drink and with the loss of my family. In the echo of each shot, I prayed a ricochet would take me.

The heat lingers into the evening like a rude guest. I am exhausted after hours of making change and smiling and ignoring the knife-blade remarks like, *Where are the guavas today, Manolo? Don't you know my wife needs to make jelly for the feast? And where were you this morning? Aren't you ashamed to be so unreliable?* But my day is far from over. I must go into the hills and tell my son Rubén the good news about the Festival, about El Gris. There should be just enough daylight for me to find my way back.

Rubén left town four years ago, the day his mother married Lars. He left a trail of orange peels so I could find him. He has never come back, not even for his mother's funeral. But each day I tell myself maybe, just maybe, he has grown tired of living alone, tired of punishing me, and he only needs an excuse to come back. Perhaps the chance to run with the hyenas for El Gris will be enough.

I leave the dirt path that runs south of the town and head into the hills. I walk for an hour, following the path I know by heart: over a field of prickly maguey and sunny trumpet bushes, across a stream where dipper birds dart underwater, up a rock face flecked with quartz. When I come to the old apple tree, I stop and call his name. Silence. I see the faintest movement of a shadow in the branches. Then an apple flies down and hits me, square on the ankle. This is what usually happens; I talk, and he throws fruit.

"Rubén," I say again. "There is exciting news from town. They have captured El Gris. He will hang at the Festival next Friday." Another apple, this time soft, rotting. It hits me on the knee and stains my pants.

I dream of bringing Rubén back into town with me; I will cook him a magnificent dinner, then we will steal a bottle of tequila from under Lars's pointy nose and share it as we watch the sunset from the bell tower, and Rubén will work with me at the stand and smile as he makes change and ignore all the complaints because he is so happy we are working together. But I have come to accept that, for now, he is a boy who lives in a tree and throws fruit at his father.

I did not always accept this. When I followed the orange peels and found him in the tree, I shouted at him, drunk and blind with anger. These are the things I said:

Come down from that tree! Boys do not live in trees!

You are bringing shame upon your family, such as it is!

You are as bad as your sister! Perhaps worse!

The lightning will hit you. San Humberto will see to it!

Squirrels will claw at your testicles, trying to gather them for the winter!

If there is a drought, the branches of the tree may weaken and break, and you might then fall and hurt yourself!

Why are you leaving your father alone?

Twice I have brought the gun here, drunk. On the day after Madalena was buried, I aimed it at my son, a shadow in an apple tree. Weeks later, on the day my daughter, Ysela, told me she was going to work in Lars's back rooms, I held it to my head. On both occasions, San Humberto prevented me from pulling the trigger. For this I am grateful, most of the time.

"Do you not want to see El Gris?" I say to Rubén. "We have never had such a famous person to hang."

Apple, apple, apple.

I turn and walk back to the road with the bruises spread–

ing under my clothes. But I have not given up. I have decided that the capture of El Gris is a sign from the saint, a sign of order restored, a sign that Rubén and I will run with the hyenas together this year.

It is pitch-dark when I pass through the south gate into town, and I swear it is as hot as it was at noon. Though my clothes are stained with sweat and dirt and apple, I go to the bar for a bottle of tequila. It is the only way I will find sleep tonight. I do not want to see Lars, but as is his custom, he sits at his desk in the loft overlooking the bar, calling out bawdy jokes as one of the girls sits on his lap and combs his thick blond beard. The sound of coins slapping the bar is as constant as the ticking of a clock.

There is a bottle of tequila on the corner of the bar, nearly full and unattended. I wonder, *Is Lars setting a trap for me?* Inviting me to steal from him while he watches me from beneath the folds of his eyelids, stroking his monkey and relishing the thought of the police dragging me away, humiliated? Well, he is right to expect me to steal from him, but he underestimates me. If I am going to steal for myself, I will not take something as insignificant as a bottle. I will steal something he loves. I do not yet have a plan, because Lars does not seem to love anything besides himself. Which is an excellent defense, I admit.

I keep my eyes to the floor and pay the bartender. I turn to leave, a new bottle in hand. "Manolo," Lars shouts from his loft. "My most reliable customer." I keep walking. Behind me I hear whispers, stifled laughs. "If you have come for a glimpse of your daughter," he says, "you should know she will have nothing to do with you."

I turn and look up. Without my glasses I see his face as a blur, but I know his expression—a scornful curl of lip under blond mustache, a creeping lopsided smile, blue eyes wide with mockery. He sits in front of a bright lamp that casts a halo around his head so that people who look up at him will think he is some kind of angel. I spit on his polished floor.

"Oh, Manolo. You must be so lonely," he says loudly. It is important to him that everybody hear. "A nice girl would comfort you more than that bottle. One of Ysela's friends, perhaps? I'm sure they would love to see where she came from."

More laughter. The door seems very far away.

I know that every man in this room has paid his money to be with my daughter. Most have not said anything to me, but I can see it in their eyes when they come to buy my fruit. Some squeeze the fruit silently and stare at the ground while they hunt for money in their pockets. Others look me in the eye too directly, speak too loudly, listen too earnestly. I do not know which bothers me more. Even Vargas took his turn, once. The next morning he knocked on my door and confessed; he said he was sorry, he was drunk, he had been fighting with his wife, and Ysela was just so beautiful, and on and on. He begged me to blacken his eyes, so I did. We never spoke of it again. If I were to hold grudges, I would soon be out of friends.

"You are an evil man, Lars," I say. I focus on a spot above his head so I do not have to meet his eyes.

Swinging from a crossbeam, Lars's monkey screeches

and bares its teeth at me. I hate that monkey, that filthy little beast in its purple velveteen coat. Lars laughs—a false, too-loud laugh that is for the benefit of everyone having a drink or waiting for a girl. "Good-bye, Manolo, and thank you for your business," he says, waving me out.

"San Humberto punishes people like you," I say. "If not now, then someday." I turn my back on him and walk through the door and into the night. He shouts something that I cannot hear, and everyone inside laughs. He has the money, he gives the party, so people laugh.

I open the bottle and drink as I walk down the road. Tonight I will not touch the gun, will not clean it, will not cradle it like a baby. I swear it to myself.

In the morning, Vargas brings news from the jail, where Ayala and El Gris sit in adjoining cells. "Ayala does nothing but cry," he says, mopping his brow with his sleeve. "He sobs so hard it is like he is having a seizure."

"Why?" I say. "He is going to live." It is our tradition that the worst criminal in the jail on the day of the Festival goes to the gallows. Ayala had been the only one behind bars; with the Festival so close, he must have expected he would hang. The capture of El Gris has spared him.

"Ayala wants to die," Vargas says. "He wants to be with Concepción."

Concepción was Ayala's wife and one of Vargas's sisters. She died of the green fever six months ago. The night after she was buried, Ayala went to the bar and drank himself senseless. When the bells tolled midnight, he jumped up and overturned his table, smashed bottles, kicked the monkey into the wall, and ran out. He went to the cathedral, where he stripped off his clothes and relieved himself all over the front steps. "I piss on your apostles! I shit on your saints!" he said. He shouted this again and again, dancing naked around the cathedral as we gathered in a crowd. He stopped, suddenly, and with a look of sudden, rapturous knowledge—as if he'd just glimpsed Truth itself—he said, "I will burn your God to the ground." The police came as Ayala was pushing through the crowd, asking people if they had any matches he could borrow.

I open a crate of sapotes that was delivered this morning. "And El Gris?" I ask Vargas. "You have seen him?"

"Yes," Vargas says. "He tries to comfort Ayala." Vargas eyes the sapotes.

"Go ahead," I say. He chooses one and cuts into the fibrous brown skin with a pocket knife.

"It is sad to see Ayala," Vargas says. "A naked man in a bare cell. Even though the police do not need him for the Festival anymore, they still will not give him his clothing. They are afraid of what he may do to himself."

"It is San Humberto's will," I say. "We live because it is our duty to live."

"You have never wanted to die?" Vargas asks. He cuts a crescent of pink flesh away from the rind.

"What we want," I say, "is irrelevant."

I, too, lost my wife to a fever—to the fever of money and power that Lars brought to our town. It left Madalena dazed and desirous and vulnerable. Her note, which was delivered to me by Lars' silk-clad coachman, made this plain: *Lars can give the children everything you cannot. He is a gentleman and you are a boor. He is a respected businessman and you sell fruit of poor quality.* At Mass the next morning, all of them—Lars, Madalena, Ysela, and Rubén—sat together, a false family looking down on the rest of us from Lars's reserved seating area—which had been the choir loft until the bishop let himself be bought. I have not gone inside the cathedral since. Does San Humberto understand my reasons? I believe he does.

Two years ago, Lars and Madalena traveled to the capital city for a vacation. He came back; she did not. Lars and his coachman claimed she was killed when a small and unknown band of rebels began catapulting boulders into the city from the surrounding hills. Whether that is true or not, Madalena is gone, and there is nothing I can do.

The white marble tombstone that Lars's unclean money bought is bigger than my house. It is a blindfolded angel pointing at the sky. When the shadows are longest, the wings of the angel darken forty-six other graves. I cannot read the epitaph because it is written in Latin. The final insult: the stone gives her surname as "De Los Pozos," with capital *D*, capital *L*. What kind of man does not know how to spell his wife's name? I asked Vargas if the stone could be corrected. "You do not have enough money," he told me.

Eventually Madalena would have come back to me. I know this. Lars made her forget what is good and what is right, but one day the great saint would have opened her eyes, shown her that Lars is like the feijoa, a fruit that rots from the inside out, turning brown and foul-smelling underneath its shiny green skin. I may be a man who blackens eyes, cleans his gun, and dreams violent dreams, but I live by San Humberto's example. I am not a bad man.

As much as El Gris deserves his punishment at the Festival, I would rather see Lars in his place, sweating and crying and helpless, knowing the floor will fall away beneath him, knowing his neck will soon be snapped and we, the true citizens of Ciudad San Humberto, will lead the hyenas to his swinging corpse. That is the picture I have in my head when I drop my coin into the well. I hear it clink at the bottom, metal on metal.

I am doubled over in the pain of last night's drink. The hot air scorches my lungs when I breathe. The shade of the fruit stand is little comfort. Hammers pound and pound from the direction of the square. The construction committee has begun to reassemble the gallows.

I am startled by my daughter's voice, suddenly close. "Those papayas are lovely," she says.

Sunlight stabs my eyes when I look up. "I sell good fruit," I tell her.

Ysela is nearly twenty, tall and slim, with graceful limbs and wide, dark eyes. She is the most beautiful woman anyone in town has ever seen. These are not the foolish words of a proud father, for I am anything but proud of her. Her beauty is simply a fact, just as it is a fact that hyenas can smell carrion from seven miles away through a crosswind. Today she wears a new-looking dress of deep carmine. It does not cover her calves.

She tucks a strand of her long black hair behind her ear. "Yes," she says. "You do your job well." I know she says this to make me feel better; she must have heard all the complaints. Even so, I thank her.

"I hope you are well," she says. "I worry."

"I do not need your worry," I say.

"How is Rubén?" she asks.

"The same. Always the same."

She looks up and down the road, then quickly opens her basket and hands me a bottle of tequila, the best Lars sells. "Tonight, at least, you won't have to go into the bar," she says. "I know Lars makes it difficult for you." I tell her I can buy my own drinks, Lars or no Lars. But I take it from her and hide it behind the stand.

She bites her lip. A habit, when she is anxious. It is the same look she had just before she told me she was going to work in Lars's back rooms.

I asked her, *Have you lost your mind now that your mother is gone?*

She said, *You can't control me like you controlled Mama.*

Do not talk to me that way. I am your father.

I will talk any way I want to talk. And I will make my money any way I wish.

I will drag you from there and beat sense into you.

I will curse you whenever someone is inside me. Whenever I am fucking.

San Humberto will make you pay.

San Humberto would pay me to fuck Him.

So now, with her lip bitten and her calves exposed, I brace myself for her news. But what she says is not what I expect.

"I want to see Rubén. Will you show me the way?"

"Rubén does not want to see you," I say. "Not while you work for that man."

Her eyes narrow, but she says nothing.

"May San Humberto guide you," I say.

"May He guide you as well," she says curtly, then turns away. I watch her walk; it is Madalena's walk, a walk of confidence, even arrogance. In my blurred vision she could be her mother, and I cannot stop watching her.

I do not even notice the two boys making off with all of my lemons until they are halfway to the square. The children are getting bolder these days.

Each day Vargas visits the jail and brings back the same news: Ayala is despondent, El Gris is strangely calm, and the two of them whisper together through the bars. I am filled with questions: Does El Gris have regrets? Does he pray? Is he perhaps conspiring with Ayala, formulating a plan that will let him escape and let our sad friend die in his place? Vargas shrugs and tells me he does not know; the bandit does not speak when anyone but Ayala can hear.

It is too hot to do anything but talk. The rumor today is that Zorrillo, who runs the hyena ranch, has starved the animals for a week; they are so hungry that one of them escaped the pen last night and ate twenty chickens before it was recaptured. People are also talking about the drinks and the meats and the jellies and pies we will share on the rooftops after the run. I want to share their excitement, but the thought of food makes me ill. I realize I have eaten nothing in two days. The heat, the stillness, the flies, the tequila—they have robbed me of my appetite.

I pull my hat over my eyes and pretend to sleep. The children will try to steal again today; they are crazy, and the Festival makes them crazier still. The gun is in my hand, hidden under my shirt. The bell at the schoolhouse rings. I wait. It will not be long.

Through the weave of the straw in my hat, I see the two boys emerge from behind the cobbler's shop and creep toward my stand. The shorter one pulls a small wagon behind him. A wagon! They are more than bold, I think, more than shameless, more than crazy—they have become animals.

They are within arm's reach of my oranges before I can make out their faces. The short one is Zorrillo's son, and the tall one is the son of the town doctor. These are not boys who must steal because they are hungry. The wagon creaks, and they hold still. They are watching to see if I stir. I am patient. I am calm. I am completely still.

But I am up quick and strong as a panther the moment they reach for my fruit. I have the muzzle of the gun pressed into the tall boy's temple before they can even pull their hands back. It is the fastest I have moved in years. They look at me, mouths open. "You are surprised?" I say. "Surprised that a man will defend his fruit?" I walk out from behind the stand and kick over the wagon. "A wagon? Were you going to steal everything I have?"

The short boy starts to stay something, so I box him in the ear with my free hand. My hand thinks for me. "Shut your mouth," I say. "Do you know what San Humberto does to boys like you?" I hit him again. I see tears in his eyes. I feel tears in mine. "Go home now," I say, "and tell your fathers what you have done." I lower the gun. "Now leave me alone." I do not want them to see an old man cry.

They are slow to move, so I hit the tall one. "Go!" I yell, and they run. I sit and wipe my eyes with my shirt. I am so tired.

Late in the afternoon, their fathers come to the stand to pay for all the fruit the boys stole. Zorrillo holds out a sackful of coins, then pulls it away when I reach for it. "In the future I would prefer that you not threaten children with your gun," he says.

"In the future I would prefer that children not steal my fruit," I say, and I wait for him to hand over what is mine.

Some nights I dream about forgiveness. I do not mean that I dream about people forgiving people. I dream about forgiveness itself, curling around buildings and nuzzling people like the cool west winds. Vargas does not believe me. He says you cannot dream about something you cannot see or touch or hear or taste or smell.

I have not told Vargas this, but when I dream, forgiveness has a smell. Forgiveness smells like limes.

．　．　．

On the day of the Festival, I close the stand early so I can visit Rubén before the run. As I pack away my stock, I sense someone nearby watching me and I look up. I do not know if it is the heat or the hangover or my bad eyes, but for an instant I see Ysela standing hand in hand with her mother. But no, it is my daughter, alone.

She holds out a pair of eyeglasses. "I found them among Mamá's things," she says. "I think they're yours."

"Perhaps," I say, although I know they are.

My eyesight has gotten worse, but the old lenses work well enough. The gallows in the square comes into focus. I feel my eyes shift again, and now I can see all the way to the east gate. I turn to Ysela, and I see thin, shallow wrinkles in her forehead that I have never noticed before. It makes me sad, to see my daughter look as if she worries so much. But she has chosen the path she has chosen. I cannot blame myself.

She is biting her lip again. "You know I have made a lot of money," she says. She waits for me to nod before she continues. "I want you to visit Mamá tomorrow. There is a surprise for both of you."

Her name, I think. Her name, the way it should be, the way she would have wanted it. I feel like dropping this crate and running to the cemetery now. But then I think: San Humberto would frown on such a tainted monument. He would curse it.

"No," I say.

She looks surprised. "It is a gift," she says. "For both of you."

"I do not want your mother's grave defiled by whore money," I tell her.

The slap hits me before I see her arm move. My eyeglasses, bent, hang from one ear. Ysela clenches her teeth and shakes with anger. "You haven't changed," she says. "You'll never change." She grabs an overripe mango and heaves it into the wall behind me. Pieces of the fruit spatter on the back of my head and neck.

"I have told Lars I am finished working for him," she says. "I am going to be the new schoolteacher."

My voice is louder than I intend. "What can you teach children? How to shame their fathers?"

She stomps away, then stops in the middle of the road. "You think you are San Humberto Himself!" she shouts. "You are not! You are an old and drunken fruit vendor, not a saint and not a father!"

I want to go after her, but I do not know what I would say. I put on the glasses again and see that people have come out onto the road to stare. I take the glasses off. I cannot watch them watching me.

I sit on an empty crate and bite into a lime. The sour juice floods my mouth. I bite again, and again. I bite, I sit, and I stare straight ahead at nothing. I do not even blink when Lars's monkey snatches the fruit out of my hand and runs away, tittering.

I am dry-throated and dripping with sweat when I get to Rubén's tree. My pulse drums in my ears. I sit on a flat mossy rock and stare up into the branches, but I can see no shadow, hear no movement. The only sound is the shrill cry of a chachalaca defending its nest. I wait, trying to think of what to say. It is difficult. I feel it has been years since I have said the right thing to anyone—not even to the saint, in my prayers. Finally, this comes out: "Rubén, I do not speak to you as your father but as a man. I am sorry for all I have done and all I have failed to do."

The apples fly. I close my eyes and let them find their marks. When I arrive home, I count the new bruises. Seventeen in all. One for each year of my son's life.

It is time. The last traces of sunset have disappeared and the gallows is lit only by the flickering torches on the roofs. We are all gathered in the square, packed in tightly, breathing on each other. I look through the crowd for Rubén, hoping, but I do not see him. It occurs to me that I might not recognize him if he were here. Would he have a beard? Would he be taller than I am? Would he be thin and weak from a diet of apples and insects? My heart drums. I feel feverish. I cannot find Vargas, either. I do not want to be here, alone in this crowd.

A young man climbs up the frame of the gallows and leans out over the crowd, holding on with one hand. This is Urrieta, who runs Lars's cochineal farm and likes to brawl in the bar. He pumps his free hand in a fist. "Give us the bandit!" he shouts. "Give us the bandit!" A twisted, gap-toothed grin spreads across his face as the crowd takes up the chant. I see Lars standing on the terrace of the hotel that overlooks the square, shouting along, beating the railing with his fists, while one of his youngest whores runs a comb through his yellow beard and the monkey bounces and screeches. Ysela is on the terrace with them, but she stands apart from them, scanning the crowd with her arms folded over her chest. I wonder if she is looking for me.

The door to the police station opens, but no one comes outside.

Underneath the shouts I hear Vargas's voice and his heavy breathing, coming closer. "Pardon me. Pardon me. Pardon me." He pushes his way into the space beside me. He is covered in sweat and dirt. He wipes his forehead, leaving a streak of clean.

"Where have you been?" I ask him.

"I had to bury Ayala right away, before the hyenas are set free. I did not want—"

"Ayala is dead?"

"Yes."

"How?"

"El Gris strangled him through the bars."

"Ah," I say. "One last kill. The demon–bandit could not resist."

"No," Vargas says. "Ayala begged him."

"Then may San Humberto have mercy on Ayala's soul," I say. "He did not deserve to be buried." I find myself getting angry. *Why should Ayala get away so easily when the rest of us have to stay here and hurt?*

"Do you want to know what I think?" Vargas says quietly, with his head down. "I think it was an act of kindness." When he lifts his head, I see tears in his eyes. He wipes them away with his fat, callused fingers and suddenly I feel very old and lost. Living was so much easier long ago—when husbands and wives stayed together, when children respected their parents, when blond strangers did not control our town, when we had nothing to fear but the infrequent visits of El Gris.

The crowd quiets as the white-haired monsignor walks slowly out of the police station and up the wood-plank steps that lead to the gallows. Swinging a censer, he chants San Humberto's Creed in the old sacred tongue. He leads us all in the Gestures of the Sacred Bones. The Festival has begun.

The mayor follows in the monsignor's path, and then the chief of police and his two sergeants. El Gris emerges from the station and plods ahead, flanked by two officers who guide him forward. His hands are shackled behind his back. He does not look so fearsome now that they have shaved his head; he looks tired, spent. Still, the crowd gasps and *ooohs* and *aaahs*, just as they did when they saw Madalena—my wife—walk down the aisle of the cathedral in the emerald-green wedding dress Lars bought her.

Vargas nudges me. "If I were in charge, I would not have cut off his hair," he says. "His name no longer fits. What is he now? He is nothing."

El Gris is surrounded by policemen on the long scaffold. One of them is young Séptimo, who played with Ysela when they were children. There have been several nights when Séptimo has woken me up in the street and walked me home. He is kind and polite, not yet corrupted by age and money and other people.

This is what I imagine: El Gris jumping down from the gallows, catching a pistol thrown to him by a comrade hidden within the crowd, then running to a ready horse, his gun blasting away and streaking the air with lead, the police awestruck and fumbling. A stray bullet ripping through both Lars and the monkey in his arms, and the two of them tumbling from the terrace and landing, twisted, in the dirt. The mare's hoofbeats resonating in my chest as she speeds El Gris to safety outside the walls of our corrupted city.

Perhaps I am the one who will throw him that gun.

But El Gris makes no move to escape. He stands still while Séptimo, on the chief's command, tightens the noose around his neck. The mayor motions for quiet. "As San Humberto punished evil, so we punish evil in His name. Before you is the infamous outlaw El Gris. Countless people have tried to bring him to justice and have failed. But we have succeeded, we, the citizens of Ciudad San Humberto, especially our good friend Lars Jarlssen and the young and beautiful Ysela María Rivera de los Pozos."

Ysela? I think as the crowd roars approval. *What have I missed?*

El Gris looks up at my daughter and fixes his eyes on her, as if he wants her to be the last thing he sees. It is possible that his lips move, but I cannot see clearly. As Séptimo reaches for the lever, Vargas squeezes his eyes shut. So do I. First there is silence. Then I hear the trapdoor slap and the rope jerk taut, and then the wood creaking as the bandit swings, dead, and the voices of the city rising all around me.

. . .

Years ago, when Ysela was a little girl, I explained the Festival to her like this: *First we impose justice as the Great Codex demands. After the hanging, we divide into four groups and wait at each of the gates for hyenas to be let in. At the sound of the gun, they run, and we run ahead of them. We act as their guides. We lead them to the dead man, and then we watch with joy from high above.*

Why?

It is symbolic.

Symbolic?

It is like we are the great saint and the hyenas are us. We lead them to justice, but we do so at great risk to ourselves. And we rejoice when they find it.

Couldn't they find the dead man themselves? she asked. *Couldn't they smell him?*

That is not the point, I said. *Someday you will understand.*

We are gathered together in front of the west gate, waiting for the signal. Jugs of dragonfruit wine are passed through the crowd. People drink quickly, in equal parts celebration and fear. Someone says the rabid ones are behind the south gate this year. Someone else says no, they are here behind the west gate, Zorrillo himself told him so. There is still no sign of Rubén.

I look down the road toward the square; though the sky

has darkened, I believe I can make out the shape of El Gris's body, swaying slightly at the end of the rope. I can hear the hyenas in their cages outside the gate, snarling, throwing themselves against the bars that confine them. I hear teeth on metal, and I realize that I am very frightened, frightened of the hyenas, of Lars, of the people around me. I am frightened that I will never see my son again, frightened that I will never again be a father to Ysela. I am becoming an old man and I am frightened of myself. The more I have learned, the more frightened I have become. The strength leaks from my tired, bruised legs. I drink a large mouthful from a jug but it does not wash away the fear. "I want to go home," I tell Vargas. "I am too tired to run."

A pistol fires from behind the gate. "Too late," Vargas shouts. He throws the jug aside, grabs my hand, and we run. The gate opens behind us, and I hear the clanks of cage doors and the hyenas' snarls turning to whoops. The muscles in my legs stretch and burn. I do not look behind me. I keep my eyes forward. My view of the city bounces crazily as my feet pound the earth.

Past the feed store, past the animal doctor's, past the bakery, a quarter of the way there. Vargas and I have fallen behind the pack, and he pulls me along with him. The air is filled with dust and with the stink of dirty, murderous fur. My breaths are shallow and I feel like vomiting. I hear the hyenas behind me, front legs long, hind legs short—*ka-thup, ka-thup, ka-thup.* Powerful jaws snapping. I have heard these sounds every year of my life. I do not want to hear them ever again.

Past the tailor, past the barber, almost halfway. Vargas is nearly dragging me. I am holding him back—fat, panting Vargas. I am so tired. I need to stop and I do not care what is behind me. Then I wonder, *Am I no better than Ayala, on his knees and begging to have his neck wrung?* Oh, but this is different, so different. It is one thing to seek death; it is another simply to accept the inevitable, to embrace the fate that snaps at your heels. Everyone will be able to see how different it was. And even if they cannot, I know San Humberto will. He will understand.

At the moment I let go of Vargas and try to plant my feet, I feel a prickly heat surge throughout my body. Just as quickly the warmth turns to ice. I think I feel myself dying.

Vargas clamps his soft hand around my arm and pulls, hard. He turns his head, and I can see by his eyes that the hyenas are close, closer than they have ever been to him before. "Run!" he yells, his high voice sharp, commanding. Without thinking I take his hand again, but I do not know how much longer I can run.

Just ahead is my stand. My stand. Where I have sold the fruit for every breakfast, every pie, every jar of jelly in this town for thirty years. In this town where people laugh at Lars's jokes and forget where their berries come from. In this town where people come to do business with me after doing business with Lars. In this town where men pay to defile my daughter and then haggle with me over the price of figs.

I feel a sharp pain in my side, and I imagine a scene as strange and vivid as one of my nightmares: Lars has shot me, and he is standing on the terrace, lowering his rifle and laughing as that damned monkey blows away the curl of smoke. "I am shot," I say, without meaning to.

"You have a cramp," Vargas says. "Breathe!"

Yes. Breathe, Manolo. Breathe. I close my eyes, shutting out the shaking city, and I concentrate on breathing—breathing in everything that is in the air, the good and the bad, the forgiveness and the dust and the stench and the ghosts of the dead, the love and the fear. We pass the stand and now I think about Ysela going there to tell me her good news, Ysela, my daughter who corrected her mother's stone, my daughter who will be a schoolteacher, my daughter who somehow captured El Gris. The pain still burns my side, but I pass Vargas and now I am pulling him along with me.

And we pass the cobbler's and the cooper's and the saddle maker's stores, and I see in my mind how it happened: El Gris heard about the most beautiful woman in the land and knew he had to see her, so he came to our town—perhaps with his hair tucked under his hat—and found his way to Lars's bar, and he told Lars he would pay many times the usual rate; he simply had to be with this beautiful Ysela, this angel of whom the whole island speaks. And Lars took the money, of course he took the money, and he sent my daughter off with this criminal, and maybe she was scared at first but she knew what she had to do for everyone else, for the larger good, so she set aside her fear, and she whispered to one of the other girls to run and get the police, and she took El Gris into her room and kept him there—he thought he was taking her, but she was taking *him*—until the police knocked down the door. Of course Lars claimed credit but that was a lie; it was only Ysela who thought of something more important than money, Ysela, who has changed, repented, who now wants to surround herself with good people and to do good things, who wants to teach children to be moral and thoughtful. And while all of this may be a story I am making up, it is my story and she is my daughter and my legs are pumping and my body is strong and the bar and the cathedral flash past and then from four directions everyone converges in the square and heads for the ladders, and Vargas and I go up the side of the hotel, and we are all safe, away from the beasts below, our chests heaving as we catch our breath.

The hyenas stop dead in front of the gallows, a pulsing mass of brown fur and coiled muscle. They hunch forward and eye the body swinging in the air. We watch them in the firelight reverently, wordlessly. We will have the rest of the night to celebrate. We will drink and dance and laugh on the roofs all the way until sunrise, when Zorrillo and his riflemen will clear out the hyenas and make it safe to come down. But now, now it is time to watch.

After the first hyena leaps onto the gallows and bites into a leg, the others fall into a frenzy, as if they had all shared the first taste of the dead. They swarm over the gallows, jaws snapping as they jump for their bounty. The body sways and jerks as the hyenas rip meat from bone. They knock each other over the side as they fight for the best pieces. They howl and laugh. We will all hear these sounds in our nightmares, and that, I realize, is one reason we do this.

Lars watches from the edge of the hotel's roof, leaning

against the railing, surrounded by three young girls, his latest recruits, who comb his beard, brush dirt off his suit, rub his back. I think about approaching him and demanding compensation for his monkey's theft, but then I spot Ysela standing with her friends across the square from us. I tell Vargas I will return and make my way around the perimeter, crossing between buildings on wooden planks and over the streets on the rope bridges, trying not to look down. I slip through the crowd and tap her on the shoulder. She faces me. Her friends tighten around her and look at me. The disgust in their gazes is obvious.

"I am so sorry," I whisper to her. "I am proud of what you have done and what you will do. I think you will be an excellent teacher."

I feel her warm breath in my ear as she whispers back, "San Humberto keep you well." She smells like her mother, like the west wind that brings the winter rains. She kisses me on the cheek and turns back to her friends, who close ranks around her. Some of them are handsome young men. It occurs to me that she could be in love with one of them and I would not know. I do not belong here with her, with them. This saddens me, but the sadness is a new one, soft and muted, sweetly bearable. Ysela has her place, and I have mine. I cross back to the roof of the hotel and rejoin Vargas. He slaps my shoulder, and together we watch the scene below.

A hyena creeps out on the crossbeam of the gallows and begins gnawing on the rope. "Ah," Vargas says. "They figured it out more quickly this year." When the bandit's body falls, there is no sound of impact; it is caught in the air by a dozen snapping jaws and pulled apart. When there is nothing left but bones, the church bells ring. It is time to celebrate.

I watch as people cluster around Lars, congratulating him for the capture of El Gris, fighting for position in his good graces. How can I expect them to do otherwise? He owns the town. This simply is a fact. Vargas and I stand by ourselves, still watching as the hyenas pace the square, licking their mouths, nosing at the dirt, gnawing bone, waiting for whatever it is that comes next. We remain quiet with each other. A light wind blows across the rooftops, cooling me through my wet shirt. It is a wind that promises a thunderstorm, a violent but merciful break in the weather, and I think of all the times I stood on a roof with Madalena and watched the sacrifice with her. When the church bells rang, she would make the Gestures of the Sacred Bones and begin to pray. Maybe it was just the bells ringing and the wind blowing through her hair and her lips forming the words of a prayer, but every time she did this, I thought, *Bless the saint, she has never been more beautiful.* For the first time I can remember her without anger. My feet throb, and I can feel the dampness of sweat in my boots. Is this is how anger drains away?

Lars is waving his arms animatedly, telling his story for all those people, collecting handshakes and pats on the back. He draws a cigar out of his jacket pocket, and one of the young whores strikes a match for him. He wraps his hand around her skinny wrist and is guiding it toward his face when someone whistles—a fierce whistle that cuts right through the wind and chatter. Lars turns toward the whistle, like a man who assumes all whistles are meant for him.

The apple hits him on the bridge of his nose, and I hear the crunch of bone. Lars recoils as if shot. Blood spills over his blond beard and streaks his white suit.

"Did you see?" I say to Vargas. "My son has good aim."

Vargas smiles, more to himself than to me, and we watch as the people around Lars wheel around and back, around and back, scanning the dark, trying to figure out where that apple came from, wondering if there will be more.

—*after "Paradise" by Alejandro Escovedo*

Vikings

~ ~ ~

W e were almost out of money, so Trace went
to steal us another bottle of something. We
were celebrating. The holiday weekend was almost over, and
the mechanic was due back in town the next morning. We'd
finally be able to get back on the road.

I sat on the rear bumper of the van and waited. Smoke
from the fireworks still hung in the air. Biggest display in
the Mojave, the posters had promised. Maybe it was, but we
couldn't tell. An hour before the show, the sky had curdled
into a clump of fog. Fog, in the desert. First time in twenty
years, someone said.

I watched the smoke and fog mingle and roll in lazy
waves in and out of the orange floodlight of the gas
station. All around me were junked cars parked at crazy
angles, cracked windshields and fallen bumpers shining in the greasy light. Buicks and Chevys and Pontiacs,

all chrome and disappointment. The dirt was speckled with pieces of broken glass. Every breath tasted like gunpowder. We were still thousands of miles from Alaska.

Trace was gone a long time, too long, and I wondered if he'd found a girl and gone off with her. That happened a lot. The last time was in Flagstaff, where he'd hooked up with a tequila-shooting girl who was wispy and tan and blonde, so good-looking that her red eyes and thick liquor-stink just made her seem game and fearless instead of sad. She told us she was from San Diego, on her way east to divinity school. At last call, I saw her lift her skirt and flash Trace her tiger-print panties, and they spent the night in her motel room. I slept in the van. "I don't understand it," he said the next day. "I'm a fucked-up-looking guy, but I always get the beautiful ones." It was true. He was fucked-up-looking—short and puffy, with a half-closed eye and a nose that looked like it'd been hit with a bag of nickels—and he *did* always get the beautiful ones. And he always seemed genuinely surprised about it. You could tell him to shut up and enjoy his luck, but that never stopped him from wondering out loud.

While I waited for Trace, I ran through the names of the places we'd drive through next: Tehachapi, Bakersfield, Fresno, Modesto, Lodi, Red Bluff, Redding. I'd studied the map, knew the route by heart. I wanted to see all these towns in the rearview, feel them as beats in a rhythm of places passed by, a rhythm as steady and soothing as tires thrumming over pavement joints.

.   .   .

When Trace came back to the van, he was carrying a baby wrapped in a threadbare beach towel. "Hey, Phil," he said. "Look what I got." He held it up like it was a carnival prize. The baby's eyes were shut, but it wrinkled its little fingers open and closed, so I knew it was alive.

"Whose is that?" I said.

"Someone gave it to me."

"Who?"

"A woman. Outside the liquor store."

"People don't just hand out babies," I said.

"This one did," he said.

"Take it back."

"I can't," he said. "She drove away."

"We have to find her," I said. "People will think we stole it."

Trace carried the baby as we walked along the road into town. He hummed softly and rocked it in his arms. I kicked at the loose gravel. "The mother," I said, "was she fat?" The other morning, in the taco place, I'd seen a fat woman chew up a quesadilla and dribble it into her baby's mouth. Like she thought they were penguins or something. It was all I could do to keep my food down, watching. I wondered if this one might be the penguin baby. I didn't want any baby, but I especially didn't want that one.

"No," Trace said. "She was skinny. Like meth-skinny."

"Even so," I said. "We have to get rid of it."

In the streetlight I could see the baby's forehead and nose were bright red. The mother, whoever the hell she was, had let the kid get sunburned. Even I knew that was wrong.

Still, the baby looked pretty happy. It wasn't crying. As babies go, this one was pretty mellow.

We sat on the curb in the liquor store parking lot and waited for the mother to come back. The baby slept in Trace's arms. People walked by and looked at us suspiciously. No one recognized the baby. After a while the store owner banged on the glass and waved us away. I pointed to the baby, trying to explain, but the guy just shook his head and kept waving.

"I knew she wouldn't come back," Trace said.

"We should call the cops," I said.

"No way," he said. "Are you crazy?"

He was right. Technically, we were fugitives.

"Let's go to the bar," he said. "I could use a drink."

I didn't have any better ideas. That's always been a problem for me.

We started walking again. "I wonder what its name is," Trace said.

"Is it a boy or a girl?"

"Either way, I'm going to call it Mo," he said.

That wasn't a good sign. Mo was his ex's name, short for Maureen. He was still stuck on her, but she was back in New York, shacked up with a guy who made millions riding the bench for the Yankees. I knew what he was thinking. He was thinking that he could save this baby, that he was meant to save it. "We're not keeping it," I said.

"We could," he said.

"We're giving it back." I was waiting for him to say something stupid like *this baby needs us.* This baby didn't need us. We were the last thing it needed. It needed anyone but us.

That whole year we'd been riding a crest of failure. In March my girlfriend left me because I threw her shoes out the window, and Mo and Trace broke up not long after, this time for good. It had been Trace's idea to leave New York for Colorado. "We'll be river-rafting guides," he'd said. "You get to help girls into their wetsuits." We got there and the rivers were nearly dry. Not enough snow that winter, people said. So we bought the van and tried to start a painting business, but we never found any customers who'd pay. It was easy to leave when the court dates started piling up. Alaska was his idea, too, and so far all it had gotten us was stuck. Stuck in a town that wasn't more than a crosshair of blacktop trained on the desert.

The bar was dark and narrow. Dim red light, like a darkroom. Red vinyl stools and booths. Two pool tables. A jukebox that played songs about trucks. I sat in a booth and told Trace to show the baby to the bartender. He held out his free hand for money. "Drinks," he said. I took off my sneaker and gave him the ten I'd been keeping for an emergency. It was the last of the money for now, because Trace's sister would only send us a little at a time. "I have my *own* juveniles to feed," she'd say. But usually she came through. She'd wire it in my name because she thought her brother was irresponsible and because she liked me from when I was a kid. Trace and I had grown up together, watched our parents' marriages blow apart at the same time, stayed close even after one strange summer when my dad was sleeping with his mom. Got closer, maybe.

The baby started to cry. Trace held up the bill and sniffed

it. "For fuck's sake, Phil," he said. "The money stinks. You got trench foot or something."

What did he expect? I'd been walking around in a desert for four days without any socks. We'd packed in a hurry.

My head hurt. I leaned against the wall and stretched my legs out on the seat and tried to pretend I was somewhere better.

Earlier that night, Trace and I had gone to the fireworks show, which was held at a football field that looked like it hadn't been used in years. No goalposts, no scoreboard, just a rectangle of sandy dirt and rocks with patchy scabs of turf. Lots of families sat on blankets out on the field. High school kids sat in the bleachers, and every now and then you'd hear a bottle fall on the gravel below or roll down the metal steps. We sat up on a little hill with some people from the bar. Trace had shot pool with some of them, and they liked us because he'd told them we were outlaws. They called us Butch and Sundance.

We drank and waited. Finally Trace shouted, "When the hell is this going to start?"

A short, bald guy named Roy passed him a bottle of bourbon. "You got somewhere to go, Butch?" Roy said. Everyone laughed. They knew we were stuck.

"They're waiting for the fog to blow through," Roy went on.

"It's not going to blow through," I said. There was only the faintest breeze.

"It'll clear up," Roy said. "We're not supposed to have

fog. We're not even supposed to have clouds this time of year." We'd met Roy our first night in town. He walked with a limp, told us he was wounded in Vietnam. Later we heard that Roy had never been farther than Barstow, that he limped because he took some shrapnel in his legs when the transmission in his VW Squareback exploded. So you didn't know whether to believe this guy when he talked about clouds.

"They should just cancel it," I said. "What's the point?"

Roy said, "Son, you don't cancel the Fourth of July. This is America."

Then the show started with a loud, crushing thud that I could feel in my stomach and throat. There was the faintest glow of green from inside the clouds. People whistled and clapped, but I couldn't see why. More fireworks went up. Some were like thunderclaps and war-movie cannons; some were smaller, sharper, like cracks of the bat, a roll on a snare drum, popcorn popping. But it was just noise. Noise, and muted flashes of light just bright enough to remind you of how much you were missing.

"This place is killing me," I said.

"As shitholes go," Trace said, "it's not so bad."

"We're supposed to be moving. That's the whole point. North."

Trace drank a long swallow. "Well," he said, "we could steal a car, if you want." He sat up straight. "I can't believe I didn't think of that sooner."

I shook my head. "We don't need that kind of trouble," I said. Although looking back, it was probably the best thing we could have done.

He lit a cigarette, nodding, and looked out across the

field. "We'll be in Alaska before you know it," he said. He passed me the bottle. "Think of all the money we're going to make. We'll save up and get our own boat for next year. We'll get a boat with one of those Viking heads on the front."

"Boats are expensive," I said. "I'm pretty sure."

"I'll find a way. I always do."

"We can't steal one."

"We'll get a fixer-upper," he said. Though neither of us was any good at fixing things. We'd proved that often enough.

Boom boom boom and clouds choking all the sparkles. It was unbearable, but there wasn't any point in leaving, either.

Around us people were talking. "They're changing the angle. Shooting lower." "That's not safe, is it?" "Keep your head down, then, candypants." Laughs.

The new angle was no better. Just louder. Now and then I saw pinpoints of colored light leak out of the clouds and shine for an instant before they burned out close to the ground. By the end, the field was a big bowl of smoke. Trace and I would be blowing black snot out of our noses for days.

Trace came back to the booth. Somehow he'd gotten the baby to stop crying. He handed the thing to me and went back to the bar to pick up our drinks. I'd never held a baby before. I froze. It wriggled and kicked inside the towel, but its eyes were open and it stared up at me calmly, like it wanted to learn what fear was by watching me. I just held tight and didn't move until

Trace came back. I made him take it out of my hands. He sat down, cradled the baby in both arms, and sucked on his drink through a straw.

"The bartender doesn't recognize it," Trace said. "He said to wait an hour, see if anyone who comes in does. After that, he'll call the cops."

Trace held the baby up to his face and smiled. He rubbed noses with it. If Mo could have seen him like this, she'd never have left him. But it made me nervous.

"Seriously, did you steal it?" I asked.

"Call it by its name," he said. "Call it Mo." He unwrapped the beach towel. Underneath it the baby had on an old, faded green sleeper. On the chest was a cartoon duckling in a rain hat and boots, smiling. A happy, happy duck.

I ran my hand across the tabletop, which was gouged with years of drunken attempts to leave a mark on the world. "Think about this," I said. "If we kept it, who would watch it while we were working?"

"Mo could. Big Mo, I mean."

"I don't think Mo is going to move to Alaska," I said.

"She might," he said. The baby slapped at Trace's glass, but missed. Trace moved the glass away. "Or Little Mo could come on the boat with us," he said. "Little Mo's a good-luck charm. I can feel it. Fish will swarm around our boat."

"Fish don't swarm," I said. "They school."

"That's not the point."

"Exactly," I said. "The point is, we have to find the mother."

We were almost done with our drinks when Roy the

shrapnel guy limped over with a pitcher of beer. He put it on the table. "My treat," he said. "To make up for the shitty fireworks. You picked the wrong year to get stuck here." Roy had been pretty nice to us. The other night he'd bought us a scratch-off lottery ticket, but it lost.

"Thanks," I said. You could smell the fireworks smoke on him. I guess it was on all of us.

He knelt down in front of Trace and the baby as best he could, with his gimp legs and all. The baby gurgled and waved its arms in happy little ovals. "And what have we here?" Roy said.

"It's a baby," I said. "You know whose it is?"

"No," Roy said, but he didn't look at me. He kept his eyes on Trace and the baby. "Is it a boy or a girl?"

"We don't know," Trace said.

"There's an easy way to find out," Roy said.

"Good point," Trace said. "We should check." He moved his drink out of the way and laid the baby on the table.

"Don't," I said. "Not in the middle of the goddamned bar."

"What's the difference?" Roy said.

"It's no big deal, Phil," Trace said. "We ought to know."

"It's not right," I said. I thought the kid deserved better. "Don't do it, Trace," I said, in the voice I used when he took things too far.

Trace picked the baby up. He knew I only challenged him when I meant it. Someone called Roy's name for the next game of pool. "The little guy looks just like you," Roy said to Trace. With his thumb and index finger, he tickled the baby's chin. Then he tickled Trace's, which was thick with stubble. "Tell Sundance to lighten up," he said. He shot me a look and walked over to the pool table.

"He's hitting on you," I said.

Trace shrugged. "I know," he said. "It keeps the drinks coming, though." He smiled a smile that said he was in control, he'd take care of everything, he'd save the day all by himself.

I knew he wasn't happy, though. I knew it bothered him that Mo was probably in bed with her utility infielder, happy and horny after a Yankee win and post-game fireworks in a starry sky over the stadium, while Trace was dead broke and stuck in the desert with Roy chucking his chin. So I wasn't surprised when, once the beer was gone, Trace went quiet and his droopy eye sagged almost all the way closed and he started looking around the place like he couldn't believe his life had come to this. And I wasn't surprised, either, when he laid the baby on the table and went to the pay phone to call big Mo.

The baby waved its arms up and down like a drunk piano player, tiny fingers pattering on the table. I kept my hand on its legs so it wouldn't roll over and fall. My father once told me that when I was little I'd fallen off a picnic table and hit my head on the cement patio. "Your mother was supposed to be watching you," he said. "It's her fault you're a fuckup." He said this the day before Trace and I saw him necking with a teenaged girl in the parking lot behind the bank.

The jukebox was too loud for me to hear what Trace was saying, but in the space between records I thought I heard him say something ridiculous like *We can be a family*. Then Patsy Cline started wailing and Trace was smashing the receiver against the phone, which answered with cheerful pings. People looked over, then looked away. "At least do it on the beat," the bartender shouted, like he'd seen it a hundred times. Trace wound up and gave the receiver one more whack, then threw it down and left it to twist and swing. He came back to the table. I assumed she'd hung up on him, so I didn't ask.

"She wouldn't listen to me," he said. His face looked red, but it might have been the lights.

"Was the Yankee there?"

"Pinch-hitting sonofabitch."

"He's no star," I agreed.

"She didn't believe me about the baby."

"You could have held it up to the phone."

"This baby's pretty quiet," he said.

"You're right," I said. "I wonder if something's wrong with it."

Trace picked up the baby, cradled it. He seemed to relax. "You have to support its head, see?" he said to me. "It doesn't have neck muscles yet."

We needed more to drink, so Trace left to find Roy. I made him take the baby with him, to show it around. Right after he got up, a woman sitting at the bar turned on her stool and looked at me. I'd seen her in the bar before, and she'd been on the hill at the fireworks show, but I hadn't talked to her. She was forty, forty-five, thin, a redhead halfway to gray. She wore jeans and a faded black shirt with the top two or three buttons open and the sleeves rolled up. She walked over, pulled up a chair to the end of the booth, and sat down.

"I hear your name is Sundance," she said.

"It's Phil," I said.

She didn't offer her name, and I didn't ask. "I hear you're running from the law," she said. She had a long, thin nose that twitched when she talked.

"Not really," I said. "I don't think they're chasing us. We just have bench warrants. In Colorado."

She asked what we had done, so I told her. I told her about Trace's DUIs and Resisting Arrests and how he missed a court date because we were up all night drinking with two girls from the community college who, it turned out, were both hot for him. And about how I popped the bail bondsman's guy with a two-by-four when he broke into our apartment a few days later. I didn't know they were allowed to break in. No one teaches you things like that until it's too late.

Trace came back to the table, balancing the baby and a full pitcher. A trail of beer wet the floor behind him.

"Whose beautiful baby is this?" the woman asked. She touched its nose, said something like *wugga-wugga-woo*, and the baby made a noise that might have been a cough or a laugh.

"It's mine," Trace said. He sounded almost like he believed it.

"Four months?" she guessed.

"Three," he said, not missing a beat. "Little Mo's developing faster than most."

"Where's the mother?" she asked.

"New York."

"That's far away," she said.

"The mother," he said, "is a coldhearted, lying, cheating, mitt-chasing bitch." Trace looked pretty drunk. I figured if he was, I must be, too.

"Some men think we all are," she said. I could tell she didn't like him at all. She looked at the baby like she felt sorry for it.

"I don't think he means that about you," I said. "Or about her."

"Of course I don't mean that about *you*," Trace said. "I don't know you. Or how you feel about mitts."

She turned to me. "How about you? Is there a woman in your life?" I watched her nose winking at me.

"There was," I said. "It didn't work out." I had been with Katie a whole year, and then one night, no warning, she told me it was over. *You want me to be just like Mo*, she said. *Well, I'm not Mo. It's not fair and I'm sick of it.* She may have been right. It's just that Mo was a lot more likable. I told her so, and she threw her shoes at me, and I threw them out the window. One got stuck in a tree. It was still there when Trace and I left town.

The woman leaned back in her chair and undid her ponytail. Her hair fell in loose rings past her shoulders. "How old are you?" she asked. "Twenty-seven? Twenty-eight?"

"Twenty-three," I said. It occurred to me that my life was bleeding out of me even faster than I'd thought.

"I have a kid," the woman said. "He's eighteen." She sipped her drink. "He went to jail this week."

"What for?" I asked.

"Joyride. Took a car from the lot at the gas station."

"That's all?" I said.

"That bastard Duffy pressed charges."

"That bastard Duffy has our van," Trace said.

"We broke down," I explained. "We're waiting for him to fix it."

"He's a bastard," she said.

It would turn out that she was right. Duffy was a bastard. The next morning he would tell me and Trace our transmission was shot and he wanted sixteen hundred to replace it. We'd say we couldn't pay that much, so he'd offer us a trade: the van straight up for a '79 Bonneville with no muffler and bad brakes and power windows that wouldn't go down. We'd take it so we could get out of town in a hurry.

Behind me I heard a pool ball smack on the floor and roll away. The baby started to cry, but Trace jiggled it and it stopped. Spit bubbled from its mouth. The woman finished her drink. I watched her neck as she swallowed. The skin around it looked a little loose, baggy. I'd never noticed that on anyone before.

"He didn't even steal anything good," she said. "Just an old Beetle, all rusted to shit. You'd think the boy would have some taste, at least."

"He's lucky to be alive," Trace said. "The transmission could have exploded."

She looked down at the floor. "The judge said I was a bad mother," she said.

"That's terrible," I said. "What'd he have to say that for?" He could have been right, for all I knew, but still.

She set her glass down on the table, hard. "I'm a good

mother," she said. "A damn good mother." Her eyes got wet. It was like she'd been waiting a long time to say this, waiting to find someone who might believe her.

"I'm sure you are," I said.

"I have to take a leak," Trace said. "Can you hold my baby?" He held it out to her.

She sat the baby in her lap and bounced it up and down. "Hello, baby," she said. "What a big baby you are. What a bouncy baby." She kissed it on the top of its head, then smoothed its thin brown hair. Maybe she was a good mother. The baby looked like it was in heaven, eyes half-closed and dreamy. It drooled a little more, and she wiped its mouth with a cocktail napkin. Her eyes were still wet, but she'd started to smile. She was pretty when she smiled. I told her so.

"You should stop hanging around with that guy," she said. "He's holding you back."

I told her I knew that. It was what she wanted to hear.

The baby grabbed her nose, and she wiggled her head from side to side. "That's a nose you've got there," she said. "That's my nose." The baby let go, but kept moving its hand through the air like it still had a nose in it.

"When are you leaving town?" she asked me.

"Tomorrow," I said. "I hope."

"Where've you been staying?"

"In the van," I said.

Her knee touched mine. "Want to stay with me tonight?" she asked. She saw me look at her ring. "I have money for a room," she said.

I didn't even consider saying no. I swept the baby out of

her arms, without thinking, without worrying, like I'd held a baby every day of my life, like I juggled babies in my spare time. That's when the smell hit me. The kid was ripe. She smelled it, too.

"Jackpot," she said.

I found Trace standing with Roy at the pool table, a fresh drink in his hand. I handed him the baby.

"Phil, this baby stinks," Trace said.

"You're going to have to change it," I said. "Maybe feed it, too. You got us into this."

He nodded, slowly. "I'll take care of everything," he said.

"For fuck's sake, Trace," I said, "why'd you take this thing? You could've said no."

He steadied himself against the pool table. "I was called," he said with a stupid smile. "I was called by forces we can't understand."

"Tell the bartender to call the cops," I said. "The mother's not coming. The mother is long fucking gone."

"I'm going to give her some more time," he said.

"I'm leaving," I said. "I have somewhere to go."

"Where? Where is there to go?"

"The motel."

He looked surprised. Then he smiled that same smile again. "Have fun," he said. "I'll be fine here."

"I can't give you any more money," I said. "We're all out."

Roy lit a cigarette and draped his arm around Trace's shoulder. "Don't worry," he said. "Drinks for the daddy are on me."

"Yeah, don't worry," Trace said, smooth and cool. "Roy's buying."

I went back to the booth. She sucked the last ice cubes out of her glass, then whispered to me, lips cold and wet, that she would leave first and I should wait a minute before following. "It's a small town," she explained. I doubt we fooled anyone. People turned to watch me as I walked out. She was waiting in the motel parking lot, money in her hand. She told me to get the room while she waited outside.

The lobby of the Desert Blossom Motel stank of curry. The desk clerk kept looking out the window, like he expected something to come crashing through it. "What's wrong?" I asked him.

"A big party," he said. "The bikers. They like to make trouble. Always they make trouble." He offered me a room on the other side of the motel. I took the key and told him good luck.

She had her tongue in my ear before we got to the top of the cement stairs. We kissed outside the room, leaning on the metal railing. "Look at that view," she said, extending her arm like she was showing me a whole new world.

The fog had blown away, but all I could see was the motel parking lot, some scattered lights, dark desert. "There's nothing to see," I said.

"That's what I mean," she said, and she kissed me again.

I had to push her away to unlock the door. The room was decorated in sad shades of brown. Brown carpet and curtains, brown-and-orange plaid bedspread, two brown-cushioned chairs, a still life of a coconut painted on tan fabric.

It was choking hot inside, and I said so. "It's the middle of summer, sweetie," she said. I kissed her long and hard because I couldn't remember the last time anyone called me sweetie. She took off my shirt. Then she stepped back. "When was the last time you had a shower?" she said.

I counted back to the day we'd left Durango. "Five days," I said.

"Why don't you clean yourself up," she said gently. "I'll go get us a bottle."

In the shower it seemed like I could smell everything that was coming off me, layer by layer, grimy souvenirs of our time on the road. Smoke from fireworks, cigarettes, and ditchweed. Sweat from the heat and the alcohol and pushing the van and losing a dozen straight hands in Vegas. Road dust. And, Jesus, my feet. I smelled like I was dying.

I got out of the shower without drying myself. I switched off the lights in the room. I turned the air conditioner on full and stood in front of it, naked, my eyes closed. At first it wheezed out warm air, but it gradually turned colder, just like I imagined the outside air would as we drove farther and farther north. I imagined me and Trace in Alaska, hauling in huge catches of salmon, soaked to the bone but free and happy in the never-ending daylight and the cold ocean spray. And I imagined myself there in winter, when I'd have a wallet full of money and a head full of stories, ready to endure the long dark and the cold, a cold so deep that it would freeze out everything but your purest self, and finally you'd understand where things had gone so wrong. I stood there in the cold air, thinking, listening to the water drops hitting the thin carpet underneath the air conditioner's sputter and grind, feeling the goose bumps rise on my arms, then my legs, then along my scalp, until she came up behind me and skated her tongue down my spine, trailed it softly with a fingernail. We made love as much as anyone could in that town.

I was scared awake by someone pounding on the door. I sat up and looked around, my heart machine-gunning inside me. It was still dark, and I was alone. At first I thought she might be the one knocking, gone for ice or fresh air and trying to get back in. Then I heard Trace. "Let me in," he said, and in his voice was something that told me he knew she would be gone, and that I should have known, too. I found my shorts in the bathroom and put them on.

I opened the door. Trace stood there, wobbling, holding the wall for support. Roy stood back against the railing, holding a case of beer and a pizza box. "Come on in," I said, "but I'm going to sleep."

The door closed and it was dark.

"I can't see," Trace said.

"Turn on the light," I said.

"I can't *see*," he said, his voice getting high and scared. "Oh, fuck, I'm blind."

I turned on the light next to the bed. Roy stood near the door, still holding the beer and pizza. Trace was lying on the floor on his side, his hands over his eyes, moving his legs like he was running. "I can't scc," hc said.

"Jesus, what's he on?" I said to Roy. "What did you give him?"

"The bikers said it was plain old crank," Roy said. "But you never really know."

I got out of the bed and knelt next to Trace. "Hey, buddy," I said, "it's me. It's Phil. It's all right." I pulled his hands away from his eyes. "You're going to be all right." I wondered if he was going to die, if maybe I should call someone.

He stopped kicking his legs. For a few minutes he didn't say anything, didn't move, but I could see him breathing. Then he blinked and looked at me. "I got us some pizza," he said. He said it like he wanted me to say, *Yes, yes, you sure did. You're a hero.*

Roy sat on the edge of the bed and opened a bottle of beer. Trace pointed at him. "That guy wants to fuck me," he said. "He wants to fuck me in the butt."

I looked at Roy. He sipped his beer and shrugged. "Well, I do," he said. "It's no secret. I told him hours ago."

"Get out of here," I said.

"Cool it, Sundance," he said. "I paid for this stuff. I'm staying until it's gone."

Trace crawled over to the pizza box and took out a slice. His hands were shaking like crazy. "Just eat, Phil," he said. "You gotta eat." And I was pretty hungry, I realized. So I went and put on the rest of my clothes, took a slice, and opened beers for the two of us.

Trace and I sat at the table next to the window, and Roy sat on the bed. We ate and drank. Roy tried a few times to make conversation, but I didn't feel much like talking, and Trace looked busy trying to maintain. Roy gave up, leaned back, and watched us, smoking a clove cigarette. No one spoke, but the room was full of sound: the air conditioner grinding away, the alarm clock humming and flipping numbers on the minute, Trace and I chewing and swallowing, Roy exhaling long streams of smoke. We heard bursts of life from the biker party outside—running footsteps, laughing, a bottle smashed, a country song belted out in three-part discord, a man and a woman cursing each other. A Harley thundered alive and revved senselessly.

"They're from Bakersfield, most of them," Roy said. "They come through here a lot. Best parties this town ever sees." Then he leaned forward and said, "Bobbi's husband is down there with them right now, you know."

"Who's Bobbi?" I asked.

"The woman who brought you here," he said. "That girl gets around. So does her husband. I hope you used a condom." Of course I hadn't. I felt sick. I felt like I'd been stuck in that town forever.

"Me, I never use them," Roy said. "I like to feel everything." Then he rambled on and on about everything he liked to feel, and everything he wanted to do with Trace, and everything was *my cock* this and *my cock* that, and Trace just sat and ate and drank and smiled like it was the best joke he'd ever heard. I got sick of it. I told Roy to shut the hell up and leave. "Look who's Mister Manly all of a sudden," he said. "I bet I could make you cry." He unbuckled his belt. "I could make you call for God."

That's when Trace threw a bottle at him. It shattered on the wall. Roy got wet from the spray.

"Settle down, Butch," Roy said. "I'm just kidding."

Trace took another bottle out of the case and threw that one, too. It barely missed Roy's head. "Leave Phil alone," Trace said.

Roy's mouth opened and he stared at Trace. "It was a *joke*," he said. His voice wavered a little, but he didn't move.

"Trace," I said. "Come on. It's no big deal." But Trace wound up and threw another one and this one thumped Roy in the chest. It made a dull, hollow sound. Roy cried out and jumped off the bed, limped toward the door. Trace kept throwing, and even as I was telling him to stop I found myself picking up a bottle and letting fly.

Roy fell once.

By the time he got the door open there was blood on his face, but I don't know if we hit him straight on or if he got cut by a ricochet. For some reason he stopped in the doorway to yell at us. "You guys are insane," he shouted, his hands in fists. "You guys are sick." I picked up the pint bottle that Bobbi had bought and I threw it. Roy ducked, and it sailed over the railing. I heard it shatter in the parking lot below. Then Roy was gone, his uneven steps thunking down the stairs, his undone buckle jangling.

We'd wrecked the room. The carpet, soaked. The bedside light, broken off the wall and dangling from its wires. The mirror, hit dead-on, angry cracks snaking out from the point of impact. Blooms of beer seeping into the walls, into the fabric of the coconut print. I stripped the sheets and blankets off the bed and Trace crawled onto the bare mattress, the only thing in the room not covered with glass.

"We should get out of here," I said.

"I'm going to sleep," he said. "I'm all of a sudden sleepy."

It was only then that I remembered the baby. I asked him if the cops had taken it.

"Oh, the baby," he said slowly, like he was remembering the night one frame at a time. "The baby."

"Where is it? Did you have it at the party?"

"I gave it to someone," he said. He closed his eyes. "Mo would want one that's her own."

Then he fell asleep. I didn't think that was a good sign. Like maybe his heart was giving out.

I know I should have tried to find the baby. I may even have wanted to. But outside was a dark town with too many people I didn't want to face alone. Inside was Trace, who needed me to make sure he kept breathing. I shook the glass off a chair and sat, watching him, trying not to think about the baby, trying not to think about my life. I watched for cops, but they never came. Neither did any friends of Roy's. No angry husband, no fucked-up bikers. No one. In a way, that made it worse.

Trace woke up just after sunrise, and we walked through an arroyo toward the gas station so we wouldn't be seen. We sat inside the van and waited for that bastard of a mechanic to show up.

We made it to Alaska, but we never got out on a fishing boat. Instead we had to work at the cannery, keeping the drains clear underneath the giant waste pipes, twelve-hour shifts in a chill rain of fish guts. I only lasted a month. I caught pneumonia and had to go home to live with my father and his new wife while I recovered. At the end of the summer, Trace moved to San Francisco with some girl he'd met up there after I'd left. A year later, he would be dead. He hit bottom, and Mo—who'd married the Yankee—offered to fly him back to New York and pay for rehab. His mom told me he hanged himself in the basement at O'Hare during the layover.

Who knew airports even had basements?

One night when we were in Anchorage, Trace won a storytelling contest at a bar. Five-hundred-dollar prize. He told the story of his first kiss—a story that I'd been the first one to hear, that he'd told me the morning after it happened. How he was eleven and she was sixteen, how this older girl had punched her tongue into his mouth and held it there, puffed up like an insult, not moving. How she'd just had lunch and he could taste everything caught in her braces: tuna salad, peanut-butter crackers, banana. It wasn't so much the story as the way he told it, smiling and flapping his arms and dancing and shining with self-deprecation, offering every word like it was his last cigarette and he was glad to let you have it. He blew the five hundred in an hour, buying drinks for all of us in the house. Trace could be a hero. You just had to be watching at the right time.

Like the day we destroyed the house he grew up in with sledgehammers. His sister and her husband had bought it from Trace's mom and wanted to redo the interior, so they hired the two of us to gut the place. I had to stop and rest, but Trace was like a machine, swinging the hammer harder and harder, grunting with every stroke, grunts that echoed louder as one by one the walls fell into rubble. I held the ladder for him as he broke apart the brick above the fireplace, where, for a few years at least, a whole family—mother, father, sister, and Trace—had hung their Christmas stockings. I watched him as the chunks of brick and mortar flew under each stroke, and before long I picked up my hammer again, believing that this was the most honest work either of us would ever do.

Jumping Jacks

~ ~ ~

The skyline of a city you've never visited blazes in night-vision green on your TV screen, and the audio track is all thumps and sirens, pippitypops and batterclangs, and you are reminded of the hiss and spit of sixteen flaming fuses on a pack of jumping jacks on that day twenty years ago when you and your best friend, Bunk, burned six acres of forest to the hot black ground.

Jumping jacks. You buy them on Mott Street from a toothless grocer who natters on about *fun-fun* and *bang-bang* beneath a canopy of decapitated poultry. You decide this man is a fool. Jumping jacks may look like firecrackers, but they don't *bang-bang*. This man knows not what he sells.

Tear open the red paper wrapping, and a fine peppery dust darkens those candy-cane swirls. The fuses are woven in a gorgeous lace of potential energy. Don't you see it? Can't you feel it?

It is a drought-stricken September after a rainless August and a dust-dry July. You and Bunk walk along the trail, kicking through brittle, crackling leaves. Bunk stops, and in his hand suddenly is one of the red paper packages. He unwraps it and says, *Check this out*, and snaps a flame from his fifty-cent Bic and lights it and tosses it into the air, where it becomes a sparkly gunpowder butterfly—eight jacks per wing on a thorax of fuse—and all this before you can say, *Wait*.

The sound? It's a cartoon sound: when a man is startled and his derby hat spins off his head. *Fweeee!* Math lesson: *fweeee!* x 16 = the shit you're in. But for a moment it equals glory: the fireworks spray spark trails of red and purple and gold and blue as they sizzle and wheel and whirl and spit and squeal. It is a chaos of motion and sound and color that to you (a thirteen-year-old suburban goodboy) is epiphany, is rapture, is power and light. And then it is sixteen spinning fire sticks MIRVing through the air.

And then it is sixteen small fires igniting around you. You try to stamp them out; you dance from fire to fire, but flames keep springing back up in the places you've just leaped away from. The air turns autumn-smoke gray. At first the smoke teases you with chestnut-cart sweetness, but then it turns to black choking guilt, and panic rises in your throat and nose. Bunk is standing still. *Let it burn*, he says, and you quit trying to stamp out all those fires, because you believe he knows something you don't. It's a moment of self-doubt masquerading as trust in someone else, that's what it is, and then the flames spread, feeding on the forest, chain-igniting, now waist-high, now chest-high, now head-high, now high-high, and you snap back into yourself, knowing that this is fucked up, something is deeply fucked up and about to get a million times more fucked up, and you are a party to all this fucking up, you've fucked up, you're a fuckup, boy howdy you have really fucked things up this time.

Let it burn, Bunk says again, and the deadness in his voice scares you. His mesmerized stare at the flames licking, crackling, devouring—that scares you, too. You don't understand the hypnotic allure of destruction. You understood that initial rush, that flood of wonder and adrenaline, but not this flat-eyed stare when everything around you is heat and blaze. Destruction scares you shitless, and you run home, alone. You change clothes. You hide your singed-hairless forearms under long sleeves.

The aftermath? You were not caught, Bunk was not caught, no houses burned, and the woods came back strong and true: first as lush, bright green life springing from the scorched ground, then as trees thicker and straighter than before. This, you think twenty years later, was exactly the wrong lesson for you to have learned. Where were the consequences? Where were the fucking *consequences?*

Today—when skylines burn in night-green, when the president's faits are accompli, when smoke rises from spent casings and molten steel and charred skin and newspaper ink and your neighbor's *Good morning!*—you imagine yourself there again, standing in the woods while the trees are burning, desperately turning to Bunk and finding him lock-limbed in a firegasm, already transformed into someone you don't know.

It is Bunk's crackly, dead-leaf voice that now rasps in your ear: *We lit that place on* fire, *man. We burned that motherfucker* down.

Twelve Portraits of Dr. Gachet

~ ~ ~

1. On the avenue des Champs-Elysées (March 1889)

The calliope chuffs merrily as the wooden horses and their child riders bob and spin. The horses are bright, newly painted, white and silver and chestnut and gold. It is warm and sunny, and the air smells of spring—of greening buds and warm gingerbread in the vendors' stalls and rich brown mud churned up by little feet. Thrushes and blackbirds warble in the trees. Laughing children ride in goat-drawn carriages. A soft breeze luffs the pennants knotted to the carousel's spire.

Dr. Gachet's head is light from afternoon brandies with Père Tanguy, the color merchant. He watches as the carousel turns, as the children and their horses disappear from view and then reappear. He is an old man, nearly sixty-one, of uncertain health, and he feels he is entitled to simple pleasures such as this: watching children and horses disappear, reappear, disappear, reappear. Always going, never gone.

Inside his black satchel (along with a stethoscope, six brown-glass bottles of Dr. Gachet's Healthful Elixir, and several packets of dried foxglove) are the seven tubes of paint and two new flat-ferrule brushes he has just purchased from Tanguy. He is not yet sure what he will paint when he returns to Auvers and sets up his easel; perhaps he will attempt that Cézanne winter landscape he has in his vault, or one of the still lifes Émile Bernard sent as payment for treating his ulcers. (Lately, he has derived far greater pleasure from copying works he loves than from wasting supplies on the capricious nothings of his own conception.) Whatever the subject, he will paint, he *must* paint. He is an old man. A lonely widower. Of uncertain health.

He is walking away when a single gunshot pops from somewhere within the Bois de Boulogne. He should not be alarmed—duels are commonplace in the woods—but a sudden panic knots his gut. Two men with guns; just one gunshot. One man has survived, and the other's time is done. This is a certainty he finds terrifying, and he breaks into a run, away from the death in the woods, away from the children whose laughter now feels shrill and oppressive, toward the safety of Tanguy's cluttered shop, with its oily air and paint-spattered floor. The outer world goes silent as his own fast breaths and pumping pulse and ringing ears fill his head.

2. In his garden with the artist, Auvers-sur-Oise (May 21, 1890)

"I am an expert in the field of melancholy," Dr. Gachet says as the two men smoke their pipes. "So believe me when I tell you that you are ill only insofar as you must be ill because you are a great artist. Melancholy afflicts all the great artists."

Puff.

"And, one suspects, it afflicts other great men as well—the great philosophers, revolutionaries, poets, statesmen, and homeopaths. Perhaps also the great chefs and botanists, vintners and swordsmen, conquerors and color grinders. I would not be surprised if the great men in all fields, high or low, were so burdened. Goatherds and carpenters, jugglers and boatswains, accountants and chimney sweeps, theologians and haberdashers, swindling gypsies and dung shovelers, trombone players and hackberry harvesters. But particularly, most powerfully, most certainly, most *inevitably*, melancholy afflicts the great artists."

He shakes the crumbs of bread crust from his plate onto the ground. A fat chicken totters over and pecks contentedly. Across the garden a duck quacks, and a rabbit creeps through a green-and-yellow snarl of moneywort. "My prescription for you is work," the doctor tells the artist. "Work, and more work. Many colors on many canvases. And, let us not forget, a soupspoon of my Elixir each night before you sleep."

He feels the artist studying his face, his eyes, the space he occupies.

"You and I are very much alike," the artist says. "Alike as brothers."

Puff.

3. Signing the work (late May 1890)

The artist delivers his first Auvers canvas to Dr. Gachet like a child bringing home a good mark from school, trembling with excitement and pride. "It is excellent," the doctor says. "Inspired and inspiring." He resists the urge to touch the brushstrokes that have been conjured into a cluster of thatched cottages on a soft golden hillside. He shakes the artist's hand vigorously, claps him on the shoulder. "I am unabashedly optimistic about your treatment," he says.

The artist's eyes are all pupil, and they tremble and jerk. "I must go," he pants. "So many things call out for my eye, my brush."

Dr. Gachet shoos him toward the door. "Go. Work is how great men make their marks."

The door slams, and after Dr. Gachet gets up to close it properly, he returns to his writing table to work on his article—an important piece, to be sure, correcting some of the most alarming provincial misconceptions about public hygiene—but he finds himself unable to concentrate, unable to stop his knees from bouncing or his feet from tapping the floor, unwilling to stop the warmth that rises in him each time he swivels in his chair and looks at the fresh canvas leaning against the wall on top of his tea table. He puts down his pen and takes up a brush.

Within a few hours, he has executed what is, to his eye, a

perfect copy. In the lower left corner, he signs his *nom d'art*, Paul van Rijssel. Then he reconsiders and brushes it out. He experiments with new signatures, rubbing out each one before adding the next, in a new color:

> *Paul van Rijssel*
> *P. van Rijssel*
> *Dr P. Gachet*
> *P.-F. Gachet*
> *Paul Gachet*
> *Paul-Ferdinand*
> *Paul*
> *Paul van R.*
> *Paul van G.*
> *Dr P. van G.*
> *Dr van G.*
> *Paul-Vincent*
> *Vincent-Paul*

When he finally steps away and shakes his head clear, paint stains cover his hands and his clothes, and a smeary blob of Verona green and ocher and burnt sienna has spread, blotting out half of a straw-colored hill. He hurls his brush against the wall, then razors the wet canvas into ribbons.

4. Contemplating the tragus (May 23, 1890)

While the renters are taking dinner in the ground-floor café, Dr. Gachet is behind the auberge with a long, paint-spattered ladder he has found in the grass. He leans the ladder against the building, tests his weight on the bottom rung. A creak, a little give, but sturdy enough. He climbs, catching a splinter in his little finger and suffering a whirl of vertigo when he dares a look down. He wriggles through the attic window, which has been propped open with a stick, and drops himself onto the floor in the room the artist rents for three francs fifty per day. It is a hot, dark, squalid cell. The walls are bare. There is a cot and a chair and a small dressing table and the lingering smell of pipe smoke and armpits and raw plaster.

On the table is a letter to the artist's brother. At the top of the page, the artist's handwriting is crisp and well-spaced, but with each sentence it becomes more cramped, anxious. Dr. Gachet leans over the table and reads. This is what a good doctor does, he tells himself. A good doctor must see how the patient is thinking, must gauge the progress of their work together. A drop of sweat falls from his chin onto the paper. He does not wipe it away for fear of smearing the ink. Halfway down the page, he finds the following words:

> I think we must not count on Dr. Gachet *at all.* First of all
> he is much sicker than I am, I think, or shall we say just
> as much, so that's that. Now when one blind man leads
> another blind man, don't they both fall into the ditch?

When the artist returns from his meal, Dr. Gachet is sitting on the cot, waiting with the letter in his lap. The artist seems confused by the doctor's presence. His pipe dips as his lips slacken. The doctor stands, and he takes the artist firmly by his thin wrist. "I have something to show you," he says, not caring that he hears an angry shake in his voice.

They do not speak as they descend the narrow stairs and exit through the café, where the innkeeper's wife, collecting plates from tables, looks up peevishly to see what all the stomping is about. Dr. Gachet tows the artist behind him as they walk swiftly up the steep, crooked streets, feels the other man's pulse quickening beneath his hand. He feels his own pulse thumping in his neck. The artist stumbles on loose stones, no doubt exaggerating his poor sense of balance. The scent of lilac is heavy in the dusky air. They pass the old church and keep walking until they reach the walled cemetery, a stone field of *Ici Repose* scored by a grid of yellow dusty pathways. The artist seems not to notice that they are surrounded by the dead; he stares off into the whispering wheat fields beyond.

Dr. Gachet removes his blue jacket and drapes it over the stone wall, places his cap upon it, then takes off his shirt and rips it in two. With half the shirt he blindfolds the artist, and while he is tying the knot, he studies the artist's nubby ear. *Lower half of left ear excised*, he notes, *by means of a diagonal incision, beginning posteriorly toward the top of the ear and cutting anteriorly through the tragus. Hemorrhaging likely was extensive.* He runs his thumb over the hardened scar tissue along the line of the cut. The artist tilts his head, leans into the doctor's hand, as if to say, *Carry this, please, carry this.*

Dr. Gachet places the other half of the shirt in the artist's hand. "Put it on me," he says, and the artist, with his long, bony fingers, blindfolds him. The doctor can smell his own sweat in the fabric as well as traces of dinner on the artist's hands—rosemary, goat cheese, some kind of berry.

They hold hands and stride through the cemetery, Dr. Gachet leading them toward the open grave in the northeast corner that was dug that morning for old Madame LaChance. They bark their shins on gravestones and trample flowers and kick-scatter tiny rocks on the pathway until at last they step together into nothing.

Inside the grave, they slip off the blindfolds. Warm pain thrums in the doctor's ankle. Dirt streaks his waxy, sagging belly. The artist sniffs at the sweetly loamy air.

The doctor gestures upward, and together they look up at the rectangle of sky in its frame of brown earth. Night is falling in a mad indigo swirl.

"A beautiful sky," the artist says.

"So you see," the doctor says, "it is not the worst thing, to fall in a ditch."

"We are very much alike, you and I."

"Stop saying that. I am your *doctor*."

A crow alights at the grave's edge and looks down at them, its head atilt in curiosity.

5. Dr. Gachet, with the heartbroken expression of our time [#1] (early June 1890)

Midafternoon in the garden. On the red garden table: foxglove in a vase and two novels by *les frères* Goncourt. My pose, he says, is modeled on Delacroix's painting of the poet

Tasso in the asylum at Ferrara, a pose that suggests that all the world's melancholy is bearing down upon me.

"I enjoy painting portraits," the artist says. "It consoles me up to a certain point for not being a doctor." I tell him not to be absurd. He tells me to hold still.

I hold myself still and listen to the music of his work, to the slap and whisper of brush on canvas. I watch the blue smoke curl from his pinched lips. I feel the air around me turning bluer and bluer. "So much blue," I say.

"Cobalt," he says.

Ah. Of course, cobalt. All around me is cobalt. I am bathed in cobalt, drenched in cobalt, drowning in cobalt. I *feel* in cobalt. As the layers of paint accumulate, my understanding deepens along with the color. I understand that all I have ever known is cobalt, except for occasional periods of ultramarine and Prussian blue and indigo and slate blue and bice blue and cerulean and king's blue and aqua and blue céleste and robin's-egg and lilac and cyanine and lapis lazuli. What I would not give to live in viridian! To dance in vermilion! To love in Paris yellow and madder lake!

But no. I am but a tiny sun-scorched face peeking out, in vain, from the greedy, gulping maw of cobalt. All the world's melancholy, bearing down upon me.

It is a wonder my neck does not snap.

6. Strolling with Henriette
(June 24, 1890)

After dinner, Dr. Gachet feels a burn in his stomach that several spoonsful of Elixir do not extinguish, so he decides to go for a walk. He heads down the hill into town with his goat, Henriette, who follows attentively at his heels, only occasionally falling behind to nibble at the irises that grow along the road. A small girl rushes out of a house to pet the goat. She feeds Henriette crusts of bread and chunks of cheese, which she offers in a grubby palm, until an anxious mother's voice calls her back inside.

Dr. Gachet and Henriette leave the road near the auberge and make their way through knee-high grass to the dilapidated barn where the artist has been storing his many new canvases. It is dark and gloomy inside. The walls are naked wood, with bits of straw poking out from between the boards. The goats in their pens call out when they smell Henriette and scrape their horns against the wooden gates. At the very rear of the barn, in a filthy hay-lined sty, are the artist's works, some on the walls, some jumbled together on the ground. The doctor sits among the canvases and marvels, while Henriette wanders through the barn, sniffing at the other goats.

Two months from now, after the burial, Dr. Gachet will stand in the same spot, choosing which of the paintings to keep for himself, the artist's brother having offered them in gratitude to those who looked after the artist in his last days. Monsieur Ravoux, the innkeeper, will claim but two—the portrait of his daughter and a rushed study of the Auvers Hôtel de Ville—before he shakes the executors' hands and leaves. Dr. Gachet, giddy at all the beauty and genius on display, will choose more than a dozen before he hears someone clear his throat and he feels compelled to stop himself because of the absurd and maddening demands of decorum. "Roll them up, Coco," he will tell his son, in whose dark eyes—heavy-lidded and deep-set like his father's—roils the same hunger for art.

But tonight, as Henriette sniffs and nibbles, Dr. Gachet just sits and looks at these images: the swaying wheat fields and the vineyards, the trees undulating in the wind, a pair of children with knowing smiles, the thatched huts and yuccas, his own twenty-two-year-old daughter glowing angelically in the garden. He sits and marvels at the greatness before him, sits and allows himself for once not to feel lonely and not to feel the weight of melancholy and not to worry about his fickle beat-dropping heart, sits and allows himself to believe—deeply, for once—that he is helping, helping this artist work and live, helping this world become more beautiful, more bearable.

He sits there until Henriette comes up behind him and licks the back of his neck, telling him it is time to go. He hums to her as they climb the hill to his house, even improvises a sprightly little song:

> *Henriette, Henriette,*
> *La plus jolie des toutes les bêtes,*
> *Que penses-tu dans la tête,*
> *Henriette, Henriette?*

And he does not care if anyone hears, if anyone sees, if anyone knows that he is an old man who sings to goats.

7. Head over basin, with daughter Marguerite (June 28, 1890)

She takes a handful of powdered saffron from the pouch and spreads it through his wet hair, kneading and stroking as the powder becomes a thin, grainy paste. She rubs small circles on his scalp, then grasps pinches of his hair, gently tugging as she works the dye in, root to tip. As careful as she is, orange stains spread over his skin at the forehead and temples and will take weeks to wear off.

An hour later, she rinses him. He regards himself in the mirror. Even wet, his hair is still several shades lighter than the artist's.

"Again," he tells her, as orange droplets fall from his face, dotting the towel wrapped around his neck. "More. Redder."

8. In the garden, at gunpoint (July 17, 1890)

The gun is Dr. Gachet's own. Last week he gave it to the artist, who said he needed it to scare away crows that were plaguing him as he painted outdoors. Each afternoon since, the pastoral quiet has been disrupted by gunfire as the artist bangs away up in the fields. And just an hour ago, the dairy farmer Jomaron came pounding on the doctor's front door in a state of vexation. That lunatic is frightening my stock, he complained, and their milk now has the bitter taste of fear. The farmer was unwilling to accept that this was a sacrifice to be made in the name of art; instead he accepted thirty francs in recompense.

And now the black bore of that very gun is inches from Dr. Gachet's face. The artist holds it with two hands that tremble with rage, the barrel tracing paths across the doctor's forehead and back, across and back. Dr. Gachet looks the artist squarely in the eye, as if there is no gun between them, and asks why he is so upset.

"The Guillaumin!" the artist says. "What else?"

The canvas in question: a portrait of a bare-breasted woman lying on a bed, which Armand Guillaumin traded for twelve bottles of Elixir to steady his own erratic heart. It is a lovely work—the artist was even moved to tears upon first beholding it—but Gachet has not yet had time to take it into Paris for Père Tanguy's man to frame it.

"Sacrilege," the artist spits. "Incredible. Nothing in this world has to tolerate more stupidity than a painting when it is regarded by fools. You are no better than the rest. You know *nothing* of art."

"I know the most important thing of art," Dr. Gachet answers. "And that is *work*. Stop behaving like an infant. Be a man, be an artist, and get on with your *work*." The artist attempts a retort, but Gachet stands, interrupting him. "I have been very busy," the doctor says, pointing a stern, steady finger into the artist's chest. "Busy with many things, not least of which is your treatment."

"You are a fraud," the artist seethes. "I am insane to think you can help me."

The doctor still refuses to look at the gun but imagines

the artist's finger softly pressing against the trigger, then lifting, pressing and lifting, pressing and lifting. The only thing
between him and death? A few pounds of force and the in-
decision of a melancholic mind. He holds his ground, holds
the artist's gaze.

A standoff then, for a long, humid stretch of time, until
a door slaps open and Marguerite emerges from the house
with the doctor's afternoon tea. Silently she sets the tea tray
down on the garden table—the doctor watches the other
man's eyes following her—then goes to the artist and rubs
broad reassuring circles on his back. The artist lowers the
gun. He tucks it into the pocket of his blue twill jacket. At a
glance from her father, Marguerite returns to the house, and
the men sit.

Dr. Gachet produces a vial of Elixir from his satchel and
hands it across the table. Obediently, the artist drinks. He
lays his head on the table. "My attacks are returning," he
says. "I see no happy future at all."

"Then you must paint more," the doctor says. "You are
an artist. That *is* your happy future."

Dr. Gachet lies awake that night, tormented by suspicions
that the artist has begun an affair with his sweet Marguerite,
his only daughter. He flips through pages of the Goncourts'
Germinie Lacerteux, absorbing nothing. He wastes his
morning pacing through the house and grumbling to himself; at noon he puts on his boots and goes looking for the
artist outside. He stomps through the cemetery, along the
edge of the wheat field, past Jomaron's jumpy cows. Turning
south, he enters a field of giant sunflowers and walks straight

through it, yanking brilliant yellow heads off their stems as he goes and stamping the flowers into the dirt. Pollen clouds the air, and he is seized by fits of sneezing—ten, eleven, even twelve at a stretch. Sweating and panting, he climbs a grassy hill overlooking the field to rest. His mouth hangs open when he looks out over his path of destruction: the trail of headless stalks has left an emerald serpentine through the field of gold. It is a stunning scene, he thinks, one that must be painted. He races back to town, nose running, lungs constricted and burning, to find the artist. An inner voice tells him that a painting of this scene might be the cure for that poor, great man. And the sooner the canvas is completed, the sooner Dr. Gachet can set up his easel, mix his paints, and create its double.

9. At the artist's deathbed (July 28, 1890)

Dr. Gachet dresses the wound, which is level with the edge of the ribs, just in front of the axillary line. The heart was not hit. "The bullet is inaccessible," he tells the artist, "but you still might be saved."

"Then I have to do it all over again," the artist says.

He dies the next day.

When the artist's brother arrives from Paris and kneels in prayer at the foot of the cot, Dr. Gachet takes out charcoal and paper and begins to sketch, his nerves ajangle, his hands excited. He sketches the sharp ridge of the artist's eyebrows, the sunken cheeks, the knobby chin, the thin downturned lips; sketches as the artist instructed him to, quick as lightning, sheer work and calculation, with his mind strained to the utmost, like an actor on a stage in a difficult role with a hundred things to think of at once. He sketches with sadness and regret and loss and all the anger and agony that come with gazing at the faces of people you have failed. He signs his finished sketch *P. Gachet*, adding his name to the provenance of melancholy, to the provenance of art.

He will give the sketch to the artist's brother, and in a few weeks will receive a letter from him. *I must tell you that it gave my mother immense pleasure to see the drawing you did of my dear brother*, it will read. *Several people who saw it found it admirable.* And Dr. Gachet will run out to the garden and toss the letter in the air and laugh in the purest joy and dance in circles with his arms outstretched while the chickens and ducks and rabbits and cats look on.

10. With the carpenter Levert (July 31, 1890)

The artist's coffin is badly made. As the pallbearers carry it up the winding road, a foul-smelling, dark liquid drips from a crack where the green wood has curled away like a sneering lip. The liquid stains Camille Pissarro's shoes. Émile Bernard turns away, gagging.

The next day, an enraged Dr. Gachet kicks open the door to the carpenter Levert's shop. He pushes the wide-eyed man—much younger and brawnier than he—to the wall, seizes the front of his apron in a fist. "I should kill you," he shouts. "You are a disgrace. An exceptional artist deserves exceptional craftsmanship."

Levert, recovering from the surprise, wrenches the doctor's hand from his apron and twists the older man, clamping his neck and arms in a firm but painless hold. "I am a fine craftsman," Levert tells him flatly. "I am also a businessman, and I was paid only enough for cheap wood."

The doctor fights against him, his legs wheeling and battering the carpenter's shins, his shoulders straining in their sockets. Pinpoints of light in primary colors fleck his vision. He sees a hammer lying on a workbench and wishes he could reach it and bury the claw in the carpenter's skull. Soon, though, he tires, and limp with grief, he begins to wheeze and sob. His tears and mucus glaze the carpenter's bare arm.

After Levert carries him to the doorway and pushes him softly outside, Dr. Gachet turns to face the bigger man and taps his thumb against his own chest. "I promise you," he says, his voice a corvid croak, "that *this* artist's bones will not molder in any coffin of your making."

A month later, thick boards of the finest Provence cypress arrive at his home, and he goes to work in the salon. The plans, which he has drawn himself—designed according to his own dimensions—are spread over the tea table. When he saws, his cuts are clumsy and crooked, and they leave jags and recesses. When he hammers, the nails bend; when he tries to correct them, they bend in new directions, until he angrily pounds them down and they protrude from the wood, gnarled as olive trees. Drifts of sawdust accumulate on the antique rug. Empty Elixir bottles clutter a corner of the room. He flings scraps of ruined wood through the open door to the garden, where they skitter and thunk on the patio bricks. Each night, his children come downstairs in their nightclothes and beg him to stop.

11. Dr. Gachet, with the heartbroken expression of our time [#2] (September 1890)

Instead of a mirror, he uses the first portrait to guide him. It is a rare gift, he thinks, to be able to paint oneself as one has been seen most truthfully—distilled, by a great artist, down to one's very essence. With a strong and sure slap of blue, he begins his work—another Gachet in Tasso's pose, at once homage, memoir, collaboration. His mind whirls and he paints, artist and subject in the purest senses.

Changes: softer sky, a less-jagged blue rain. Remove the Goncourt brothers' books—those cadmium yellow blocks—a distraction, a xanthopsic redundancy—for is not the essence of brotherliness already concentrated in this very act of creation, this self-portrait of portrait? The foxglove must remain, though—yes, those sprigs of *Digitalis purpurea*, those twinned stems of indigo teardrops—it remains—remains—as does all the world's melancholy, always bearing down—

Outside the sun sinks, and the shadows in the room deepen. At one point, his brush hand shakes and tingles so badly that he has to pause to fetch a fresh bottle of Elixir. It is night when he finds himself watching himself from above, watching in the guttering lamplight as his hand, firm and steady, signs the canvas *Vincent*, watching as his body collapses into a chair, watching as this one iteration of him falls into a long, deep, holy sleep.

12. At the Folies Bergère, watching Loïe Fuller (March 1892)

He watches her dance, this American sensation, this ethereal sylph. She pirouettes and spins, her flowing white costume awhirl about her, diaphanous veils fluttering and flaring in light that spins and flashes and wheels and washes in soft creamy white and in cool complementary pairs: pink and pale green, orange and cyan, purple and yellow. She is an unfurling flower, then a flame, then a butterfly.

The music ceases. A barrage of applause then, and the dancer disappears behind the brocaded curtain. The stage is dark, empty, but Dr. Gachet still feels her shining, sinuous grace, feels it as surely as if it were a thick impasto sky under his fingertips.

Closing time is called, and although around him chairs are sliding and groaning on the wooden floor, feet are shuffling, elbows are nudging, and voices are prodding barmen with *One last drink, please*, Dr. Gachet sits quiet and still, his eyes closed, colorful circles and swirls burning the dark inside him. He feels time's fingers curled around his fragile heart, pinching and releasing, pinching and releasing, teasing and teasing him; one day they will clamp down and crush it in a fist. He sees himself stretched out in a white nightgown while his son sits at his bedside sketching his pale dead face. He sees his son and daughter growing old and silent and alone together in the house at Auvers as they sit and watch the red pigments in the artist's paintings fade to bloodless pink. He sees a newborn rabbit, finger-sized, squirming in a patch of thistles in the garden, blind and helpless and moist and new.

A strong arm guides him out into the night. Colors streak and voices yammer and nothing makes sense until he spots that stunted, drunken Toulouse-Lautrec under a gas lamp, wobbling on his cane and addressing a small circle of laughing men and painted women. Dr. Gachet pushes past all the bodies and, breathing heavily, presses a bottle of Elixir into the tiny, crooked man's hand.

"What's this?" the painter asks. "Why are you—?"

"I can help you grow," the doctor says.

The Monkeys Howl,
the Hagfish Feast

~ ~ ~

I t is past midnight. The kid is tired after a long day of marching and slashing through undergrowth and dodging ambushes, but he has been forbidden to sleep. He would like to swim in the cool ocean, but he has also been forbidden to swim or dip or even wade. Nor may he remove his boots to wrinkle his burning toes in the spent waves that bubble over the sand. He has been forbidden even to sit. He has strict orders, from the general himself. He must stand and guard Sergio's head.

The kid does not understand why the head must be guarded. Who would want it? It is a dead thing, caked in blood, with a sour, meaty stink that the ocean breeze cannot carry away. Flies buzz dizzily around it, then alight and prowl its terrain.

The head rests in the dry sand, well above the tide's reach. The kid nudges it with his boot, rolls it facedown. He finds its weight disconcerting. He tamps it solidly so it will not roll back. The flies resettle upon the head as soon as he takes his foot away.

Looking out over the rippling black waves, he reaches into the pocket of his worn canvas trousers and with one finger traces the scalloped edge of the photograph of Alvaro's *novia*. The photograph is the prize of prizes, coveted by all, and now it belongs to him. He wants to take it out to admire her, but the night is moonless—and, in any event, he cannot afford to be seen with his attention on anything but the head. Still, the image of the woman is clear in his mind, feels like something rare and vital. He has been running through forests and jungles and scorched plains with the rebels since his voice was high and thin; he has never tasted a secret kiss in the shadow of a giant yucca, or peeled off a blouse steeped in cool feminine sweat after a climb up the volcano, or raised a skirt in the salty dark under the wharf.

He touches himself through a hole in his pocket and is pleased to encounter his own warmth. He handles himself tenderly, with slow, deliberate strokes of his thumb and forefinger, keeping his arm still so that anyone watching him will see only a soldier attentively performing his duty. In the water, creatures phosphoresce, wink.

Farther up the beach, Alvaro lies open-eyed on his plastic tarp, which crinkles beneath him as he rolls over and back, over and back. He cannot sleep. His feet are covered in sores and blisters and fungus. The sand fleas are biting. The saraguate monkeys are howling in the forest. Most of all, he is angry about the photograph. He is unaccustomed to losing. He is a gambler who leaves little to chance.

Earlier that evening, after the general had given the order, the entire army circled around Sergio and chanted a countdown from ten; on the beat of zero, Alvaro swung his bolo knife, and the blood arced high and misted dozens of dirty faces. The men clustered around the two pieces of Sergio and watched the blood winding through the sand toward the ocean. They placed bets on how far the blood would run.

He should not have risked the photograph, but he could not resist; he could tell the other men were going to guess poorly, planting their sticks high up on the beach, underestimating how much blood there is in a man. His bet raised the stakes, forced all the others to search their packs and pockets for their things of greatest value. Then Alvaro silently computed the coagulation time, the slope of the beach, the absorbency of the black volcanic sand, the temperature and humidity, the speed of the wind off the ocean, and he drove in his stick at the water's edge.

He should have won. Something was wrong with Sergio's blood.

The kid took away quite a haul: two kilos of foot powder; a pocket watch and four rings; a silver revenge charm; dozens of cigars; a necklace of monkey teeth, all polished and sharpened; a vial of bone dust looted from some old saint's reliquary; many grenades; a glass eye; and the photograph. This kid! So young he can't keep his hands off himself for five minutes at a time! The photograph must be retrieved soon. It won't be long before the kid splashes himself all over it.

Around him, a hundred dark lumps on plastic tarps taunt him with their snoring.

In his tent, the general drinks. He can afford to be giddy, even though ammunition is scarce and trench foot has taken its toll. His power has grown immeasurably since he eliminated Sergio. It will grow even more when he delivers the head to his enemy, the Queen. He imagines catapulting it over the castle walls into the garden while the Queen is entertaining guests. He laughs as he imagines a startled servant spilling a tray of canapés into her royal lap.

The general holds out his flask so that he can see his reflection in the polished steel, angles it back and forth, regards himself up and down. Though his belly lolls over the waistband of his shorts, though wiry black hairs sprout from his shoulders and knuckles and ears, though he suffers innumerable tics and twitches, though his nose is but a cone of tin secured by leather straps, he knows that the men all recognize him as a commander of the highest caliber.

He takes a final drink, emptying the flask. He unbuckles his nose and places it in the leather case that also holds his teakwood chessmen. He stretches out and closes his eyes and fine-tunes his battle plan for when they reach the capital: if they surprise the Queen, a swift fianchetto akin to the Catalan Opening; if not, a frontal thrust reminiscent of the Falkbeer Counter Gambit. He imagines the Queen at his feet, defeated. He takes his stiffening cock in his hand and begins to pump furiously. Most nights this is the only way he can fall asleep.

In the photograph, the woman is knee-deep in the ocean, caught in a posture of surprise as a cold wave slaps against her bottom. Her back is arched and her eyes are wide, her thin brows raised high. Her elbows are tight against her sides, and her hands are at her face in a girlish half clench. Her lips are puckered in a tiny perfect o. Splashes of sea foam blur in the air around her. Her swimsuit reveals more thigh than the kid has ever seen. Her nipples jut, pressing against taut fabric. The photograph is sepia-toned, and she is the color of honey.

Nothing in the picture shows scale. No swimmers, no birds, no trawlers or tankers or banana boats, just a blurred horizon, dimly streaked light and dark. The kid wonders if she is taller than he is. He must meet her. He believes he will, someday, believes that she will receive him, that his possession of the photograph connects them in some way they both will honor if not fully understand. Such mysteries, he believes, are the very workings of love.

There is a curved shadow of a finger creeping in from the left border. The kid imagines the finger is his own, that he is the one who snapped the picture. He imagines he can feel the cold water winding around his calves, tickling and numbing. He imagines a softly tugging undertow.

Alvaro, fully cocooned in his tarp, feels another sand flea bite his ear. He is being eaten alive. He unrolls himself and dances in the sand, a furious chorea of swatting and scratching. A man lying nearby sleepily calls out, "Shut up!" and Alvaro tromps toward him and steps on his neck. The man sputters; his legs wheel, his arms flail, his fingers clutch. Alvaro leans harder, feels his bare sole grinding against cartilage, and then releases. "Next time," he says through his teeth, "I will snap it." The man clutches his throat and begins to weep, softly.

Alvaro sees the kid faintly outlined in the dark and slips over the dunes toward him. Lessons must be taught. The gambler is not a man to be trifled with.

In his tent, the general dreams:

He is younger, not yet so thick around the middle. He wears his medals, bright reminders of all he has done in the Queen's service. Night. A whispered, vespertine invitation unfurled in the royal arbor. Tight shadows hiding pearly ankles. Bougainvillea and damiana, creeping ivies, the most fragrant of honeysuckles. Later, a surreptitious climb to her chambers. His legs wobble. His meaty lips quiver. His nose— still years away from the day it is torn off by a bullet—itches. (His nose! What a glorious nose it was, long and full, with an amiable bulb at the tip!) He tries the knob, and it turns.

Hinges creak. Then silence: a long, swollen moment. The scrape and hiss of a match, and one by one, three candles light. The Queen lifts the white sheet, inviting. She is wonderful to discover. He is forced to twist his neck. Vague sensations of galloping and trotting, advancing and encircling. She spins, a slippery diagonal glide, playing herself like the Ponziani Opening. She thrusts out. He tries not to gasp but does. The moment scares him, because he knows what will come next, what comes next every night, what comes next both in the dream and in the memory from which it steals—her jagged, mocking laugh as she grasps him by the throat, nails sharp in his flesh. *With one word, with one wave of my wrist,* she says, *you will have nothing. You will walk along the wharves at midnight, in rags, alone, longing. And you will come to like it there, where the air reeks of waste and rotting shellfish, and where the only girls are toothless whores who beg for needles full of grace and then flick open knives, go straight for your pockets, and say "Surprise" as they slit your throat.* She climbs off him, and he lies there, discarded, shrinking, and helpless, listening to threads popping as she tears the medals from his tunic.

The general awakens long enough to wonder if the traitorous Sergio had similar dreams in the nights before his head came off. It has long been said that all men who have loved the Queen are fated to dream of her.

Sergio remains silent, caught, as he was, on the wrong side of the bolo knife.

The head. The sand. The sea glowing yellow-green. Monkeys howling in the dark.

"You weren't paying attention," Alvaro says. "I could've stolen the head. Easily."

"I heard the sand moving under your feet. You're lucky I didn't shoot."

"If you lose the head, you will die. The general will demand it."

"I'd expect nothing less. This is my duty to the cause."

"Listen closely, kid: there is no cause. This whole war is about the general's cock. He'd call a cease-fire in a flash if the Queen offered him another night in her bed. Do you even know why Sergio was killed? Why it's *his* head upon which your life depends?"

The wind picks up, and palm trees rustle, urgent. The kid mumbles no. He hadn't thought to ask.

"The general believes Sergio was the Queen's lover," Alvaro says.

"That's impossible."

"Exactly: impossible. When could it have happened? Sergio never laid eyes on her. He was with us from the beginning, spent every night sleeping beside us. It's as likely that *you* have fucked the Queen."

"You're saying I couldn't?"

"Shut up, boy. I'm saying the general is a delusional fool. He imagines rivals and traitors all around him. Today it was Sergio. Tomorrow it could be you."

When the kid speaks, his voice flutters. "The general is a great leader," he protests.

From inside the tent, a moan escapes the general's throat. It drones softly on the swift salt breeze.

"The general's mind was carried off along with his nose," Alvaro says. "Listen. Do you hear? That's him, huffing and puffing and yanking his cock. You've never heard it before? Every night, three, four, five times. Someday it'll break off in his hand. And you speak of greatness!"

"Then why are you his *teniente*? Why do you fight at all?"

"I fight because I enjoy killing," Alvaro says. "I enjoy it greatly."

Heavy waves bully the shoreline. The kid is silent.

Alvaro smiles into the dark; faith is so easily stolen, and it is so rarely recovered. His hand shoots out to pluck the photograph from the kid's pocket, but the kid blocks him, holds fast to his wrist with strong fingers.

"It's mine," the kid says.

"I don't like you thinking about my girl like that."

"Like how?"

Alvaro drives his knee into the kid's groin. "Don't play innocent," he says. "You're among men."

The kid writhes in the sand and finds himself looking into Sergio's wide and dead and fly-spotted eyes. The pain, the sight, the stench, all unbearable.

"I could just take her from you, if I wanted," Alvaro says over him, "but I'm a sportsman, so I'll win her back. I'll flip a coin. If I win, you give her to me."

The kid rolls away from the head and retches, once, twice, a third time. "If I win," he manages, "you tell me her name. And where she lives."

"Happily," Alvaro says. "So. Will it be heads or castles?"

The kid staggers to his feet and steps away from Sergio. "Castles." He's had enough of heads for one night.

. . .

The coin is in the air, spinning.

Even if the beach were bathed in moonlight, the kid would not have noticed that Alvaro had two coins in his hand, flipping one while tucking the other against the fleshy mound near his thumb.

Even if there were moonlight, the kid would not notice that the coin is now spinning from head to head, creating a blurred and fluttering but uninterrupted image of the Queen.

Even if there were moonlight, the kid would not notice Alvaro producing the second coin to show him a head and a castle, to prove that the game was fair.

And because there is no moonlight, the kid will not be able to steal one last glimpse of the photograph before handing it over.

"I hope you've kept the picture clean," Alvaro says. "You'll owe me if you've soiled her."

Already the kid's image of her is coming apart. He can recall a length of thigh, eyelashes, nipples, a glistening forehead, a mouth calling to him in a language composed solely of o sounds, but he cannot put them all together to make a woman. "I'll win her back someday," he says.

Alvaro laughs. "Enough. I'm tired, and you and Sergio have a long night ahead."

The kid sniffles. "But the flies," he says. "The smell."

Tears roll down his face, and Alvaro has to stifle his urge

to catch one on his finger so he can taste the shame. Instead, he drapes his arm around the kid's narrow shoulders. "You want some advice? The head won't smell so bad if you rinse it in the ocean."

"I don't want to touch it."

"I will carry it for you. A courtesy between men. Come with me."

Together they walk toward the ocean, the kid kicking sullenly through the dark sand, Alvaro buoyantly swinging the head by its long, stringy hair. At the water's edge, before the kid can grasp what is happening, Alvaro winds up and hurls the head mightily over the waves. The kid hears a faraway splash. He scans the ocean, hoping to spot the head floating in the flickering, luminous water. Hoping even to see ripples. But the head is gone, swept away by the riptide.

Gone. The head is gone. His life is over.

"Adios, kid. It would be best if you started running now." Alvaro smiles. Victories are rarely so complete.

The kid turns slowly in circles, as if considering a direction to run, as if the high, humid forest were not his only option. A sound comes from his throat, and it reminds Alvaro of a baby chinchilla crying for milk. Then, after a few stutter-steps in the sand, the kid sprints up the beach, taking a wide arc around the sleeping army.

Once the kid has disappeared into the trees, Alvaro strolls back to his tarp and settles down to sleep with the photograph buttoned safely inside his shirt pocket. Tomorrow he can go back to selling glimpses of his girl to the men for cupfuls of foot powder, and he can get some relief for his goddamned ruined feet.

In his tent, the general awakens to the soft light of dawn. He buckles on his nose and goes out to greet the men. The morning sky is pink and gray. A barnacled black crab scuttles past his feet. Wood smoke tickles his sinuses as he watches his men rise and drift zombielike toward the fire, lining up for coffee with tin cups dangling from crooked fingers. The general takes a stick of salt-cured meat from his pack, bites into it, and chews contentedly, feeling kingly. *That Alvaro*, he thinks with admiration, *he is a bad bishop in an extreme sense. And these men are my strong pawn center. And Sergio, a captured knight, is off this board for good.*

But where is the kid? Where is the head? Where, god-damnit?

His eyes whirl out of focus. He bites his lip until he tastes blood. Is there no one he can trust? Has everyone been witched by the Queen? How many heads will he have to take? Where will he keep them? His armies will be slowed, so loaded down with heads will they be! There will be a great volley of heads over the castle walls! He will need many more catapults!

He shouts Alvaro's name, demanding answers. A wet shred of meat falls from his mouth into the sand. He bends to retrieve it, puts it back in his mouth just as Alvaro arrives.

"I am appalled," Alvaro says. "I thought the kid was one of us."

Bits of sand grind the general's teeth, but he continues to chew, loudly, adamantly. "Find him," he says.

Alvaro salutes crisply. "You will have his head by noon."

The general returns the salute and watches Alvaro walk among the men, choosing his tracking party. He notes with satisfaction that over the years, his *teniente*'s clothes have gone from a clean olive color to a deep rusty brown. This is the kind of man a general wants in his army, a man who has been flecked, spattered, daubed, smeared, and soaked with the blood of thousands. This is a man who can be believed in.

Summoning calm as only a seasoned commander can, the general gathers the rest of his men around him. He draws the day's troop movements in the sand with a stick, pointing out each of the moves the Queen's army might make in response and sketching countermeasures for each. Afterward, he kicks the sand clean, leaving no trace of his strategy.

Alvaro leads three other men through the forest, all of them wiry and mustachioed, eyes red-rimmed and gleaming. His pounding feet feel strong and new; he is only dimly aware of the burst blisters oozing in his boots. He stops and scans the forest around him. The kid is good, better than he expected—he has left no trail, no footprints in the wet black soil, no broken twigs, no trampled paths. Alvaro must follow his own animal instincts, and he leads the posse through barriers of fallen oaks, snarls of hyena weed, and buzzing clumps of hungry insects. He plunges through a dense thicket of saint's-whip, and the razor-edged leaves and thorny branches slap his face, raising welts and thin, stinging cuts. He races on. This is the part he likes best.

The kid comes to the edge of the trees, many miles north of the rebel camp. He hears voices, and stops, crouches, tries to breathe softly, though his lungs are howling for air. Through the branches he can see a beach. The yellow sand is bright and unfamiliar. Playing in the waves are four young women in frilly pink suits. The water level is at their chests; when waves come, up to their necks. They laugh and splash and toss an inflated ball.

He assumes these girls have been taught to fear the rebels. He knows he must look feral and dangerous, his skin torn, his clothes heavy with black jungle muck, and he knows he must be giving off the myriad stinks of war. But still: what if he shed his cover and approached them? Even if there are men hidden nearby, guarding them—fathers and brothers and uncles, perhaps, armed with guns and knives and scythes and mauls and mattocks—how much worse could his chances be with them? To stay in the jungle alone is to be tracked relentlessly by Alvaro, a man who doesn't just know the odds but *sets* them, a man who shakes fate in his fist as if it were a pair of weighted dice. Play long enough, and you will lose.

He watches. The girls bob in harmony with each lap of wave. He parts the branches for a better view and reaches into his pants; fear—or hope, or both—has stiffened him.

On the beach, ready to decamp, the general regards his men, who stand before him in a sloppy, imprecise line. Only the ones who have filled their boots with precious foot powder are standing still; the others hop from one foot to the other, their toes and heels and arches all in a misery of burn and itch. "Soon," the general promises, "there will be powder for all. My friends, our victory shall yield endless supplies of foot powder—plenty for you and all your loved ones!"

"*Friends? Loved ones?*" some whisper in confusion. "*¿Qué son?*"

The general cuts short his inspirational speech and raises his eyes; he watches, transfixed with wonder, as the southern sky fills with orbs of color: olive and gunmetal and the white of bones. Thin cords extend from each orb, and from each set of cords hangs a man, and together the orbs and their men drift downward and sideward and downward through the blue with the unhurried grace of jellyfish in the deep. Attached to each man is a gun. Angels! Yes! Heavenly reinforcements delivered to him by a higher power whose existence he has never considered! The angels are beautiful, and their firepower much needed—although he wonders, briefly, if a heaven-sent fighting force can be as ruthless as he needs them to be.

His men shout, but he does not hear. They break for the jungle, scattering as they run. Sand flies in lovely rooster tails from beneath the flapping soles of their boots, many of which were recently stripped from the feet of corpses, as they soon will be again.

Only when he is alone on the beach and the gun-toting angels have shed their deflated orbs and are rushing into the jungle and across the beach toward him does his paretic mind absorb the truth. *"Puta de muelle!"* he barks, cursing the Queen. *Wharf whore!* It is her army! Pinning him into a corner with the rarely used but potent Schwarzschild Skewer! A savvy endgame modeled on the Karagoosian Mate! Oh, he understands his position: he is in trouble, he is faced with the zugzwang to end all zugzwangs. He should never have sent Alvaro after the kid! Alvaro would have seen this coming! Alvaro would have orchestrated a lethal counteroffensive! He unholsters his sidearm and races toward the nearest thing he can kill.

The battle is a rout. The general's men are slaughtered, chased by the Queen's army through the jungle, across rivulets and swamps, through gauntlets of venomous tree snakes. One by one, they are fallen upon and butchered like boars. The jungle echoes with truncated, blood-choked cries of *Mamá, Mamá, Mamá.*

The general is taken prisoner, bound at the wrists and ankles with barbed wire that has rusted in the humidity. The Queen's general approaches him with a shining knife, each serration polished to high gleam.

"My orders," the Queen's general says, and the general nods, and his ears are sawn off.

"My orders," the Queen's general says, and the general nods, and his eyes are carved out.

"My orders," the Queen's general says, and the general nods, and a grenade is forced into his mouth. The pin protrudes like a pacifier. Shards of the general's broken teeth litter the black sand and look at home among the pebbles and the shells and the yellowed remains of tiny crustaceans.

His tin nose is unbuckled, taken for a trophy. Someone grabs his hair and holds his head steady as the Queen's general pulls the pin. The metallic *snick* reverberates in his skull. The sand spray of fleeing feet stings his lips and his raw eye sockets.

He does not become a reflective man in his final moments. He does not reminisce about the pet espada monkey that he, as a boy, trained to accompany him on guiro while he played marimba. He does not contemplate the futility of war and pillage and politics and rape. He does not even count down the precious seconds he has left with his head in place. All he thinks about is the Queen and her latest rook, writhing in white sheets and candlelight and mating mating mating mating mating.

And what of Sergio's head? It is several miles offshore, carried by the southeast current that each spring deposits tons of flotsam on the white-sand beaches of some small, nameless cay. The picked-clean skull will, in time, end up on the shore amid a pile of fish remains, desiccated jellies, carapaces of murdered sea turtles, and sour-smelling kelp, all of which will be coated in rainbow slicks of diesel fuel.

Years ago, Sergio might have been saved and resurrected by friendly Nereids. A trio of them might have recovered the head and spirited it away to a shimmering grotto, where they would have conjured a new body—complete with an implanted underwater breathing apparatus—and returned life to him, all the while fondling him gloriously, and he would thereafter have lived with them in benthic bliss. Alas, the Nereids are all gone, scooped up by the trawlers, pressed and vacuum-packed in their own oil.

Instead, the head is feasted upon by marine creatures. Hagfish rasp away pieces of the salt-softened flesh. Spinner crabs twirl their claws and grind off bits of bone. Screw-fanged eels chase each other through the lank weeds of black hair.

Alvaro hears the explosion. It is but a tiny pop in the distance, filtered through thick layers of vegetation, but Alvaro knows war too well to mistake the sound. "The general is dead," he tells the tracking party. "We shall need a new one." He points to a thin man tugging at the ends of his droopy mustache. "Flaco," he says, "you are now the general."

"Not you?" Flaco asks. Age-browned scars are cross-hatched into both his cheeks, severe reminders of some earlier war. Or perhaps this one. Who can remember?

Alvaro shakes his head. He has no interest in titles, in the burdens of formal command.

"In that case, I would like a hat," Flaco says. "Something with a plume. I would have respected our general more if he had worn a hat with a plume."

"We will find you a hat," Alvaro promises. "With a plume. I will hunt the bird myself, once our mission is complete."

Flaco stands straighter as the power takes hold. "A brightly colored bird," he orders. "Preferably orange."

"The most beautiful, orangest bird on the island. I swear to you."

"And also, as I am the general, I demand a peek at your *novia*."

Alvaro smiles. "This time it is a gift from me," he says, unbuttoning his shirt pocket with one swift flick of the wrist. "But a good general knows he cannot just take. Like the other men, he must pay, or he must bet."

The new general nods quickly, comes to him, takes hold of the photograph with greedy fingers and greedy eyes. He angles it back and forth in the sunlight that drains through the trees, as if he is trying to catch a glimpse of the girl from behind, as if he does not understand the laws of two dimensions.

Looking over the new general's shoulder, Alvaro notices a flaw on the surface of the photograph—a spot in the upper-left-hand corner where the image has no gloss. A daub of what might be the kid's dried spunk, marring the horizon behind the wave-slapped girl whose name he no longer remembers.

The kid! It is a shame he can only be killed once!

He snatches the photograph from the new general's hands. "Enough," he says. "We have a mission."

"We have a mission," the new general echoes.

Alvaro runs his thumb along his knife to test the blade, opening a perfect, thin, shallow cut from which no blood leaks. And then they run.

The kid steps out from his hiding place and crosses the beach slowly, with neither stealth nor authority. He removes his shirt and boots, drops his gun in the sand. He is unashamed of his tenting trousers. When the girls spot him, their ball falls uncaught and drifts along the gentle shore break. They watch him closely as he wades out to them.

The water is warmer than he expects. He can feel tiny fish at his feet, tasting the salt from his toes. He holds his hands above his head, palms open and empty. It is, he hopes, a gesture of peace. "Ladies," he says, and it is a difficult word, one that makes his tongue feel parched and clumsy. "Ladies," he says again. "Please don't be afraid."

They are silent. They goggle. The tallest and fairest-skinned girl folds her sun-pinked arms across her chest, as if she must shield from his gaze not just her small, pointed breasts but the ruffled pink fabric that covers them. And yet didn't another girl, the shortest, just now push herself higher in the next wave so that he could see more of her? Didn't she?

They do not speak. He wonders if they are not local, then realizes he is the one who is far from home. Do they understand his accent? Or has his tongue failed him? Or did he forget even to speak those words aloud? As he pushes himself deeper into the water, he hears shouts—male voices, from a boat he now sees moored off the tip of the cove. The men gesture, hustle about the deck, raise anchor, gun the engine.

"Are—?" he asks the girls, but gets no further. "But—" he says, trying again. Then: "I—"

The boat speeds toward them, trailing a violent wake. He tries to read the girls' smooth faces, but he cannot; their expressions offer him nothing he can understand. Will he be driven back into the jungle? Will he die, bullet-riddled, here in the shallows? Or taken in, fed and nursed, led to a bed? He closes his eyes and waits, listening to the motor's roar and the shouts and the breaking waves and the girls' pink silence. Arms high in the air, he delivers himself unto them, hoping.

Splitters

H. A. Quilcock's Profiles in Botany:
A Lost Manuscript Restored

~ ~ ~

Edited by Jonathan Parker Kingslee, Ph.D.[1]

Editor's Introduction

Nineteen sixty-eight marks the centennial of the birth of Hartford Anderton Quilcock,[2] one of the true pioneer botanists of the American West, although it is unlikely that this event will be widely celebrated, or even noticed. Marginalized by the academic Establishment, Quilcock was generally ignored in the botanical literature of his times, with mentions of his name usually relegated to footnotes and nearly always paired with a pejorative. (Examples include:

---

1. Professor of botany at Mulholland University and director of Kingslee Memorial Herbarium, Ventura, Calif.
2. Hart, to his (few) friends.

"irascible," "foul-tempered," "ceaselessly aggrieved," "deranged," "choleric," "vulgar," "disordered," and "unstintingly opprobrious.") Most contemporary texts ignore his work completely. To the extent that he is known today, it is not for his taxonomic efforts—which were extensive and serious, if not always accurate—but for his sensationally inappropriate "Profiles," a series of vituperative attacks on his colleagues. Quilcock's Profiles are now the stuff of chatter at departmental cocktail parties, of lore passed around collecting-trip campfires—sometimes exaggerated, often misconstrued, and utterly unrecognized as the revealing historical and scientific documents they are. In part this is because few people have ever actually read them.

Quilcock intended to publish these profiles in an omnibus volume titled <u>Botanists in the Age of Quilcock: A Field Guide to Frauds, Fools, Thieves, and Demagogues</u>, but he failed to do so before his death in 1931. One suspects he delayed publication because he never viewed the series as complete, as there would always come some new affront to his botanical sensibilities, which would drive him back to his cluttered desk, poison pen in hand.

Most readers will be surprised to find my name listed as editor of the project, since my late father, Philip St. John Kingslee, was the target of Quilcock's most impassioned attacks and most virulent animosity.[3] Further, my mother, the late and much-beloved Anna Sophia Parker—a talented but

---

3. I am not convinced that my father ever took him seriously enough to return his intense dislike.

under-appreciated botanist in her own right—was briefly and unhappily married to Quilcock in her youth. So: how did this man's papers—and thus his legacy—become my responsibility?

Unbeknownst to me or my father, my mother had remained a trusted figure in Quilcock's increasingly sad, difficult, and isolated life. It was only after her own passing three years ago that I discovered she had been the executrix of his estate and writings, as well as the curator of the remains of his personal collection of herbarium samples.[4] All of this she stored in the remote mountain cabin to which she retreated after she divorced my father and quit the academic life. In her will, she expressed her hope that I would publish the papers once everyone about whom Quilcock had written— including herself—was dead.

Understand, reader, that this is an obligation I never sought to take on. Obviously my father would disapprove; one imagines him straightening in his chair and puffing on his pipe, silently but disdainfully, refusing even to dignify the topic at hand with speech.[5] My mother made her wishes clear, though, and I have spent the past three years im-

---

4. Not surprisingly, my mother sought to keep her collegial relationship with Quilcock a closely guarded secret. For one thing, she was married to my father—a towering, imperial presence—but she was also a woman in a male-dominated field and could not afford to be seen as having anything less than a complete commitment to the academic orthodoxy and social pecking order of the day. It was a time, she lamented more than once, when even the most brilliant scientific work would be ignored if it was known that a woman had done it.

5. If you were a student of his, you surely will remember the difficulty of facing him in such moments!

mersing myself in Quilcock's work, reading through the entire corpus of his writings; his field notes; correspondence by, to, and about him; and contemporaneous news reports of his time; as well as giving close examination to his herbarium sheets, both those that have been kept properly in the Kingslee Herbarium at Mulholland and those from his private collection, which came to my mother in a grievous state of deterioration and which she had tried, with limited success, to restore.[6] I have compiled and annotated Quilcock's profiles with the goal of showing that their author was no mere crank, but rather a scrupulous and dedicated man of science, albeit a remarkably disagreeable one.

Before I turn to Quilcock's infamous Profiles, let me present a brief sketch of the man himself. He was born on September 22, 1868, in Dawson County, Nebraska, according to church records. Little else is known about his childhood, as he went to great lengths to conceal the details of his humble origins. One might speculate, perhaps, that he toiled on a family farm, driven hard by a foul-tempered taskmaster of a father, and that he fled this life as quickly as he could, eager to reinvent himself.

Our first record of him as a young adult comes from the payroll logs of the Murchison & Reno Railroad, which shows

---

6. The dispute as to where his collection would be kept was one of Quilcock's last and greatest battles. See profile of Fitzgilbert, infra.

that he signed on in Omaha and shuttled to the west coast and back for several months—all the while marveling at the expanses of frontier land, with their vast and unstudied inventories of flora. He appears to have been dismissed for insubordination and put off the train in Carbondale, Colorado. For the next few years he worked menial jobs in the area, each just long enough to finance his next excursion into the wilds of the western states.

His entry into the world of formal botanical scholarship came as he was working as a handyman at the Strater Hotel in Durango in early May 1892. The legendary Aeneas Scottwell-Scott and his field team spent a night at the hotel en route to collecting in Arizona's Verde Valley, and Quilcock seized the opportunity. "New boy attached himself to us quite forcefully in Durango," Scottwell-Scott wrote. "Possibly a halfwit, but eager to please & thus useful. One hopes he doesn't eat or talk much."[7] By the end of their journey, though, Quilcock had demonstrated both competence and motivation; he was attentive, careful in his treatment of collected materials, and strikingly knowledgeable for a self-taught botanist. Scottwell-Scott himself was an up-by-the-bootstraps sort of fellow, and he may well have seen Quilcock as a younger version of himself—his initial comment about the lad's sense (or lack thereof) notwithstanding.

---

7. The Complete Field Journals of Aeneas Scottwell-Scott, edited by P. St. J. Kingslee (Boston: Stamen Publishing, 1924), p. 141.

Quilcock apprenticed himself to Scottwell-Scott for the next decade, traveling and collecting extensively with him, preparing his samples, and assisting him in publishing his findings, which would be among the most important of the man's illustrious career.[8] Quilcock was utterly devoted to his mentor, and he would come to adopt many of the older man's mannerisms, speech patterns, and habits of dress,[9] his pugilistic tendencies and indifference to hygiene, and—most important—his species concept and his approach to taxonomical change. Quilcock took extreme umbrage whenever any element of Scottwell-Scott's taxonomical work was questioned—let alone corrected, as it was in more than a few cases. Indeed, he reacted more violently to such affronts than he did to challenges to his own work (which, admittedly, tended to arise more commonly). Whether or not Scottwell-Scott returned an equivalent devotion to his as-

---

8. These include his magnum opus, the three-volume <u>Scottwell-Scott Manual: Higher Plants of the American Southwest</u> (1901). A review of both men's field notes proves that Quilcock's contributions were significant, although Scottwell-Scott did not highlight this fact in the publication itself.

9. Scottwell-Scott wore white—all white, always—and his clothing usually bore the stains of his earthy trade. "His only concession to sartorial splendor," Quilcock wrote, "was the monogram he had stitched in blue onto every shirt he owned. Sadly, though not surprisingly, this monogram was a source of great amusement to his rivals and their callow students. In tribute, I have had many articles of clothing stitched with my own initials, also in blue." Of course, this, too, produced snickers in the hallways at Mulholland; indeed, I recall my father delighting in the use of the epithet "hack" on the rare occasions H. A. Quilcock was mentioned in our home.

sistant is unclear—but, one suspects, unlikely, as mentors
are usually reluctant to allow their protégés to emerge from
their long shadows.[10, 11]

---

10. Consider, for example: Quilcock long assumed that he would be the obvious
choice to serve as Scottwell-Scott's official biographer. Instead, the elder botanist chose my father, whom Quilcock had always seen as an interloper as well
as a rival for Scottwell-Scott's approval and respect. Quilcock thought a grave
injustice had been done to him, although he contrived a variety of rationaliza-
tions to place the blame for this upon my father and not upon their mentor. By
this time, it should be noted, my father had already published his Willis Gray
Patterson Prize—winning <u>Endemic Plants of the Sky-Islands of the San Umberto Archipelago</u> (1912), and Quilcock's own reputation was falling to tatters
in the wake of the Cates incident (see profile of Slade Cates, <u>infra</u>) and my father's devastating review in <u>Stamen</u> of his rushed, poorly organized <u>Flora of
Coahuila</u> (1913). Quilcock, for his part, insisted that his manuscript had been
"butchered and bowdlerized" by an overzealous editor who surely had been paid
off by one of his nemeses.

11. A bit of explanation <i>in re</i> taxonomical matters may be in order for lay readers.
Taxonomists in any field generally fall into one of two categories: "splitters" and
"lumpers." In botanical scholarship, acrimonious debates rage over whether
physical differences between two individual (though similar) plants are significant enough that the current definition of the species must be <u>split</u> (i.e., that the
two plants should <i>not</i> be treated as identical in a taxonomical sense) or if these
differences merely illustrate an acceptable amount of individual variation within
a species whose current definition remains valid (i.e., that the two plants should
be <u>lumped</u> together taxonomically). Scottwell-Scott and Quilcock generally pre-
ferred <u>not</u> to split species absent overwhelming evidence of difference, and they
were suspicious of their colleagues who continually racked up publications de-
fining "new" species and bestowing them with names of their own choosing. As
you will see in the profiles, Quilcock detested "knee-jerk splitting"; he saw in this
practice evidence of not just shoddy scholarship but arrogance, self-indulgence,
even hubris. "To name an organism," he wrote in a letter to my mother, "is to
arrogate to oneself the power of a deity, to attempt to stamp the natural world
indelibly with one's mark. Splitters are vile, irredeemable self-servers and pre-
tenders to the divine. The thought of how greatly they outnumber the sensible
people in our field often causes me great anxiety, which then produces grievous
dysfunction of the bowels (specifically mine)." Letter to Anna Sophia Parker,
October 22, 1927.

. . .

The following pages contain selections from the 462 profiles Quilcock wrote for <u>Botanists in the Age of Quilcock</u>.[12] They are presented chronologically in the order that Quilcock wrote them. I hope, reader, that you will find this work informative, that you will be as taken with their author's rebellious spirit as I have been, and that my annotations will offer illuminating context.[13]

—JONATHAN PARKER KINGSLEE, PH.D.

August 4, 1968

Ventura, Calif.

---

12. Note to prospective publishers: the full manuscript of Quilcock's profiles and my commentary will be made available upon my receipt of appropriate remuneration.

13. I had hoped that this compendium would be accepted for publication in <u>Stamen</u>, which has, for better or worse, been the journal of record for botanical scholarship for the last century. I thought it would be fitting, as the journal had never recognized Quilcock during his own lifetime. The only mention of him in its pages? The briefest of obituaries—two paragraphs that fairly dripped with the schadenfreude that plagues academia in general and botany in particular. My hopes for Quilcock's redemption in <u>Stamen</u> went for naught, though, as its editorial board appears to be populated with the ignorant, complacent descendants of the insufferable fools against whom Quilcock so justifiably railed.

Profile #1[14]

Aeneas Scottwell-Scott

I shall begin my series of profiles with a sketch of the botanist to whom all the backbiters, bullies, dullards, and thieves who rule our field ought to compare themselves, so they can see how glaring their deficits are.

Aeneas Scottwell-Scott did not care what others thought of his academic credentials or lack thereof. He did not care what others thought of his scientific conclusions, so confi dent was he in his species concept, his accurate observations

---

14. Quilcock appears to have written this piece within days of his mentor's death on August 4, 1916.

and measurements, his encyclopaedic knowledge of botany and the history of its study. He did not care what others thought of his wardrobe or his failure to marry or his quickness to raise his fists. He did not care what others thought of his disinterest in politics, sport, or washing. He did not care what others thought of his approach to teaching, which was demanding, acerbic, and stern, and which occasionally made use of ear-boxing as a tool for emphasis.

Because he was an autodidact and an iconoclast, he was never embraced by the white-haired panjandra of east-coast botany.[15] These fops and frauds, in their towers of ivory (and ivy), were too busy listening to each other's clarion-blasts of flatus to hear the voice of a brilliant man in the wilderness, a man who routinely risked his physical and financial health trying to bring taxonomic order to the flora of the American West.[16]

Scottwell-Scott improved those of us who studied with him. He taught us to observe meticulously, to avoid the small but disastrous errors that issue from hasty or careless work, and to be upstanding, honest, and truthful in all matters—

---

15. One doubts he would have fared any better in the academic environment of the present, considering the institutional hostility to my Quilcock Project. If certain ultimata from certain deans are to be taken seriously, today's academic may not choose to pursue innovative scholarly writing if there is to be any cost to his "traditional publishing record," "commitment to undergraduate instruction," "grooming," or "maintenance of regular office hours."

16. Scottwell-Scott suffered from a variety of physical ailments, including migraines and debilitating back pain, which caused him to retire from fieldwork far earlier than he wanted. Quilcock's notes suggest that he felt unjustly robbed of his mentor's presence and support.

botanical, financial, personal, or any other. He was a father to me—to all of his students, I once thought—and if he occasionally withheld approval, validation, warmth, or rewards, he did so with our intellectual and personal maturation in mind. (He was not, for example, one of those people who use each opportunity to name a new species as currency for bestowing thanks, building egos, or begging for funds. He most certainly did not bestow such favors on us, his students, except in one instance (<u>Ptimorus kingsleei</u>). In the interests of history, I asked him on several occasions to explain this aberration. I suspect he did not recall, for his mind had dulled a bit with age and infirmity, and he was never forthcoming with a convincing answer. [17] In any event, he never bothered to petition the Society for renaming the offending <u>Ptimorus</u>, which is unsurprising; he was a man of fieldwork, not "paperwork.")

Our field has suffered in recent years because Scottwell-Scott's lessons have fallen out of vogue—even among some of his former protégés, such as the klepto- and ego-maniacal Kingslee and the spineless Fitzgilbert. I have maintained my mentor's high standards and, like him, I have suffered as a result. However, these brief biographies are not the proper venue for detailing my mistreatment by my "colleagues" and by Mulholland University, and thus I shall not do so herein.

---

17. According to Quilcock's diary, an in-his-cups Scottwell-Scott told him that my father received this recognition because "he doesn't need it so damned desperately." In the diary, the quote is followed with brackets that contain twenty-three question marks and a fair number of wild ink spatters.

Profile #19

Clark Sydney Grimshaw

Word comes that Grimshaw has gone and died, although it is hard to fathom how anyone noticed. He had published no work of value for decades. We should be grateful, I suppose, for the prolonged moribundity of his career, as it leaves us with less of his willfully obtuse scholarship to undo.[18]

---

18. Bear in mind that Grimshaw <u>wasn't</u> one of the many botanists with whom Quilcock had quarreled. Quite the contrary: Grimshaw was the best man at Quilcock's wedding to my mother in 1903, and I have found no evidence that the two men ever had a falling-out, personally or academically.

Profile #64

Colton Cates

How Cates escaped this life without being formally repudi-
ated as the serial plagiarist he was[19] is one of the earth's great
mysteries. I suspect a wide-ranging scheme of bribery and/
or intimidation.

Of course, even his meager output of ostensibly honest
botanical work was execrable. Recently I was going over

---

19. Quilcock believed that Cates had presented work by Petitfour, Prim, Schupe,
and Woolforke as his own. Readers should note that Quilcock had no particular
love for any of these four; he simply believed that everyone was entitled to fair
dealing.

some of his final leaflets, and I read his treatment of <u>Amor-</u>
<u>ifera maldita</u>, which makes one feel like planting a specimen
of same on his grave so he can spend eternity studying it
more carefully.

Still, Colton Cates's greatest crime came not in his
work but in his decision to reproduce. The less said about
his offspring—in particular the reprehensible Slade Cates—
the better.[20]

---

20. Quilcock's references to various details of the Cates affair appear <u>infra</u>, in
Profiles #297 (Simoneaux), #298 (Prim & Gjetost), #299 (Brompton), #415
(Tenterhook), #416 (Jones–Anhinga), #417 (Tumressel), and #418 (Cates <u>fils</u>).

Profile #96

Maximilian Unterdorf

Another botanical irritant, this one of the Teutonic variety. Unterdorf splits species left and right and left again, finding dramatic differences where none exist.

What on earth could account for this thuggish Hun's rampage across the hallowed grounds of responsible taxonomy? With most splitters, the cause is usually arrogance, leavened with a wholly inappropriate sense of certitude, although in Unterdorf's case, ineptitude may be an equal factor. Support for this hypothesis can be found in his abhorrent dichotomous key for <u>Lamides</u>, which induces its unsuspecting users to misidentify <u>L. dorothyi</u> as <u>L. bettyi</u>, and vice-versa. (I shall not even waste ink to point out how vulgar it is to name one's botanical discoveries after whichever comely "volunteer assistant" happens to be in the field with one at the moment.)

Unterdorf somehow has no shortage of young and curvaceous dabblers to accompany him as he roams the West whilst allegedly botanizing.[21] One imagines that in the musky air of his laboratory at the University of California–Lake Elsinore, these foolish girls clutch to his tweeds, sigh about how <u>fascinated</u> they are by his <u>work</u>, only to return from the wilds sullied, red-faced, and full of his gametes. At most recent count, sixteen children on this continent (and devil knows how many in the Old Country) call this man Father. One fears one can scarcely put one's pencil down before one will have to pick it up again to mark the score-sheet as another poor lass's cries of labor pain fly to the winds in Tucson or Provo or Ensenada or Heidelberg or wherever else Unterdorf has set foot in his quest to name everything his lizard-lidded eyes fall upon, regardless of whether it is in need of naming.

A hopeless, vile, and unrepentant splitter; as many bastards as he has produced, he has notched ten times that number in bastard species of the botanical variety.

---

21. Ironically, this sounds like the way Quilcock met my mother. She was a junior at Mulholland and a recent student of his when she signed on to assist him and Scottwell-Scott with their summer fieldwork in the Sierra Nevada. They were married in the fall. As mentioned earlier, the union did not last; they separated the following July while collecting at Anza Borrego with a team that included Scottwell-Scott, Fitzgilbert, and my father (who had recently arrived out west, Harvard Ph.D. fresh in hand). It appears that Quilcock was right to have pegged my father right away as a rival not just for Scottwell-Scott's attention but for my mother's as well. "I was awfully young, and I'd never met anyone as passionate as Hart," my mother told me. "When your father showed up, well, he was passionate, too, and he was a man of better moods and cleaner habits and better prospects. Hart wasn't a bad man, but <u>you</u> try living through a winter with him. . . . Besides, Scottwell-Scott didn't want anyone competing for Hart's attention, anyway." (Interview with Anna Sophia Parker, Grizzly Meadow, Nevada [October 1, 1965]).

Profile #121

Guy-Laurent Petitfour

In the human sense, Petitfour's accidental death[22] in 1919 at the age of forty-three was a tragedy. In the botanical sense, it was a blessing, and it ought to have been celebrated with a great feast, much dancing, and that jubilant ritual the Mexicans refer to as "pinyata."

His limitations as a botanist aside, he was also a demented little man. Of his behavior in the field I can say little without risking much emotional distress to myself. To those of you who have heard the whispers that he customarily used

---

22. While collecting in the hills above Tierra Blanca, Petitfour was mistaken for a Villista revolutionary and felled by a <u>federale</u>'s bullet.

his plant press in the service of onanism: I shall not be the one to disabuse you of this notion. Since our first and only expedition together, I have refused to handle any specimen collected by him or his assistants.

As if that were not enough: one morning when we were camped on the banks of the Rio Hondo, he delayed our departure by claiming extreme impaction of the colon, owing to a quantity of Mexican cheese of dubious provenance which he had ingested the night before. (I had not partaken, having the sense to limit my diet to tinned foods while in that primitive land.) He then volunteered the information that he needed to "dig himself out." Perhaps I misunderstood his intentions, owing to his tortured English and lazy diction, but the image that his words conjured will haunt me until they plant my bones in the ground.

The former Mrs. Quilcock always professed respect and admiration for the constipated Frenchman, which I always found baffling, but then, she makes it a practice to search for the best in people. A rare quality indeed, especially in this line of work.

Profile #179

Earl Godfrey Orr

Even at his advanced age, E. G. Orr persists at inflicting his imbecilic work upon us. His "contributions" to systematic botany in general—and to the study of the family <u>Proboscaceae</u> in particular—can only be described as pestilential. An indefatigable supporter of Kingslee, he is also said to be a pederast.[23]

---

23. Quilcock's basis for this assertion remains unknown.

Profile #222

Percival Pickwick

Pickwick was Scottwell-Scott's nemesis and an enemy of science itself. Of his many offenses, the most grievous was his assault on my mentor's reputation with allegations of academic perfidy (not true), clumsy passes at the wives of colleagues (unverified and unlikely), sadistic treatment of assistants (never), and excessive ingestion of both spirits and the various plants sacred to southwestern cave-dwelling tribes (exaggerated, and none of Pickwick's damned business, regardless). I shall not discuss any of his accusations further, as they belong in the ash heaps of history and not to works of academic integrity such as this.

Proof is still being gathered, but I believe that Pickwick sent minions out to infiltrate various herbaria to destroy the type specimens of many species described by Scottwell-Scott so that these species could be recollected, redescribed, and renamed by the dastard himself (e.g.: <u>Involvulus pickwickii</u>, <u>Zosum pickwickii</u>, <u>Pflugeria pickwickii</u>). Also, like that villain Gjetost,[24] Pickwick used his connections to money and power shamelessly. He obstructed Scottwell-Scott's funding, added my mentor and me to the secret blacklist at <u>Stamen</u>, and arranged for the publication (in <u>Stamen</u>, of course) of Kingslee's traitorous review of Scottwell-Scott's magnum opus, <u>An Omnibus Guide to the Western Flora</u>, in which he made great sport of pointing out minor errors in the manuscript.

One of these, the manual's confusion of <u>Claemium bakerii</u> and <u>C. minor</u>, was, in all candor, a result of my own carelessness as I helped Scottwell-Scott prepare the manuscript. I am not above admitting my mistakes, and in any event, Scottwell-Scott delivered to me a reprimand that has served me well in all of my work since, emphasizing as it did the importance of meticulousness. It should be noted that the mistake is a common one; as I demonstrated in <u>Flora of Coahuila</u>,[25] these two species never should have been separated to begin with. In that volume, I proposed that the proper "lumped" species be named <u>S. aeneii</u>, by way of honoring my ailing mentor, but my suggestion (like most of my

---

24. See Profile #298 (Prim & Gjetost), <u>infra</u>.

25. Quilcock, <u>Flora of Coahuila</u>, pp. 96–129.

work) has been studiously ignored by the despots in our field and the henchmen on their payrolls.

But I digress. In the wake of Pickwick's and Kingslee's calumnious campaign of mockery and destruction, <u>An Omnibus Guide to the Western Flora</u> was pulled from publication. Scottwell-Scott was never the same, withdrawing into seclusion, keeping even his allies at a great distance, and sitting idle as his mind and body deteriorated. He had always said he wanted to die while still doing his work—"in the harness," as it were—but these villains robbed him of the ability to do so. I have vowed not to let them grind me down in the same way.

Profile #298

Axel Prim and Per-Fridtjof Gjetost

Together, these photographs of Prim and Gjetost make a dip-tych of thievery, mendacity, and manipulation: Prim, an un-repentant thief and a festering wen on the nether parts of honest botany; Gjetost, a monied but morally bankrupt fool and four-flusher. These two Norsemen worked together so closely that one wonders how they could tell whose trouser pockets were whose.

For decades they perpetuated their slander of me by re-peating ad nauseam all the hoary falsehoods about my part in the Cates debacle and my claim of primacy with respect to the species of <u>Ptimorus</u> discovered on that expedition. No doubt they did so at the direction of that other botanical criminal, Kingslee.[26] (If only any of these men had put a tenth as much effort into their scholarship as they have done in maligning me!) Their damnable fictions have obstructed the funding of my work, which has caused me much anguish and gastrointestinal misfortune.

Prim, at least, has gone and relieved us from his presence. On a visit to Bergen last autumn, he strode into the path of an onrushing taxicab. (No doubt he believed that people and machines alike were obligated to keep clear as he strolled importantly through the city.) Gjetost, the now-hostless parasite, was last seen crying in his lutefisk and writing the inevitable obituary-cum-hagiography for Prim in <u>Stamen</u>. The sooner he, too, strides in front of a heavy conveyance moving at great velocity, the better. We shall all release a long-held sigh.

It cannot fail to dawn on one that Norwegians, who preserve their fish with lye, preserve their careers with lies. (I customarily leave punning to less serious scribes, but here I cannot resist.)

---

26. Quilcock's basis for tracing any conspiracy <u>in re</u> the Cates affair back to my father is unclear. In the absence of same, I find the accusation difficult to credit. He is no more specific with respect to his allegations that my father ever perpetrated an act of academic dishonesty.

Profile #315

Mrs. O. O. Beard,
née Miss Helen Fair

I cannot think of a single female botanist who possesses any of the conniving, mean-spirited, and destructive impulses that we male botanists have "in spades" (as the young people say). Of course, many botanically inclined women have produced embarrassingly half-witted work (e.g., Mrs. Beatrice Hilpert of Modesto, Calif., in her treatment of the genus Catherwoodia [Stamen, 9:1 33–36] and Mrs. C. P. Grüntz of Fredericksburg, Texas, in her Flora of Gillespie County [1924]), but incompetence alone is no sin, merely an irremediable condition. Incompetence twinned with treachery, however, is responsible for much of what is so damnably wrong with American botanical study today.

Miss Helen Fair is no incompetent. She is without doubt one of the most talented and dedicated herborizers around, with a vast knowledge of flora from <u>Adastra</u> to <u>Zyxum</u>. I have known her since she was in her early twenties, a bright spark of a girl who had not much interest in the mundane business of woo and courtship—not as long as there were <u>Rynesia</u> blooming in the desert! Not when the world lacked a definitive dichotomous key for the vast and complicated <u>Modicaceae</u> family!

Miss Fair has gone ahead and gotten herself married, to my heart's sorrow, taking the vows with Mr. O. O. Beard, the genial (if rather epicene) scion of a zinc-mining family and also a passionate lover of ferns. (I was unable to attend the wedding due to my rigorous botanizing schedule, but the former Mrs. Quilcock attended and reported that a spirited time was had by all.) This marriage will produce no issue, obviously, but their wealth has allowed Mrs. Beard to pursue her scientific inquiries free from interference. <u>Brava</u>, I say.[27]

---

27. My research suggests that she was the only woman other than my mother to whom Quilcock ever declared his love. His selection of her, though, was unfortunate; as her scandalous late-life memoir, <u>Pistils at Dawn: An Erotic Life in the World of Botany</u> (1961), made clear, her attentions were reserved for members of the fairer sex.

Profile #331

C. B. Hoyt

C. B. Hoyt was referred to by his colleagues and students at Easterbrook College, Baltimore, as "Ol' Beans and Tape." Though the origins of the sobriquet are obscure, common sense suggests that "tape" derived from his insistence on proper techniques (i.e., no glue!) for specimen preservation on herbarium sheets. (Compare, at your peril, Petitfour's likely choice of adhesive.) As for "beans," I do not know; I shall limit myself to pointing out that Scottwell–Scott and I must not have been alone in thinking him a "windy" old gasbag.

Indeed, Hoyt was a past master in the use of hot air, as he demonstrated ceaselessly while chairing the North American Botanical Fellowship star–chamber proceedings against me, which were held in early 1916 in the aftermath of the Cates outrage. In the same proceeding, Hoyt and his footmen denied my claim against Prim <u>in re</u> primacy <u>in re</u> the discovery of <u>Ptimorus "catesii."</u> (Of course, in my writings I have referred to the species by its rightful name, i.e., the one I had chosen for it: <u>P. annasophii</u>.)[28] Scottwell-Scott, in his pained and miserable last days, roused himself from his sickbed to appear on my behalf, but he was in too compromised a state to make his points forcefully. I remain to this day convinced that I heard back-row snickers from Pickwick, Unterdorf, Prim, and Gjetost while Scottwell-Scott—frail, toothless, tubercular, and aphasic—valiantly defended my character and honesty. Reader, you should understand that a man does not easily forget such vile mistreatment of his mentor.

After the sham proceedings, I pursued remedies against Kingslee, Prim, Hoyt, and the Fellowship in the American civil court system—a Sisyphean endeavor if ever there was one. I served as my own attorney and, with a year or two of study, mastered tort law, in particular the case law regarding defamation, fraud, conversion, trespass to chattels, intentional infliction of emotional distress (and, in a later action, loss of consortium). Sadly, the legal system is also full to the brim with lickspittles, cowards, and toadies, and my efforts were fruitless.

In botanical matters, I find little fault with C. B. Hoyt's work. He would have ranked among the field's finest if he had not styled himself a gray-flanneled despot, lording over the world of plant taxonomy from his Baltimore throne. Power corrupts, yes, but it is only the corrupt who seek power in the first place.

---

28. Imagine my father's reaction when he first heard of Quilcock's attempt to name the species after my mother!

Profile #367

Timothy Edward "Ted" Conklin

Conklin is a well-meaning and eager young pup, but to call him even a mediocre botanist would be a colossal act of charity. He is also a damnably persistent writer of missives to men of science whom he imagines to be his mentors.

I allowed him to accompany me into the field once, to my great disadvantage, because my contracted assistant had quit on the eve of the trek, citing the revelations in the Cates fiasco (which, again, will not be dignified with comment herein). I warned young Conklin as we prepared for our explorations on the rocky outcroppings of Lower California's San Renaldo Bay that the terrain would be difficult, the weather unpredictable, the fauna hostile to our presence. He reassured me he was man enough for work, bouncing about on his toes and fluttering about the room and incessantly chirping gramercies, all in a mode of behavior unrecognizable to me as having any connection to masculinity.

In any event, off to the rocks of San Renaldo were we, and all was promising, as the area had recently enjoyed many steady, nourishing rains. We were crossing the first of many ridges when the boy suddenly cried out in pain, hopping ineffectually on one leg while a copperhead (known in the local jabber as "la vibora") dangled from the other, its fangs firmly implanted in the meat of his ankle. I cried out myself (in exasperation), plucked the snake from his leg, decapitated it with my shovel, made a prompt and neat incision at the site of Conklin's injury, sucked the poison out, applied a clean bandage firmly to the wound, and carried the hysterical child on my shoulders to the nearest malodorous pueblo, where I was forced to wait as he drifted in and out of consciousness.

When little Teddy finally could speak again, he said, "Professor Quilcock, you saved my life!"

"Quite so," I said, "and you ruined a perfectly good day for herborizing."

Despite such incontrovertible evidence that he lacks the tenacity and fortitude required for serious field botany, Conklin has persisted in his pipe dream of joining the ranks of credible plant taxonomists. I recently received word that he had described a new species and named it in my honor: <u>Yuthremides quilcockii</u>. This is unfortunate, as I can see no rational basis for distinguishing this from <u>Y. pubescens</u>, which was ably described by Scottwell-Scott while I was by his side at Cinco Fuentes in 1903.

Well, at least Conklin has successfully joined one group— that of the infernal splitters. Foul company, to be sure, but company nonetheless.

Profile #400

Anna Sophia Parker,
formerly Anna Sophia Kingslee,
formerly Anna Sophia Quilcock,
née Anna Sophia Parker

While prone to both hard-heartedness and questionable judgment <u>in re</u> her personal affairs, the former Mrs. Quilcock is an excellent botanist, and I have always had great respect for her intellect, field technique, taxonomic restraint, native-Texan "can-do" spirit, wavy chestnut locks, and graceful stride. Her career at Mulholland advanced nicely over the last decade,[29] as she was amply rewarded for playing second fid-

---

29. My parents came to Mulholland in 1919, when Fitzgilbert, in his capacity as dean of sciences, recruited my father to take over as chair of the biology department.

dle to her second husband. I have recently received word, though, that she has left academia, ended her marriage, and taken up residence in the wilds of the Sierra. No doubt speculation abounds as to which of her husband's perfidies has driven her to take such dramatic action; propriety forbids me from making my guess publicly. (I will observe, though, that their son, the aspiring botanist Jonathan Parker Kingslee,[30] has received his doctorate from Mulholland and begun his career promisingly with his excellent dissertation on the genus <u>Ataraxidopsis</u>, and that his mother need no longer worry about maintaining the appearances of the nefarious elder Kingslee's career for the boy's sake.)[31]

Further the affiant saith not.

My mother received an assistant professorship as part of the arrangement. Quilcock, of course, took all of this as evidence of a conspiracy to drive him out of the university. Grimly defiant, he held his ground for six tense years, until he was undone by his erratic behavior. See Profile #424 (Fitzgilbert), <u>infra</u>.

30. Imagine my surprise to see my own name mentioned in Quilcock's profiles—and without derogation!

31. When I asked my mother if she understood what Quilcock was insinuating here, she called her nurse for more morphine, then smiled at me and made a cryptic and garbled reference to my eyesight. I did not pursue the matter further. In point of fact, my eyesight is generally excellent, although I do sometimes use corrective lenses to help with some mild farsightedness.

Profile #418

Slade Cates

Slade Cates was a reprobate, a grafter, a thug, and an even bigger fraud than his father, the infamous Colton Cates. Young Cates's career in plant study was inexplicably encouraged by some who ought to have had more respect for the sanctity of our efforts (i.e., Prim, Gjetost, Kingslee), but it was cut short by his fittingly pathetic demise in a Wenatchee snowbank at the age of twenty-six. The barkeep who tossed him outside at closing time made a great contribution to science in doing so.

I was introduced to Cates <u>fils</u>—then a gawky, fuzz-faced stripling of nineteen—in San Diego in May 1915 by those subarctic scoundrels Prim and Gjetost, who had hired him (without my consent, and at my shared expense) to drive the wagon, cook, and manage the gear on the ill-fated trip expedition to Valle de Panza. I was told that the boy had a desire to follow in his late father's footsteps; I suspect, too, that Prim, who had been offering comfort (so to speak) to the recently widowed Mrs. Cates, was doing her a favor by taking the brat out of her hair for a few weeks.

No doubt you have heard this story, reader, but you have heard it only from people with "axes to grind." I shall attempt to clarify the record once again.

From the outset of the expedition, it was clear that Cates had no intention of performing his duties with any degree of effort, fairness, or respect. He was a ceaseless jabberer and a prolific user of the youthful vernacular that sets an educated man's teeth on edge. He ignored my needs utterly, preferring to follow Prim like a puppy, practically drenching the tall Norseman's field tweeds with sycophantic slobber.[32] I finally pulled him aside and told him that since I was paying a third of his wages, I expected a full third's worth of his efforts, and I would be happy to whip him with my own fists if he did not "shape up." The chastened scapegrace made no further argument for the moment, and afterward, he toned down his toadying mildly—although he made great sport of mispronouncing my surname (sophomorically using a short "o" in-

---

32. Prim was, apparently, a man of great patience. Had I been in his boots, my first act would be to call for a burlap sack, a length of rope, and a raging river to hurl the pup into.

stead of the Anglophilic schwa, such a rapier wit was his) throughout the rest of the trip and, indeed, the rest of his blessedly brief career.

We were five miles west of Lago Romesco, traipsing through the foothills, when I spotted a striking indigo <u>Ptimorus</u> growing in the brush. I did not recognize it, even though I had quite recently made an exhaustive study of the entire <u>Hobaceae</u> family. A closer look revealed that it was, in fact, a new species— the first such discovery that was truly my own. I called a halt to the team so I could collect it. The plant (about 16 cm high, branched at the base, with a 14mm corolla, widely bell-shaped) was in plain view twenty yards off the trail. In my excitement, I made the grave error of calling their attention to the specimen. Their suspiciously muted response should have alerted me to the conspiracy that was then forming between them.

On our way home, we stopped in Tia Juana on a Saturday night and managed to find a respectable inn managed by a white couple. I slept soundly, well pleased with all of my finds, particularly the <u>Ptimorus</u>. We all had agreed to stay over until Monday so as to avoid botanizing or traveling on the Sabbath, but in the morning, Prim was rushing around, saying he had urgent business in San Diego. He would take Cates and the wagon, he proposed, and Gjetost would wait with me until the boy returned for us the next day, if I did not object. As I have always been a man who is respectful of others' needs, I agreed. I passed the day playing some senseless Scandinavian card came with Gjetost while he prattled on about fjords and <u>ski</u> and warm woolen undergarments. Only later, back in Ventura, did I realize what Prim's urgent business in San Diego had been: stealing my discovery by sending the plant to Pickwick to have it published before I could attend to it.[33]

Cates did not return until Wednesday, and he showed up with his older brother, "Archie Boy," who was ugly, ill mannered, and of staggeringly subnormal intelligence. They passed by me in the hotel café without saying a word—just giving me the ojo malo, as it were—and went straight up to Gjetost's room. I knew trouble was brewing, so I went to my room, fetched my six-shooter, oiled it, and loaded it with fresh ammunition. I went down to the street and hitched up the team, hoping to ensure my safety with a quick getaway. My three companions emerged from the hotel, though, all shouts and threats—Gjetost, oddly, still wearing some sheeny night garment, though it was noon—and Archie Boy jumped in front of the horses, took them by the bits, and drawled semi-coherently that I would not be going anywhere until I paid my bill in full. I informed him that the bill was not due until we reached San Diego, and in any event, his impertinent and slack-jawed brother had failed to earn even a fraction of my share of his pay. I leveled the gun at the thick-necked dolt. He foolishly tried to climb into the wagon to get at me, so I shot him in the leg and he fell into the Mexican dirt. Slade shouted at me, so I shot him in the leg, too, then gained control of the spooked horses and left the three of them to "hoof it" across the border, limping like the cloven-

---

33. Adding insult to Quilcock's injury, this plant was named—at Prim's suggestion— Ptimorus catesii.

footed devils that they were. (Gjetost, cowardly fop that he is, fled at the mere sight of my weapon. Ever since I discovered the theft that Prim and he had orchestrated, I have wished that I had put some lead into his legs, too.) I am proud to say that neither the Cates boys nor the treacherous Vikings ever succeeded in extracting a cent from me.

The story that these "men" told to the San Diego Union reporter when they arrived was just the first of many mendacious accounts of the event, none of which acknowledged how the lot of them had wronged me. The only person who defended my account of the facts in print—and who stands by it even today, I believe—was the former Mrs. Quilcock. She is a far better woman than Philip St. John Kingslee has ever deserved; that much is certain.

Profile #424

Leslie Foxworth Fitzgilbert

The sad tale of Fitzgilbert's decline is emblematic of the problems that plague the study of botany today. In his younger days, he was a hawk-eyed and methodical collector, a resourceful thinker, and an able steward of taxonomic consistency and decorum. This, lamentably, is a rare combination in our field.

Fitzgilbert, eight years my junior, joined me on the faculty at Mulholland in 1911, a time when the university and the department were held in the highest esteem worldwide. I appreciated him as both a colleague and confidant, just as I had when we were in the field together with Scottwell-

Scott. His work in developing a coherent taxonomy of the family Tulaphyllaceae was top-notch. It remains uncontested, and rightfully so.

Unfortunately, Fitzgilbert was insecure as a man and as a scientist, and he fell victim to the siren call of Advancement. In 1911, when he took over the position and the spacious, well-lit office of the dean of sciences (replacing D. B. Plotz, who had died in that same office while "in the saddle" with a second-year coed, a detail that the newspapers still have not got hold of), he ceased to be a serious botanist and became instead a bureaucratic lickspittle and a coward.

I have little regard for lickspittles, and I believe cowards to be the lowest of the low. Yet these days, people of this miserable ilk obstruct the work of serious scientists, instead pledging their spineless fealty to the university or the donors or the trustees or the police, and leaving men of passion and integrity to twist in the wind. I shall never forget the day that "Fitz," my former friend (and my subordinate on Scottwell-Scott's expeditions!), appeared in the doorway of my office—costumed perfectly as the ascendant functionary that he was, in his new suit and polished shoes (which were, to my untrained eye, of a quite feminine style)—and informed me that my presence in the department—and, indeed, on the campus—would no longer be welcomed if I continued to "persecute," "harass," and "spread lies about" Professor Kingslee.

I was aghast. "Kingslee is a fraud," I said, "and I will not allow the foetid stink of his dishonesty to fall over this university, this department, or my own achievements." I informed him that he and his campus overlords in the Main Building ought to <u>thank</u> me for having the courage to defend the institution's integrity.

"Look," Fitzgilbert said, avoiding my eyes, "this isn't personal."

"The hell it isn't," I said. "Botany is nothing if not personal."

"Yes, well," he said. "I don't know about that."

"Of course you don't," I informed him. "You've prostituted your soul. You've abandoned your work on <u>Aeolia</u>, which was not half-bad, so you can cavort with high-hatted moneymen who want university buildings named for them."

"Yes, well," he said. He made some noises about asking Anna Sophia to join us in the office, as if her presence would make his betrayal of me less odious.

"Leave her out of this," I said. "This has nothing to do with her."

"Doesn't it?" he asked.

I had visions of strangling him. "You know," I said, "there was a time when you had the potential to be mentioned in a breath with, if not Scottwell-Scott, and if not with the few other great men in our field of study, then at least with those about whom, upon their death, one can say with a straight face, 'He was a damned fine botanist.'"

He asked if I was threatening him, an accusation I ignored. "And now?" I continued. "Now you can't even distinguish between <u>Aeolia altimontii</u> and <u>A. brachyloba</u>!"

"That was one mistake in a treatment of a large genus,"

he simpered. "A man makes mistakes. You of all people should understand that."

"I have made mistakes, but handing garland after garland to a filthy cheat will never be one of them." Our discussion went on for some time and, I admit, at some volume.

This is what Bureaucracy does to science, reader. Be warned.

In the following weeks, it became evident that Fitzgilbert and Kingslee would exact their revenge in the financial arrangements in re my personal collection.[34] and I will not tolerate any further delay in holding these fiends to their promise. Even if the courts do not vindicate me (for they have been as emasculated by cowards and lickspittles as has the academy), I shall go down fighting. Scottwell–Scott would have done no less.

On my final visit to the Mulholland campus (15 February 1925), I was walking through the halls of the biology building when I was accosted by Fitzgilbert and one Officer Raymond Calabash of the Ventura Police Department. They told me that a student had reported seeing me "brandishing" a weapon in the washroom. I informed him that I had been doing no "brandishing" whatsoever; I had merely been cleaning and oiling my old six-shooter, a practice of good maintenance

---

34. Fitzgilbert had promised in 1917 that the university would purchase Quilcock's collection at a reasonable price upon his retirement, and Quilcock had planned to live off the proceeds. As Quilcock's mental and physical health declined over the years, his home fell into disrepair, and many of his samples suffered from exposure and infestation. A "reasonable price" for a collection in such a state would no doubt have seemed a pittance to Quilcock.

and responsible firearm handling, not to mention an activity that I find calming. Officer Calabash shook his head—such condescension from a supposed public servant!—and asked me why smart people insist on making "stupid" mistakes.

"Excellent question," I answered. "I take it, then, you've read Fitz's work?"

With Fitzgilbert watching at a distance, clucking his approval, I was roughly ejected from the university to which I gave the best years of my life.

My weapon went unfired, which is unfortunate, as the situation presented an excellent opportunity to impart a few last lessons. In the struggle, though, the officer suffered several sharp kicks to the shin and knee, which must have raised some painful contusions. Just like the Cates boys, Calabash had to limp away from his encounter with H. A. Quilcock, Ph.D. One learns, with age, to take pleasure in one's small triumphs.

I am grateful that the former Mrs. Quilcock was delivering a lecture at the time of this confrontation and did not have to witness such a miscarriage of justice. Philip St. John Kinglsee was off receiving an award in Geneva—a convenient alibi for someone wishing not to leave fingerprints at the scene of a crime he has orchestrated.

Profile #461

Philip St. John Kingslee

Some may purport to enjoy Kingslee's company and behave as if his academic work is anything more than a latticework of lies, but this is only because Kingslee has been given the keys to the castle by the monarchs of our realm, which makes him a strategic ally for any up-and-comer. In truth, his overweening opinion of himself is, to any objective observer, repellent.

Of my dealings with him much has been said, written, narrated around campfires. I have attempted to set the record straight as much as my pledge to the former Mrs. Quilcock allows me, and if the world continues to turn a blind eye to the fact that Kingslee has never set foot within five hundred miles of the sky-islands of San Umberto, and refuses to examine more closely the itineraries of the former Mrs. Quilcock and her occasional botanizing companion, Mrs. Beard, in the spring of 1911, well, in the end there is not a thing I can do about it.

It is far from satisfying to limit myself to this brief profile of botany's greatest disgrace, and I plan to devote an entire volume to Kingslee's perfidious life once I can no longer do fieldwork. (That is a young man's game, and lately I have not been feeling at all like a young man. The old digestive problems have returned with a vengeance, I feel flushed with fever, my heart is racing, my teeth feel loose in my gums, and my ears are ringing maddeningly with high-pitched tones. It is time, I believe, for me to leave my writing desk, pour a tall glass of Scottwell-Scott's favorite Scots whiskey, and turn out the light. As the former Mrs. Quilcock was fond of reminding me, perhaps tomorrow I shall feel better.)[35]

---

35. Hartford Anderton Quilcock died in his secluded and dilapidated cottage in Bondiga Springs, Calif., on October 30, 1931. Unless my collection is incomplete, this was the last Profile he wrote.

S. J. Comerford & Sons
200 Madison Avenue
New York, N.Y. 10016
November 12, 1969

Dr. Jonathan Parker Kingslee
Department of Biology
300 Kingslee Hall
Mulholland University
Ventura, Calif. 93003

Dear Dr. Kingslee,
Thank you for submitting the excerpt from your
manuscript, H. A. Quilcock's Profiles in Botany: A Lost
Manuscript Restored.
I regret to inform you that it does not suit our present
needs. In short, I do not think the arcana of bygone rival-
ries in the world of plant taxonomy will be of interest to lay
readers. I do think there is a home for this manuscript,
although I believe it will be with an academic and not a
commercial publisher. Surely you have options other
than Stamen? I am no expert in academic life, but surely
it is better to publish in a second-tier journal than not to
publish at all.
I am curious, though: Do you mean to imply that your
father represented your mother's work on those "sky-
island" plants as his own, and that she remained silent
about this fraud? Why would your mother agree to cede
credit that was deservedly hers? For his benefit? For yours?

In her own self-interest? How much did Quilcock know about this deception, and why would he—for the most part—maintain her secret?

You ought to make any such claims explicitly; contemporary readers have neither the time nor the inclination to engage in a great deal of inference. If you do choose to add more "sizzle" to the interpersonal relationships about which you write (as Mrs. Beard certainly did in her recent memoir!), then perhaps a publishing house less established than ours will take a chance on your manuscript. Stories of treacherous father figures, long-suffering mothers, and their fractured families are very much in vogue, are they not?

Of course, if I am "off-base" and you have no such doubts about your father's life and work, please forgive my lack of grace in offering these suggestions.

Warmest regards,

Spalding J. Comerford, Jr.
Editor and Vice-President

The Candidate in Bloom

~ ~ ~

The candidate is so tense he cannot walk without crutches. Renata grimaces as she walks behind him through the hotel lobby. Her job is to make him glimmer, and she has been in the election racket long enough to know that when the legs fail, the heart soon follows.

He enters the warm whoosh of the revolving door and fumbles his crutches. The tip of one catches in the door behind him, and the door jars to a stop, trapping him inside. Renata watches through the glass that separates them as he tugs and tugs on the crutch, watches his face darken and puff with toddler frustration. She sighs, then pushes backward on the door, using all her weight to create an inch of space that frees both crutch and man.

He galumphs out through a receiving line of three slouchy bellhops in brass-buttoned red uniforms and incongruous fezzes and makes his way to the rented yellow bus. The door of the bus creaks open, cranked by the driver, who doubles as the campaign's district coordinator of yard signs.

They have a long night ahead, a night of riding in the yellow bus beneath the arc lights of the city. Renata has disapproved of the bus from the beginning. It reeks, she believes, of pale and bloodless populism; it is a desperate, flailing stab at aw-shucks bonhomie, and it is doomed to fail, message-wise. The bus is also a fat, slow-moving target for scorn and bullets, and the campaign has already endured much of both. (Sixty-two bullets, by her count. The scorn is unquantifiable.) But the candidate insisted. "Everyone loves school buses," he said. "We all rode them and sang the same bus songs." Such dreamy evocations of youth are part of his voter appeal, which is limited but passionate. He plays well among registered voters who self-identify as seeking that which cannot be reclaimed.

So, this bus. Idling in a blue diesel haze, it looks as ragged as the baggy-eyed, sag-cheeked candidate himself. Inside, dried gum polka-dots the floor, duct tape has been peeled away from green vinyl seat backs to reveal filler that looks disturbingly like hair, and seat cushions are minefields of sprung coils. She smells an exhaust leak, imagines her lungs turning shriveled and blue.

She and the candidate share a seat, and they lurch forward together as the driver pops the clutch and stalls out. He stammers out an apology to them and jerks the bus into traffic. Angry horns blare all around them. (Seven horns, she counts; seven new votes for the candidate's opponent.)

They rattleclank and rumblebump through the city,

potholing with great frequency. The district coordinator of yard signs is a terrible driver.

West of Main and south of Jefferson, they stop for a photo op at a day-care center. The bus unloads them in a weedy, cracked-concrete playground, where a dozen small children run in circles in the failing light, all shrieks and pounding feet and corduroy squeaks. One boy, freckled and lean and exuding the mirthless aggression of a bully, runs past the candidate and kicks out one of the crutches, sending it scuttering across the macadam. The candidate wobbles but does not fall, thank god, and as he clings to his remaining support, Renata looks daggers at the boy. The boy stops in his tracks, chastened and submissive. He retrieves the crutch and hands it back to the candidate, who tousles the boy's hair and calls him *scamp.*

The press, unfortunately, is nowhere to be seen. She hands disposable cameras to the center's staff: two spent-looking and gray-skinned women who reluctantly stub out their cigarettes to accept the gifts. "For posterity," she tells them.

"Who's Posterity?" one woman says, but she doesn't wait for an answer. The two of them snap pictures as the candidate hands out green lollipops to the children. One little girl bursts into tears, and the candidate looks to Renata with the expression of a drowning man. Renata kneels next to the girl, asks her what's wrong. The girl says she doesn't like green. The candidate looks hurt. Green is his favorite.

Renata asks if she can keep a secret, and the girl snuffles

and nods. Renata tells her that her green lollipop isn't green at all, it's a special new kind of lollipop that looks green and tastes green but is really red. "Really?" the girl asks, and Renata says, "Really," and the girl skips away, happy again. Renata looks to the candidate, expecting to find gratitude. Instead, he looks at her with hangdog credulity: a special new kind of lollipop? Why didn't she tell *him* they had one? And why on earth did she give it away?

Back on the bus. Renata watches as the candidate smiles and waves to the people outside. The sky darkens to purple-black and he waves. Traffic thins and he waves. The law-abiding return to the fragile safety of their apartments and he waves. Crotch-stained drunks teeter in front of liquor stores and he waves. Floppy-jean homeboys flip him the bird and he waves. He waves and waves even when no one is in sight, waves to televised ghosts flickering behind slatted blinds and iron bars, to lampposts and their bright sodium moons, to traffic signals winking amber, to retracted awnings and squat blue mailboxes and bags of trash left out for morning pickup.

The bus stops at a red light. On the sidewalk is a street singer, a bone-thin white kid with a face picked raw by speed-freak nails. He is spitting rapid-fire rhymes in a jagged tenor, punctuated by harmonica lines that punch and squawk and accuse and cry. His shoulders twitch and jerk. At his feet is a cigar box with its lid open; a few coins gleam like miracles in the streetlight. Renata wants to stay and listen, wants to fill his box with coins and tell him that he is beautiful—or someday may be, at least—and that his music, though dissonant and violent and frantic, is in a way beautiful and he has made the world more beautiful than it seemed moments ago (which is to say, wholly unbeautiful, beautiless, beautiempty, beautibereft), but the traffic light turns green, and the bus lurches forward and belches a diesel cloud, and the kid and his music are lost in the engine rumble and the whine of wheels.

She looks at the candidate. His eyes are closed and his head bobs up and down; he is lost in a different rhythm, in a song that, from first note to final echo, exists only in his own head. He soon falls asleep, his forehead resting against a window scratched with childish obscenities: I DID HEIDI G and FAT LARRY FUCKS ASS and assorted stick figures sporting inflated cocks that remind Renata of birthday-clown balloons. She covers him with the powder-blue blanket she carries everywhere in a canvas tote bag. These days he seems to doze off before finishing anything.

There is a snap and a crack and a pop as a bullet passes through the bus, in one shatterproof window and out another. Renata pulls the candidate into her lap, shields him with her own body. He stirs. "Thank you," he says into her skirt.

At the hotel is a phone message from her sister, a woman who has a gated estate, four gifted-and-talented children, and a husband in perfect prostate health but still clutches to the sisterly rivalry of their teenaged years. *Looks like you hitched your wagon to the wrong horse this time,* the message says, the sneer in the words amplified by the desk clerk's meticulous script. What her sister does not understand is that *none* of Renata's horses are the wrong ones. Renata does not lose. Never has. This is why she is sought after, consulted, handsomely compensated, kowtowed to at pancake-and-prayer breakfasts.

With the candidate safely in bed, Renata reads his draft of the speech he will give at tomorrow's fund-raiser with the riverboat-casino kingpins. She is shocked; his mind has slipped even further than she thought. In strong black ink he has written at the top of the first page: *America. It is indescribable. It is so vast that even if we could grasp It by the lower jaw and wrench Its head free, we still could not fathom It.* Then thirty minutes' worth of delusions and outrage and paranoia. The conclusion, double underlined: *America is in trouble today not because Her people have failed, but because She is a voluptuary, screwing everything in sight. Because Her shot of nostalgia was administered with a tainted needle. Because tomorrow it will rain and We will die.* She sighs and opens a fresh notebook. Words spill from her as soon as pen touches paper. It is effortless; she is just the medium, the translator, the messenger to the Messenger.

Seventeen cigarettes, six cups of coffee, and two bowls of frosted cereal later, she is finished. She reads over her work with pride. She has assembled all the right words in their ordained ritual fashion: compressed nuggets of ideas and opinions and stances, crunchy and wholesome, glazed with a honey-sweet slurry of metaphor suited to the crowd: "chance" and "fate" and "the inside straight," "split the aces" and "double down," "loosest slots" and "five-percent vig," "box-cars" and "baccarat" and "a hard ten on the hop." It's a winner. She'd bet her life on it.

The next day, it rains.

A red tarp has been stretched over the deck of the riverboat. Hundreds of chairs are filled with the polyestered bottoms of men and women who fix the odds on slot machines and break the thumbs of card counters. A brass band plays a Sousa march. The tarp billows in the breeze.

Renata takes her place in a chair beside the dais. She is sleep-deprived and feels cotton-headed from seasick pills—she is not one for the water. She watches the small group of supporters gathered on the pier behind crowd-control barricades. Some hold umbrellas and/or children. Some hold home-painted signs, most of which—though her tired eyes can't read clearly at this distance—appear to lack both verbs and sense. GOD COUNTRY PIE, one seems to say. Others: WE PEOPLE ORDER FORM; LEADSHIP TOMORROW; VALLEY SHADOW OIL ROD; and, curiously, CANIDATE. She listens as raindrops paradiddle on the red plastic above her head, barely notices as the candidate crutches past her and takes his place at the lectern. The band stops, but the tuba player misses the cue and blats out an unaccompanied B-flat.

The candidate comes across as a new man. Invigorated by the words she has fed him, he delivers the lines impeccably—

some incantatory, some gruffly barked, some lilting along with the bob of the riverboat itself. Renata, seduced by her own words, has to stop herself from mouthing along. His skin shines with the fervent sweat of a revivalist. Someone says hallelujah; someone answers with amen.

After a final fist in the air, he casts away his crutches and hops down from the dais to the deck, as if he has been healed by his own spirit. There are handshakes and thumbs-ups, ties beating frantic semaphores in the wind, applause like cannon fire. The sun comes out, as if on cue, and casts a blush of red light over everyone.

Renata checks her watch. Five minutes to absorb the glow, then the moorings will be untied and the paddle wheel will turn and they will power down the river while lunching belowdecks. She hopes he does not overeat; at three-thirty he must Charleston at the senior center. She relaxes, lets her head swim freely.

She does not notice the youth lurking in the gangway. He jumps into the candidate's path, brandishing a sword as rusty as the ideology he will later profess to the TV cameras. As the sword cuts its arc through the air, the candidate's legs freeze; he swivels his head, looking for Renata, seeking direction. But what can she say? *Run? Get away?*

The hack is a savage one. The candidate slumps to the whitewashed deck. His mouth opens and closes without a sound. The horror—or the revelation, she can't tell which—in what she is witnessing is this: the motion looks purely mechanical, a clockwork of mandible and maxilla winding down, coming to rest at half-past-gape.

Renata weaves past the writhing pile of men that pins the assassin to the deck. She pushes numbly through the people who, crying and shouting, surround the candidate. As she kneels in the pooling blood, she sees something rise from the corpse, something curling like smoke in the red light. It plumes straight up to the tarp, then winds outward and escapes into sky, tracing a shape that reminds her of a calla lily blossom. She tilts her head and watches, a strange calm warming her like bathwater. She does not feel herself being jostled, does not hear the keening of grief and the roar of panic; still kneeling, she watches as the candidate blooms into mystery, into romance and tragedy, into something she can make holy.

What Is Mine Will Know
My Face

~ ~ ~

I drove Trace to the hospital the day they tried to fix his eye. At the time, I was driving a delivery van for a man called Smiley. It was glossy white and cursed on both sides with a caricature of Smiley's face, in profile, with a gaping comic-book grin—strangely toothless, and scooped out so deep that his ear looked like a hinge on which his whole head depended. SMILEY FLORISTS, it said, and underneath that, *Send a Smile to someone you love!*

Trace was waiting for me in his uncle's garage, which was his home on the nights he didn't stay with his girlfriend, Mo. The garage door was open and Trace was sitting at the foot of his bed, lit by the morning sun. Blue smoke curled up from his cigarette. Around the bed were rakes and bags of potting soil and a rusty seed spreader. Clothing hung on a Peg-Board alongside trowels and shears. He got up and slung the garage door shut behind him. He shook his head at the van. "I can't believe you drive this, Phil," he said, getting in. "I can't believe I'm riding in it."

His bad eye was barely open. It'd been a few weeks since he got kicked, and the swelling was gone, but the skin around the eye hung slack and was smudged with yellowing bruise. The surgeons were going to replace cracked bone with smooth plastic. They'd told him he might lose sight in the eye. There was always risk, they said. I was the one driving him to the hospital because Mo had gotten stuck at the rehab center where she worked nights. One of the anorexics had opened up her own wrists with something sharp, and Mo had to pull an extra shift to do grief counseling.

"How's Mo?" I asked. "Did she sound all right?"

"Don't worry about Mo," he said.

"A girl died," I said.

"Mo will be fine. She's trained for things like that. Whereas I could go blind today, and I'm not trained for that at all."

"Half-blind," I reminded him.

"That's not the point," he said. "The point is, Mo should be here. I got kicked in the face for her. You'd think there'd be some gratitude."

"Think of it this way," I said. "Those girls need her more than you do. They don't even know to eat."

He nodded, then flicked the butt out the window. He leaned forward and examined his eye in the visor mirror, ran a finger along the bone below his eyebrow. "I'm just nervous," he said. "Thanks for the ride."

"I have to go there anyway," I said. "I've got deliveries."

He turned in his seat to check out all the flowers in back. "None of those are for me, are they?"

"Of course not. You're an outpatient."

"Nobody loves me," he said. He slumped in his seat and lit another cigarette.

"Tell you what," I said. "If any of these people turn out to be dead, I'll save their flowers for you."

"Let me see the names," he said. I handed him the clipboard. He read the names aloud, then sucked on his cigarette thoughtfully. "Popovich is the one," he said. "My money's on Popovich."

The van bumped over frost heaves left by the hard winter. We drove past the high school we'd gone to—I'd graduated, he'd been kicked out—and we drove through the double-S turn that killed our friend Crockett while Trace and I were passed out in his backseat. We drove past the golf course where we'd both gotten laid for the first time, up on the thirteenth green, which on clear nights had a view of Manhattan. We drove past the house my parents had to sell when they split up for the first time, and past a marsh where Trace and I had rescued an injured heron when we were little. It was strange, I thought, how much of our lives you could see from this one road.

"You missed some action at the bar last night," Trace said.

"Was Katie there?" She'd left me, and I was avoiding her.

"She was," he said. "She called you a useless fuck."

"Which way did she mean that?"

"Whichever way is worse. She was pretty hostile."

"She's a hostile person." The night she left, she'd thrown her shoes at me, and I threw them out the window. She walked away barefoot. She wanted to go that badly. Her feet were salmon-pink under the streetlights.

"This is one way we're different," Trace said. "I need Mo. You do better alone."

"That's not true," I said. I didn't want it to be true. It was April and warming up, and the smells of the wet piney morning and the flowers in the van made me feel like possibility was in bloom.

The hospital was a concrete tower the color of good teeth. While Trace finished another cigarette—for all he knew, he said, it could be his last—I took the metal cart out of the back of the van and loaded it. Most of the orders were Smiley Healthy Wishes arrangements. The glass doors of the hospital swung open, and we walked in together: Trace, the patient, about to receive a plastic miracle in his head, and me, the messenger of hope.

"Thanks again," he said. "Mo will pick me up when it's over."

"Do you know that for sure?"

"How much grief counseling could those girls need?"

"They're at-risk," I pointed out.

"Fuck," he said, "aren't we all?"

That made a certain kind of sense. "Good luck with your eye," I said.

"I don't need luck," he said. "What I need is less trouble."

It turned out none of my people were dead. Mr. Popovich

did look pretty bad. He was groggy and his room smelled like creeping fear, but he was still breathing away. His sunken eyes tracked the shiny Mylar balloon that came with his flowers. You could tell he liked the way the sun was shimmering on its surface. I spun the balloon a few times so he could watch it send disco-ball lights sweeping over the walls.

After that I delivered Smiley Business Is Blooming! baskets to all the suites in the office park out on 128, a *Merci!* Bouquet to an overperfumed real estate agent, and a cross made of white snapdragons and daisies to the funeral home. In the parking lot behind the funeral home, I shared a bent, skinny joint with a guy I knew called Black Swede, who worked there keeping the carpets clean and the bathrooms sparkling for the grief-stricken. My last stop on the morning run was at a gated estate up on Whippoorwill Road, where I brought fresh irises to a gray-haired lady who was wearing yellow gloves and polishing her silver. She told me she was hosting a prayer group dinner that night, and I guess I said that was nice. She tipped me a twenty that she slipped inside a glossy pamphlet. On the cover, in red block letters, it said, WHAT IS MINE WILL KNOW MY FACE.

"Do you understand the title?" she asked me.

I considered. "Does it mean that things work out in the end?"

"In a way," she said. "As long as you believe."

She waved from her window as I backed the van down her narrow driveway. She was still wearing her rubber gloves.

I pulled into the parking lot behind Smiley's just before noon. The store was sandwiched between a beauty salon and a Chinese restaurant, and by that time of day the air stank of burned hair and fried food. I rolled up the windows in the van, so that the flower smell would stay in. One of the Chinese waiters was outside feeding scraps to a skinny gray cat. I yanked open the steel door, freshly tagged with some word I couldn't make out, and sat at the workbench in the back room.

Smiley was at the counter with a customer, a tall girl in her mid-twenties, a vision of summertime two months early. She wore a white sundress and had a store-bought tan that made her look orange. She was crying, and Smiley was talking to her softly. His words were lost to me in the refrigerators' hum, but when he walked her to the door, she hugged him. Smiley was smooth. He knew the things to say.

Smiley came into the back room and tossed a dozen red roses onto the workbench. "Now, that was a sweet girl," he said. "Nice-looking, too. I'd tell you to chase after her if I didn't think you'd fuck her up even worse."

"She was orange," I said.

"Nice attitude," he said. "One of many reasons you're not getting laid." He opened a cabinet, took out a can of black spray paint, and flipped it to me.

"You want me to kill these flowers with paint?"

"They're cut," he said. "They're already dead."

"But what's this about?"

He spread his arms wide. "It's about love," he preached. "Love and desire and jealousy and hurt feelings and orgasms that make your ears ring for days and resentment and bliss and painful but treatable infections and comfort and yearning and our inevitable exposure as the fickle, craven frauds we all are."

I shook up the paint can and aimed the nozzle at him. "Are you done?" I said.

"Of course, that's just one school of thought," Smiley went on. "There's another that says it's just about some dickhead named Chip who got caught screwing someone he shouldn't have."

The front door chimed open with the first notes of "Edelweiss," and Smiley went to help the customer. I picked up a rose, wrapped a paper towel around the top of the stem, and sprayed in short bursts while I spun the flower slowly in my hand. Then I rained black on it from above, aiming into the folds where I could still see slivers of secret red. I watched from inside a sweet cloud of fumes as color turned into slick, inky black and paint clogged the soft petals, puddling where I'd oversprayed. I laid the roses to dry in a straight line down the edge of the bench. Twelve dead soldiers. My fingers were covered in paint. I should have thought to wear gloves.

I walked out front, where Smiley was misting the tulips. I was feeling spin-headed and a little numb. I wiggled my black fingers at him like a cartoon wizard. "Fear me," I said. "I am evil."

He snorted. "You wouldn't know evil if it crapped in your mouth. Now go clean your hands before you get paint all over my store."

The paint wouldn't come off. I scrubbed and scrubbed, but I was marked.

．　．　．

Business was slow, as usual. Smiley's ex-wife Charlotte had opened up her own flower shop a few blocks away, just to ruin him. Smiley was fighting back—he undercut her prices, had his friends phone in fake orders, put sugar in her delivery van's gas tank. Neither place was doing very well. People could sense that both were trading in spite.

The roses were still drying, and I didn't have any other deliveries, so I told Smiley I was going for a walk. He told me to check behind Charlotte's store and see if any packages had been left there.

"I'm not going to steal anything from Charlotte," I said.

"There's a fifty in it for you," he said. His eyes looked lidless, reptilian.

"Forget it," I told him.

I walked a circle around downtown. I watched a swarm of boys play kill-the-carrier on the middle school field until one kid got tackled on his face and came up bloody. I walked past the bank where Katie worked, but I didn't see her car in the parking lot. I looked into Charlotte's flower shop and saw her sitting at the counter, her chin in her palms, the place empty except for her. I called the hospital from a pay phone to find out about Trace, and when the girl asked if I was family, I said I was his brother. She shuffled some papers and clacked some keys and told me they didn't have any information yet. When I got back to the store, Smiley was in the back room, laying the black roses to rest in a long white box. He put the last one in, fitted the lid on, and tied the box with a black bow. I could see he was having fun.

"These are ready to go," he said. "Got another one for you, too." He passed me a delivery tag. It was an order for a dozen roses, red, long-stemmed, in a Deluxe De-Lovely decorative vase. The tag said the roses were for Mo.

I was about to ask Smiley if Trace could use my employee discount, so maybe he could get back some of what he'd paid, but I stopped myself. Trace couldn't have ordered these roses. Not while he was laid out in a white room with masked people looming over him and wielding lasers and blades, all to fix the damage done by a steel-toed nobody he'd caught pissing on the rug in Mo's bedroom during a party.

"Who ordered these?" I said.

He went out to the counter and came back with the sales slip. "Guy named Archer," he said. "You know him?"

I didn't. I'd never met any Archer.

"Here's the note," Smiley said. He handed me a sealed envelope. *Maureen* was written on the front in bold blue ink. On the other side, this guy had drawn a blue heart over the flap, like it was a seal. He'd drawn badly. The heart was uneven, distended on one side like it had a valve about to blow.

"Can we open this?" I asked. "I need to read it."

"I can't do that," Smiley said. "It would be a serious breach of professional ethics." He took an electric hot pot off one of the shelves above the workbench and filled it in the bathroom sink. He set it in front of me. He plugged it in. "You, on the other hand," he said, "are not bound by any such code."

The water bubbled hot and I waved the envelope gently in the rising steam until I could peel the flap open. On the card inside, the guy had written Mo a poem. A poem that rhymed. Heavy with the platitudes of love. The last line: *Til the next sweet time our bodies meet.* The whole thing was one big sloppy overshare. I'd have been embarrassed for the guy if I didn't already hate him, whoever he was.

"That's some of the cheesiest shit I've ever read," Smiley said over my shoulder. "She ought to dump his ass on principle. Though I do admire his rhyme of 'lilacs are mauve' with 'plush treasure-trove.'"

"Is this a joke?" I asked. "Are you behind this? Is someone fucking with me?"

"What's the problem?" Smiley said.

I told him what the problem was. How Mo was *Trace*'s girlfriend, how they'd been together for some crazy number of years already. How Mo, who was older and had money, had bought us alcohol since we were way before legal, and she hadn't ever minded cleaning me up whenever I got sick on myself or talking me down when the night suddenly turned hopeless. How the two of them had written a toast for me to give at my dad's fourth wedding when all I wanted to do was curse everyone there. How, as combustible as they could be, Trace and Mo were the one thing I could count on anymore. How there wasn't any room for some rhyming motherfucker named Archer.

"Hmm," Smiley said. I knew he'd quit believing in borders like these a long time ago. "The guy paid with a credit card," he offered. "I'll give you the number, if you want."

I told him I needed the rest of the afternoon off. He put his hand on my shoulder. "I'll make you a deal," he said. "Take these to your friend, and deliver the black ones, too, and then you can call it a day. Take the van home with you, just in case

Charlotte's thinking about slashing the tires again." Then he disappeared into the front room, carrying a pail full of lark-spur and Queen Anne's lace.

I stood at Mo's door, holding tightly to the smooth female curves of the vase. The day remained cloudless. A bluer sky never existed.

I rang the bell three, four times. I knocked. I called her name.

She answered the door in a thick green terry-cloth robe big enough for a boxer. Her face was pink and small and her hair was wet. She smelled like lavender.

"I was in the bath," she said. "I was thinking."

"You've had a hard day," I said.

"Like you wouldn't believe."

I handed her the flowers. "Maybe these will help."

"They're beautiful," she said. "Thanks, Phil." She led me into the living room and set the flowers on the coffee table. The air was cool and sweet. Ringo, her German shepherd, was lying on his side in a rectangle of sunlight. He was an old, old dog, arthritic and crooked. Around his head was a plastic cone to keep him from chewing himself open.

"How long does he have to wear that?" I asked.

"Until the end," she said. "Which is probably going to be soon."

"That's sad," I said. "He's a good dog." All around the house were photos of Mo and Ringo growing up alongside each other.

She closed her eyes and smelled the flowers, and while

she was doing it I counted the seven freckles on her nose. I'd been counting her freckles for years. Usually I did it when I was loaded, to reassure myself that things in the world outside my head were still the same.

"Thanks for the roses," she said. "And thanks for driving Trace this morning."

"Aren't you going to open the card?" I said, pointing. It was tucked between the stems, announcing itself whitely.

"How did I miss that?" she said. She plucked it out. She used her palm to hide the blue heart and the ink on the card.

I watched her read, thinking, *Please don't bullshit me, please.*

She looked up when she was done. Her eyes were blue-gray and revealed nothing. "Oh," she said. "They're from my dad." The top of her robe had come open, showing a triangle of smooth, pale skin. With one hand she guided it closed again.

Ringo started to whine. That dog understood things. I got up and brought him a chew toy, a length of thick rope with a knot tied in the middle. He gummed it and looked satisfied.

As I was sitting back down, Mo took hold of my wrist and steered me into the loveseat next to her, smiling like nothing was wrong, like a girl wasn't dead, like Trace wasn't maybe blind by now, like she and I weren't sitting together on a couch where she'd probably screwed a guy named Archer.

"So," she said, "are you going to tell me why your fingers are black?"

"I have been implicated in many things today," I said. "Today I feel cursed."

"You should try turpentine."

"You're changing the subject."

"No, I'm not. Not if the subject is all this paint on you, which it is."

"The subject," I said, "is Archer."

Mo was quiet.

"Archer," I reminded her. "I'd describe him for you, but I don't know who the fuck he is."

She turned her head away slightly and bathwater glistened in the wings of her nose, and I thought she was going to say something to make things better. But she didn't. "That was pretty manipulative," she said, "not telling me you knew."

"I didn't know what I knew," I said.

Across the room, Ringo struggled to his feet and slowly padded into the kitchen. It was a good thing that nothing was chasing him.

"You have to let me tell Trace myself," she said.

"Maybe," I said. I've never been good at thinking on my feet.

"It's very complicated," she said.

"It's not complicated at all," I said. "There are rules. You play by them."

"Don't lecture me about relationships, Phil. I know you. I've seen you alone for years, and I've seen you with Katie, which was even worse."

Outside, an ice cream truck tunefully drove by. I didn't know they even had those anymore.

"Please let me tell him," she said. "Today's not the day. He's having his surgery, and it's been a tough day for me, too. I saw a girl die this morning, Phil. I spent all day trying to get twenty-five more girls not to die any quicker. I'm tired."

"Tell me about her," I said. "The girl who died." I was out of other things to say.

So she told me. She told me about how the girl's father had started molesting her when she was eight, how he liked to go to titty bars and teach her the dancers' moves when he came home, how the mother was a boozy mess, how the girl had quit eating and gone to the hospital near death, all bony and jagged, covered in fuzz like a duckling. How the girl had been getting better in rehab, until this.

"That's the worst thing I've ever heard," I said.

Mo's cheeks had lost their bathtub glow. I could see how exhausted she was. I pulled her into me, and she hugged back, and I said maybe I didn't have to tell Trace today. I could have sat there forever, basking in her aura of bath oils and gratitude. *You know me*, I thought. *You know my face.*

And this is what I thought about as I nuzzled into her neck: I thought about easing my hand under the collar of her robe and rubbing the back of her neck, and then tracing small circles all the way around to the exposed skin at her throat, and how everything would be quiet except for breathing. I thought about sliding my hand down to her chest and underneath the robe. I thought about kissing her, our faces so close I wouldn't be able to see the seven freckles. I thought about all those things. But when I put my hand on the back of her neck, she said, "Don't. Phil? Don't." And I said, "I wasn't," but she had felt it somehow—in my fingers, maybe. So I put one hand back on her shoulder, and the other on the arm of the sofa, and we sat. Then I thought about Trace, and I thought about how sometimes loyalty is the one thing keeping you from dropping to your knees and howling like a poisoned animal in all your aloneness.

There was a lazy jingle of dog tags from the kitchen, and Ringo reappeared, tottering over to us. He put his front paws on Mo's knees and tried to lift himself into her lap. His rear trembled with effort. Mo pulled away from me and helped the big dog up. She poked her head into the cone and let him lick her face. "You're a good dog, Ringo," she said. "That's my baby." She stood up with the dog in her arms. I was surprised she could carry him. "He needs to go outside," she said. She was fumbling with the back door when the phone rang, and she asked me to get it. I answered and got Trace's voice in my ear.

"Phil? Did I call you? I meant to call Mo." He sounded half-asleep and confused.

"I'm at Mo's," I said. "I had a delivery nearby."

He didn't question. "I'm ready to go," he said. "It went well. They tell me it's art." Which turned out not to be true. Even though they kept the socket from collapsing in on itself, his eye would always look half-closed and droopy.

"You sure you want me to get you? I'm still driving the van."

"That fucking van," he said. "Let's drive that thing to Mexico, the three of us. We'll sell it down there and party with the money. We'll all learn how to surf. We'll find you a señorita who will let you sip tequila from her navel."

"I doubt Mo's up for that," I said. "She seems pretty tired."

"Let her rest, then. And get here quick. This place is full of dying people."

I joined Mo outside. The lawn was a hearty chemical green that matched her robe. The dog was in some tall grass along the fence, whimpering, straining to squeeze out some relief. I told her I was heading out to pick up Trace.

"You're going to bring him straight back here, right?" she said, and I told her yes, I would.

"Why don't you take the roses with you," she said. "You can do something good with them. Surprise someone."

On the way to the hospital, I stopped at a red light and saw a little boy in overalls in the car next to me. He looked at Smiley's face with its demon grin and burst into tears. Who could blame him?

Trace was standing in front of the glass doors when I pulled up. His eye was covered in gauze. He got into the van slowly, like an old man.

"Your hands," he said.

"Tell me about it," I said.

He pulled down the sun visor and looked in the mirror. He fingered the bandages. "Want to see what it looks like?" he said. "I do."

"I think you should keep that on," I said. "It's probably holding something in place."

He flipped the visor back up. I put the van in gear, but Trace held up his hand and told me to hang on. He reached into his shirt and pulled out two surgical masks. He handed one to me. "Put it on," he said. "So no one will know it's us in this ridiculous fucking van."

"I have to do a delivery," I said. "I have to bring some guy black roses."

"All the more reason," he said.

So we put on the masks. All you could see of his face was the one good eye. "Let's get some smoke first," Trace said. "I'm an eye patient. It's medicinal." The mask tented and pocketed around his mouth as he spoke.

I drove us to Galactic Mary's house, and I handed Trace the twenty I'd gotten from the rich old lady with the Jesus pamphlet. He went in, still a little wobbly, and came back out with a bag. We smoked in the van. I drove fast into town, racing the high, but Mary's stuff hit fast and hard. It was good. It was just the thing.

My mind was liquid by the time we got to the art-supply store where Chip worked. I opened the back of the van and saw both sets of roses, the vase of red and the box of black. I could have taken in the red ones instead, but I knew that wouldn't solve Chip's problems.

Trace got out of the van. "I'm coming with you," he said. "I want to see what happens when this poor bastard's heart breaks."

We walked into the store together. There was a balding guy in a starched white shirt at the counter. "I have flowers for Chip," I said.

"Chip works in framing," he said. "I'll call him." He

switched on an intercom and said, "Hey, everyone come up front. Chip's getting flowers."

"You didn't need to call everyone," I said.

"What's with the masks?" the guy asked.

"There's something going around," Trace said.

People gathered around the counter: a few girls my age, a few middle-aged women in floral-print dresses, some guys who were probably musicians by night. A spaniel-faced guy in a skinny tie walked up to me. "I'm Chip," he said. I pictured him and the orange girl together on a beach, contentedly sipping rum drinks. It seemed possible. I thought about pulling the box away, I swear I did, but Chip had his hands on it, firmly, hopefully. I tried to whisper that he should open it in private, but he couldn't hear me because of the mask and because his coworkers were chanting his name.

I turned to go, but Trace grabbed my arm.

"Chip and Alice," somebody sang. "Sitting in a tree."

Chip opened the box, and there they were. All twelve of them, black as Bibles. Everyone shut up. A few people noticed my hands. Chip stood there with his mouth open. I felt grateful not to be him. I may have laughed, from relief.

"What's wrong with you?" the bald guy said to me. "Why would you do this to someone?"

Before I could say anything, Trace put his finger in the guy's chest and said, "Don't shoot the messenger, fucko."

I watched Chip. Understanding crept into his face in a deepening red. "I think," he said quietly, still looking at the roses, "I think you guys should get the hell out of here."

I led Trace away. Someone called us assholes.

"Hey," Trace said as we pulled away from the curb. "That guy stiffed you on the tip."

"Plenty of people don't tip me," I said. "This guy had a reason not to."

"It's a matter of respect for the working man," he said. "You have mouths to feed."

"I have mouths?"

"I'm kind of hungry," he said. His good eye crinkled up. Under the mask, he was smiling.

"To the diner, then," I said. "My treat, I guess."

"Ah, don't worry about it," he said. "Right now I should be with Mo. She and I both had to stare down Death today."

We were on an overpass, and beneath us cars flew brightly down the parkway. I said, "We could be in Mexico in three days if we headed south right now."

He lit the pipe again, passed it to me. "We can't go without Mo. Especially since she's the only one who knows Spanish."

I exhaled. "Do you know anyone named Archer?" I asked.

"Don't think so. Who's that?"

"It's just a name I heard," I said, and I thought, *Just a name, just one name standing in for all the men who are better than you and me.*

Mo was sitting on her front steps, dressed, waiting and smoking. Trace thanked me and got out. I was going to tell him to take Archer's roses and give them to her, but I decided Mo was right: I ought to use them myself. I deserved to.

I watched as Trace hugged her. She touched his bandage

gently, and he said something I couldn't make out and they laughed. I honked as I pulled away from the curb, and they waved at me.

This was my plan for the roses: I would go back to Smiley's and get Alice the orange girl's address out of the files. I would bring her the red roses and show her that her bad luck had boomeranged into good.

I drove to the store and parked the van in front, because Smiley bolted the back door after hours. I unlocked the front door and stepped in over the electric eye that triggered "Edelweiss." The light was on in the back room. I heard a clatter and a yelp, and I ran to the doorway. I saw Smiley on top of Charlotte on the workbench, pumping away. They were naked. They looked pale and waxy under the fluorescent light.

Smiley stopped and looked at me, a smirk creeping up from the corner of his mouth. Charlotte tilted her head back over the edge of the bench and looked at me upside down. Her blond hair reached almost to the floor, where clothes and scissors and ribbon rolls and stems of baby's breath were scattered around. I could still smell paint fumes, faintly.

"I'll just go now," I said.

"Bright and early tomorrow," Smiley said. "No more of this late shit, okay?"

"No more," I said. "I swear."

"*Hasta*, then."

"Good-bye," said upside-down Charlotte.

・ ・ ・

That night I went to a bar a few towns over, where I didn't know anyone. The place was quiet. I was sitting by myself, tracing wet rings on the scarred oak, when a guy tapped me on the shoulder and started grunting at me. No words, just sounds, nasal and urgent. I told him to leave me alone. The last thing I wanted to do was try to figure someone else out. But the guy just got louder, more insistent, and he started jabbing his finger at me. I was about to knock him down when I realized he was pointing behind me, pointing at two women sitting at the end of the bar. Late thirties, both of them, and they looked like they'd seen some hard miles. One had straight brown hair crimped into little rows of waves. The other one wore a shade of bright pink lipstick I'd once seen on a dead old lady Black Swede showed me in the basement of the funeral home. These two women were staring at the TV, which was announcing the lottery numbers that nobody had matched. I turned back to the guy and he was smiling and making his noises, happier-sounding now. He pointed at me, then at himself, then at the women. I finally got it. He was deaf. "You want me to talk to them for you?" I said. "For us?"

His hands tightened into happy little fists, and his head bobbed up and down—yes yes yes. I pitied him. He thought he'd found words in me.

Little Reptiles

~ ~ ~

Let us strive to do what is in our power and guard our-
selves against these poisonous little reptiles, for the Lord
often desires that bad thoughts afflict and pursue us
without our being able to get rid of them. Sometimes He
even permits these reptiles to bite us.

St. Teresa of Avila, *The Interior Castle*

I. Boomslang

On an after-hours tour of the natural history museum,
my friend the herpetologist shows me the laboratory in which,
fifty years ago, the division's curator gathered with several
colleagues to puzzle over an African tree snake that the city
zoo had sent for identification. Thirty inches long, bright
green and black-beaded, with folding rear fangs: it was almost certainly a boomslang, they agreed, but for the matter
of the anal plate, which ought to have been divided but wasn't.
The men were confounded; this snake was a taxonomical im-
possibility. The curator picked it up for a closer look, but he
took his grip too far behind the head and the snake whipped
around and struck, burying those rear fangs into the soft

flesh at the base of his thumb. *That it was a boomslang was dramatically manifested by its behavior*, the curator would write. Still, they all agreed, the snake was young and had been in captivity for some time, so it wouldn't possess venom in enough quantity or potency for the bite to be fatal. The curator did the old cut-and-suck, then retreated to his office to chronicle his symptoms as the hemotoxin pulsed through his body.

By two-thirty, the area around the puncture had blackened. By four, he had developed chills that shook him as he donned his overcoat and headed for the suburban train. On the train, he noted waves of nausea. At home, in bed with heating pad, pencil, and notebook, he recorded continued nausea, a fever spike, bleeding from the mouth. Midnight: blood in urine. Later, just blood—no urine—plus abdominal pain and violent nausea. In the morning, heavy-lidded and sore, he paused in his writing and asked his wife to call the museum and say he'd be back at work the following day. *Mouth and nose continuing to bleed, though not excessively*, he wrote. This was his final entry. He fell into a coma. By three-fifteen p.m., he was dead. His colleagues, though saddened, told the newspapers that a good herpetologist never misses an opportunity to record a case study. His wife's thoughts on this subject were not reported.

The office that once belonged to the late curator is locked (and it has someone else's nameplate on it, besides), but I linger there, one hand on the dark-grained wood, and I imagine him in his office that afternoon, in his creaky chair behind his bulky desk, staring at his hand as he flexes his swollen thumb.

Along one wall are maps of southern Africa, India, the Pantanal; along another are two tall and packed-tight bookshelves. At his back, a window open to the lake breeze. On his desk, a gila monster's skull serves as a paperweight. Perhaps he has a moment of doubt. Perhaps he finds himself with the telephone in his good hand, about to connect to the hospital, but he turns his gaze to the clock on his wall (brutishly plain, as institutional clocks are, with cold black numbers on a white face and a second hand that buzzes, insectlike, as it sweeps its arc) and decides he can catch the next train home if he hurries.

The air around me is chilly and spiced with formaldehyde. My friend calls from down the hallway, tells me to hurry up because we have much more to see in the museum tonight: the lab where a *T. rex* is being reassembled; a fearsome collection of shark jaws; the insane menagerie that is the birds-of-prey specimen room. I let my hand drop from the curator's door, suddenly sheepish. I am forty and graying; by now I ought to know what, if anything, I will give my life to, or for.

In the distance, down some other hallway of the vast museum, a floor polisher thrums and thrums, getting the place clean for tomorrow's visitors.

II. Galliwasp

Christopher, the best man, is on his fifth rum-and-Coke when the music stops and the stage is cleared and his thoughts turn to Jamaica. To the inn in Montego Bay where he proposed to the woman who is now his wife. To the garden where

they had their breakfast the following morning. To the creature they saw darting across one of the flower beds. The
strangest thing: a lizard head on a thick, stubby-snake body
with cartoonishly tiny legs and feet. It paused on a flat rock,
and they admired it until the gardener, a dark-skinned man
in flawless white linen, crept up to the creature and smoothly
decapitated it with one strike of his shovel. "Galliwasp," the
man explained to them. "Most dangerous ting on de island.
Got venom in dey teeth." He scooped up the two pieces of the
reptile with the shovel and carried it away, whistling, leaving
them to their plates of ackee fruit and saltfish and their
stunned silence. What they found out later, back at home,
surprised them even more: galliwasps aren't venomous.
Aren't dangerous at all. The lore is a lie, and the damned
things are nearly extinct because of it.

There's another piece of island wisdom about the galliwasp: If one bites you, you're supposed to run for the nearest water. If you get to water before it does, then you'll live
and it will die. If it gets to water first, you'll be dead before
the next sunrise.

Christopher wants to share this with the guys at the
table—it feels important, somehow, in his rum-fogged
mind—but they're all busy scoping out the lap-dance talent
and conferring with each other on same, and the groom-
to-be is already blind on tequila shooters, and now there's a
new girl on stage and the music starts pumping again. He
couldn't make himself heard if he wanted to.

He looks around the table. Eight men. They've been
friends since they were teenagers; they've screwed some of

the same girls; they've boasted-slash-confided about sloppy-drunk hookups, about each of their Top Five Blowjobs lists, about conquests in bathroom stalls and faculty offices and graveyards and parking lots and airport hotels and delivery vans and dank basements while parties thump away overhead, about the demure girls who fuck like wildcats, about walks of shame and cold sores and amoxicillin, about the I-swear-I'll-call-you-agains and the Ones That Got Away. And now he understands why his thoughts are on Jamaican galliwasps instead of the C-cup cowgirl pole-dancing ten feet away: all of them spent the first two decades of their adult lives treating sex like a galliwasp bite. There is the bite, and then there's the running. You might be the reptile or the human, you might be the biter or the bitten—you might not even be sure which one you are—but the barest fact of it remains: Jaws sink into flesh, and then you're both running for the water. All those bites, all those sprints, all those deaths by sunrise. But it's different, he thinks, now that they've gotten older, now that they're settling down. It's different. Isn't it?

This feels like a question that should not be contemplated with an empty glass. He raises his hand and tries to catch the eye of the bone-skinny cocktail waitress, who for some reason is dressed like a matador.

III. Argus Monitor

The Argus monitor, a.k.a. *Varanus panoptes*, is a diurnal metaphor and an important predator in today's global biomeme.

. . .

In Greek mythology, Argus Panoptes was a giant with a hundred eyes who was assigned by Hera to guard a white heifer from Zeus, that crazed rutter.

The Argus monitor has sharp claws for digging, climbing, and ripping apart aesthetic distance.

The Argus monitor is a major employer in most American cities and towns, but it is nervous and quick to startle.

When scanning its environs, the Argus monitor will often "tripod"—i.e., raise itself high on its hind legs and tail. It sees all. Keep your shoes shined, your underthings clean, and your paperwork up to date.

A powerfully built, rapacious eating machine, the Argus monitor is the "bottomless pit" of the animal kingdom, feeding on snakes, insects, corn syrup solids, rodents, birds, consent, *The Fountainhead*, frogs, rage, synecdoche, arbitrage, apathy, wounded dingoes, Tibet, that new car smell, situation comedy, marketing majors, Bowery river crab, restraint, theocratic impulses, the Rule Against Perpetuities, wonder, exhaustion, degenerate art, collateralized prey obligations, the missionary position, phenomenology, cake, the proposed

Trans-Afghanistan pipeline, and, in times of scarcity, other monitors.

Off camera, Marlin Perkins would refer to the Argus monitor as "a bad mamma-jamma."

The Argus monitor's droppings are superconcentrated pellets of hope and bones, prized as trophies by some and as protein sources by others. More precise demographic breakdowns remain unavailable, however, due to budget cuts at the research facility.

The Argus monitor pays well. Sweet rutting Zeus, does it ever.

On March 14, 1983, an Argus monitor urinated on Johnny Carson's shoulder during a live broadcast of NBC's *Tonight Show*. When they cut to commercial, it tore off and devoured both of the TV host's legs.

The Argus monitor offers many opportunities for internships as well.

Venom? Damn skippy!

It prefers to bask in the morning, with a two-gallon Mono-lithiGulp™ of coffee, a raw goat, a bowl of white phosphorus, and the *Wall Street Journal* it has swiped from its neighbor's driveway.

The Argus monitor has a forked tongue and a vomeronasal organ in the roof of its mouth, which is why one should not speak ill of it. And also on account of it pays so well.

Its underside is cream-colored and surprisingly soft.

IV. Daboia (The Lurker)

Last night, S.——, a thirtyish man, dreamed that he was sitting on the couch with his wife—not his real wife, but a dark-haired dream-understudy whose face he was never able to see clearly. They were watching a show called *Hot Herps* on the Circle Of Life Channel, which was following up a feature on "Lizards That Eat Their Young" with a profile of a species of viper called the daboia (whose name comes from Hindi for "lurker"). In one clip, an Indonesian field-worker presented with a daboia bite on his hand. The wound was blistering, the arm swollen to more than twice its normal size. A real-time computer simulation reenacted the bite, showing a daboia being held—much as that infamous boomslang was—with fingers carefully arranged around the head, pinning the jaw. Then: a flash of movement, a whip-flick of brown and black, and suddenly snake and hand were attached by a pair of long, curved fangs. *Normally, bites like this are due to careless handling or inattentiveness*, the narrator said, *but not in this case*. The simulation ran again, in super-slow motion, revealing the snake's secret: unable to break the man's grip, it had struck the only way it could. It had *bitten through its own lower jaw* to get at the man's hand. S.—— backed up the DVR, and he and his dream-wife watched the simulated strike over and over, rapt, alive with this glimpse of the pure, concentrated menace of the natural world. He put his hand on her neck and felt her skin warming.

Perhaps they should not have watched any further; perhaps S.—— ought to have tried some lucid-dreaming stratagem to take control of the narrative and cause his dream-self to pick up his dream-wife and carry her to bed, where they would whip themselves about, dangerous and sharp, driven by the intense, atavistic passion so rarely unleashed from its tight coils inside their reptilian brains. But S.——'s real-self didn't have that kind of power. Instead, his dream-self sat with his dream-wife and watched as a lab-coated Austrian discussed the physiological effects of the daboia's extremely potent venom and noted that a dilute form of it is often used in an in vitro diagnostic test for autoimmune disorders.

At this, S.——'s dream-wife ripped herself away from him, curled herself up at the far end of the couch, hid her face in her hands, and convulsed with sobs. He—dream-self and real-self both—tried to tell her, *We can try again, we can try again*, but the words wouldn't come out clearly. He knew she wouldn't have heard them anyway; everything was drowned out by those jagged, bloody, apocalyptic sobs. And he felt afraid to go to her, afraid to touch her, so he curled up on his side of the couch and covered his ears and told himself he'd wake up before too long. He tried to comfort himself, by imagining the face of the dream-baby that had been taken from them, but he couldn't do it. The baby seemed to belong to another dream altogether, and everyone knows that the membranes that divide our dreams, while they may appear thin and translucent, are in the end impermeable.

V. Gharial

Lately, every time you finish a story, the gharial that lives under your writing desk darts out and bites off one of your toes, then scutters back into the shadows. To ask how it knows you've finished is pointless; it just does. Anyway: it's sad, how little work you finish, but it's understandable. A person needs to walk, after all.

When you limp into your psychiatrist's office, he asks what's the matter.

"I have a gharial problem," you say. You wanted to bring a photo to show him, but every shot you've taken has come out as a murky, blurred nada. The creature is surprisingly quick. Why, if it weren't for your lost toes and the dark-red spatters and swirls on the hardwood floor of your office, you would doubt its existence yourself.

He admits he knows next to nothing about this species of reptile, apart from the fact that gharials have narrow jaws and long snouts that are ideally suited to their piscivorous feeding habits.

"They're native to the Indian subcontinent," you offer, because you've looked it up. "Although apparently they can thrive indoors in central Texas, too."

"Yes," he agrees. "And also: they rarely if ever attack humans. But if one were to, it makes a degree of sense that it would choose a writer."

You ponder this. "Is it because they can sense the dread in our blood?"

"Precisely," he says. "Studies have shown that dread is sweet and umami-rich."

He gives you a referral to a specialist, an old college roommate of his who runs a semi-licensed snake farm on a ranch road outside Wimberley. You ask if your insurance will cover your consultation with the herpeculturalist, explaining how, on account of, you know, money and your utter lack of it, and also how these days the things you get paid for—stories—require body parts from you (even if they are minor ones), etc. "Almost certainly not," he says, but he hands you a sackful of benzodiazepines, which you interpret as an expression of empathy.

You arrive at the snake farm late in the afternoon under a seasonal-affective-gray sky and find the man sitting in a recliner on a spacious screened porch. Around him are chunky metal filing cabinets, the drawers all open and spilling out loose papers. "Come on in," he says, having heard your un-even footsteps as you scuffed your way up the gravel drive. At the door you peer through the screen and sense motion everywhere, dark shapes creeping and pulsing and darting along. Snakes writhe around on the floor, slither-twist over and around the man's boots and his faded-denim thighs and his faded-tatt arms, wrap themselves around the brim of his ten-gallon hat, curl in and out of the file drawers. You catch glimpses of bushmasters and taipans and banded kraits. Armored lizards jostle and grunt and snap as they raid a trough full of meat that smells like steak fajitas. A snapping turtle lies in wait inside a Scooby-Doo kiddie pool, sizing up a fat feeder frog. Caimans and crocs prowl the inner perimeter and regard you in ways you do not like; the screen looks too thin to hold back a thousand pounds of reptile on the attack. Your phantom toes start to itch inside your new steel-toed boots, your latest attempt to up-armor.

"Come on in," he says again. "Don't be a stranger."

"I'll stay out here," you say. "I just need to know if you can help me with my gharial problem."

"Depends," he says. "Do I get to keep the critter, or are you looking to eat it?"

"Eat it?" Something about the idea appeals to you. Vengeance, perhaps. Or irony. But the itching flares up, hotter now, maddening, and you tell him you don't care what happens to it, you just want the damned thing gone.

"Gharial grills up nice," he says, and it sounds like he's smiling, but you have trouble seeing his face because of the steady traffic of snakes traveling across it. He says he'll need cash in advance, and you pay eagerly. You figure you'll make the money back with, two, maybe three new stories. Driving back to the city as the last daylight leaks out of the miserable sky, you take off your boots, set the cruise control, and scratch scratch scratch all the way home.

Two days later, he rings your doorbell. Wings of white hair poke out from under his hat. Without snakes obscuring his face, you can see he's handsome in that leathery, half-a-century-of-Texas-sun kind of way, as long as you overlook the scarred-over puncture wounds that cover his cheeks like a bumpy purple beard. He has left his truck idling in your driveway, and you admire that kind of confidence, wish it were contagious. He drops his cigarette and grinds it out with the toe of his boot on your welcome mat. "So," he says, "where's the little reptile?"

You lead him to your office and point under the desk. "It lives down there," you say, "although I can't be more specific than that."

He shines a flashlight on the floor, around the wall moldings, behind the desk, inside the drawers, over the tangled wires that snake out from your CPU. "Ain't no gharial here," he says.

"It's here," you tell him. "It comes out when I hit Control+S. When I'm saving the final version of a story. It bites off my toes."

"Welp," he says, "then I guess we need to lure her out. You'd best get down to it. My time ain't cheap."

"You mean write? Finish? Hit Control+S?"

"Hell yeah, if that's what makes her hungry."

You settle into your desk chair, crack your knuckles, wiggle your remaining toes. You turn on the computer. You open a new document. You get ready to write. You listen to his truck's engine grumbling in the driveway. You wonder how much gas it has in the tank.

The man puts his flashlight between his teeth, adjusts the coil of rope on his hip, pulls a mesh net from a deep pocket, and crouches down to begin his vigil over the dark beneath your desk. His hands hold the net perfectly still— they don't tremble, they don't twitch—and you know that when (if?) the time comes, those hands will strike with precision and purpose and cold-blooded quickness.

You could pretend you have hands like that. Maybe that's all you need to do, is pretend.

Astronauts

~ ~ ~

J o floats naked on the inflatable chair. The tennis ball, blackened with dirt and dog spit, bobs in the water next to her. The dog sits at the edge of the pool, fixing her with smoky eyes and waiting for her to throw. She is tired and a little drunk and she just wants to close her eyes, but she gives in. She has only a few more days with Shane, a sleek black lab from a long line of movie dogs. She wishes he were her own. It takes so little to make him happy.

"Last one, baby," she says, picking up the ball. She throws it as hard as she can, spilling her beer on herself and nearly capsizing the chair. Shane spins and bounds into the yard, hurls himself skyward to snatch the ball at the apex of a bounce, then takes a celebratory tumble through the dry grass and dirt. He trots back to the pool, tags jingling, and drops the ball in the water next to her.

"No more," she says. "The girl needs to rest." The dog

cocks his head and eyes her curiously. Jo avoids his gaze and instead looks at her pink hi-top Chucks at the far end of the redwood deck. One of them has her car keys tucked inside. It's not too late to drive out to Stockton to see Wayne, like she promised him. It's really not. She could still get there in time for dinner.

Shane barks—a staccato, scolding burst—and she closes her eyes, forces herself to count off the reasons she can't go, shouldn't go:

One. It's over. He needs to understand this.

Two. She's had four or five or maybe six beers.

Three. Her car can't make the trip. The transmission is screwed up. She lost fourth gear yesterday.

Four. She invited Spencer to come over and hang out after his shift. She could change her mind and he wouldn't complain, but still.

Five. She has the test tomorrow morning all the way down in Gilroy. It's her last chance at getting certified. She should get a good night's sleep, show up fresh.

No, the best thing she can do is forget Wayne, forget the test, forget it all for now. Concentrate on the warm sun on skin, the cool tickle of sweat, the sweet haze of alcohol and early summer. The beer in her hand is warm now, but she shakes the last sip into her mouth anyway, swallows, shifts her weight in the chair, relaxes her shoulders.

Shane gives a squeaky yawn and pads off to lie in the shade under the bougainvillea that overhangs the deck. Jo lets the can roll from her fingers into the water, where it floats with the other empties, glittering silver flotsam. Within minutes she is asleep.

· · ·

When Jo had awakened in the Crenshaws' canopy bed that morning, she'd lain still for almost an hour, feeling spent and washed out, ignoring the phone whenever it rang. She finally got up to go to the bathroom, where she swallowed three aspirin. In the kitchen she made a pot of coffee and filled Shane's bowl with water. She did the dishes from last night's dinner, threw out the empty wine bottle, put away the bottle of Mr. Crenshaw's scotch that she hadn't remembered taking out.

When the coffee was ready, she poured it into the mug she'd been using every morning for the three weeks she'd been there. It had a photo of Shane on the side—a Halloween snapshot of the dog dressed as an astronaut, sniffing at a jack-o'-lantern. The costume looked professionally made: a shiny silver suit, NASA patches and all, a plastic helmet (without a face shield, so his snout could poke through), a jet pack on his back. What Jo loved about the photo was not that Shane looked cute, which he did, but that he also looked serene, like he was calmly weathering an indignity that he knew would be temporary, that soon it would be over and he would be able to go back to fetching balls and chasing squirrels. Jo had decided a while ago to take the mug with her when she left. Tell the Crenshaws it broke.

The answering machine in the hallway flashed three new messages. She carried the mug with her, burned her mouth on the first sip, and pressed PLAY on the machine. The first message was Rafael, her boss at JavaPlenty, telling her she wouldn't be getting any shifts for a week, maybe more. The second was Missy Crenshaw, Jo's best friend through high school—soon to become *Dr. Crenshaw*—calling to see if her parents were back from their trip yet. As an afterthought, Missy added a quick "Hi, Jo, if you're there." Jo didn't mind; it had been a long time since they'd had much to say to each other.

The third message was Wayne, telling Jo he'd taken a fuckload of pills the night before and had to have his stomach pumped and he just wanted her to know.

Later she would guess that she had gone into shock, because she felt nothing. Played his message again and still felt nothing. Nothing. The next thing she'd notice feeling would be frustration—the door-slamming, wall-kicking kind—as she searched the house for her car keys, and after that, disgust when, with keys in hand, she realized she was about to do exactly what he wanted her to do. She played the message again and heard something she hadn't heard before, a quiet hitch in his throat just as he hung up, a sound that could have been the beginning of a laugh or a sob or something else entirely.

She sat on the floor in the hallway with her sneakers on but unlaced, running her thumb up and down over the jags of the ignition key. Her eyes drifted to the potted snake plant, which was now a sickly yellow, and she realized she hadn't watered anything in two weeks, maybe more. Water the plants, water the flowers, water the lawn, Mr. Crenshaw had said, pounding his fist into his palm, joking but strangely worked up, too. Mist those bromeliads. Soak that mossy-looking thing near the kitchen sink. Water the herb garden.

Hear me, Jo? Water, water, water. She hadn't forgotten, really. She just hadn't done it.

She sat for a long time, staring at the dying plant and nursing several pangs of failure that all bled together, until Shane jingled into the room like a wind-chime breeze and blew his dog breath into her face.

Spencer's reedy voice, calling her name. She sleepily calls back to him, then remembers she's not wearing anything. She rolls off the floating chair into the safe embrace of the eighty-degree water.

He walks down the stone steps to the pool, carrying a twelve-pack. He looks a little like John Lennon in his *Imagine* phase: long and stringy brown hair; little round glasses; thin, sad face. He's short and slight—Wayne could put him out with one punch. She probably should've called someone bigger and tougher, just in case, but Spencer's the best friend she has these days. She watches him closely as he negotiates the steps; he has a problem with one of his ears and his balance often deserts him. Afraid of distracting him, she waits until he is safely seated and swirling his feet in the pool before she says anything.

"Close your eyes a second," she says, breaststroking to the ladder. "I'm nude."

"They're closed," he says.

Jo climbs out of the pool, her back to him. She knows he's peeking but she doesn't care. She's grateful that he's here keeping her company, and it's not like they haven't ended up in bed together before. A glimpse of ass isn't such a big deal—maybe it's even a small way for her to say thank you. As she wraps herself in a towel, though, she finds herself smiling ruefully, because really, it was her ass that started everything going so wrong with Wayne: they're at a bowling alley in Lodi on fifty-cent longneck night—Wayne's already in a bad mood, he couldn't find his keys earlier, and she really rode him about it (hypocrite!)—Jo does a happy butt-wiggling dance back to the seats after she picks up the eight and ten, some button-down jerk-off in the next lane says something rude, Wayne shouts back as the pins reset, there's glaring across the plastic seats while Jo laughs to herself and swigs her beer, and then there's a volley of fists that ends with a bottle cracked over the scoring desk and a spray of red over the varnished wood. Assault with a deadly weapon. No prior record? Nine months. *Bang.*

Jo wraps the towel tighter. She's going to have a hard time sleeping tonight, that's for sure.

She walks across the deck to Spencer, kneels and hugs him hello, the smell of roasted coffee still in his hair, in his JavaPlenty T-shirt. He opens a beer and hands it to her.

"You burned," Spencer says.

She shrugs.

"Feeling a little better?"

"Not feeling much." She takes a long, slow sip. "Thanks for coming," she says.

"No big deal," he says. "I like you." It sounds rehearsed, like he was practicing on the drive over. He's totally into her but is afraid of pushing too hard and scaring her off; she pretends she doesn't know. It's simpler that way, for both of them.

She walks to the glass-topped table on the deck and sits, rocking back on two legs of the metal chair. "That prick Rafael didn't give me any shifts this week," she says. "Or next."

"Why do you care?"

"What do you mean?"

"You don't need him anymore. You're the goddamn Queen of the Road."

She hesitates. "I failed the driving test," she tells him. It's the first time she has said it aloud.

"Oh," he says. "Sorry."

I'm not stupid, she wants to tell him. She's not, she's got the inspection procedures down cold, knows S-cam air brakes inside and out, can double-clutch with drumbeat precision. It's just backing up that's the problem. "You ever drive a tractor-trailer in reverse?" she says, trying to make the words sound casual, fluid, not defensive. "They make you go between all these cones. It's hard."

He shakes his head, raises his beer in sympathy. "At least you tried."

"I get one more chance," she says. "Tomorrow. If I fuck it up again, they might still let me be a dispatcher." But she doesn't want to be a dispatcher, she doesn't want to live down in the Sunbeam Tomato Freight dormitory and wake up every morning just to go sit in an office. She wants to be out on the road on her own, hauling tomatoes through the western states, doing speed to stay awake, making the thirty-five thousand dollars per season that the brochure promised. She wants to live her life like that Little Feat song, driving her rig from Tucson to Tucumcari, Tehachapi to Tonopah. She wants to *drive*. She finishes her beer, throws the empty in the pool. "But I'll probably fuck it up again," she says.

"Hey," he says. It's supposed to reassure her. He stands up quickly and takes a step toward her, but he wavers, arms circling almost comically as he tries to gain his balance. She calmly realizes she won't be able to catch him if he topples over, so she doesn't move, just watches, hopes for the best.

He rights himself, then turns away from her and stares into the water. "Tell the Crenshaws to have the pool cleaned," he says after a few seconds of silence. "It's growing cans."

"What?"

"Forget it. Dumb joke. I suck."

Can't you please just relax, she wants to say. The last thing she needs is anyone else to worry about.

The phone rings while Jo is changing. She yells from the bedroom for Spencer not to pick it up. She is surprised by how loud her voice is.

She walks into the hallway half-dressed and stands in front of the machine as Wayne leaves a nightmare of a message, careening from anger to calm to weepiness to anger again: he can't believe she didn't come see him this afternoon, but maybe she's not answering because she's already on her way, and he really doesn't like to get so fucking mad but she doesn't understand how bad things have gotten for him, and what's wrong with her that she can't or won't understand, and she owes him, she owes him, she has to at least understand that she owes him the simple fucking courtesy of talking to him and it'd better happen soon.

She walks into the kitchen, where Spencer is dropping ice cubes into the blender. He nods toward the phone. "Crazy," he says. She nods and sits at the kitchen table, watches him make the margaritas. Happy drinks, he calls them.

"Do you want something extra? To take the edge off?" he asks.

"Like what?"

He holds up a small baggie full of yellow pills. "Percodan," he says. "I bought them off my brother."

"Do it," she says.

He drops some of them into the blender. How many, she can't say.

Spencer pours the drinks and Jo thinks about the first time the two of them slept together. It was a Tuesday night, she remembers—evening visiting hours at the jail—and she'd really meant to go because she hadn't for the last three weeks. She never missed the visits intentionally, but it was an hour and a half through traffic, and it was hard to see Wayne in there in those orange coveralls, and she hated having to wait in the lounge with all those people coming to visit the real criminals, and she especially hated the security patdown and the way the guards eyed you so suspiciously that you'd begin to wonder if you really *were* up to something. So, instead, that night after work she'd gone for a quick drink with Spencer and the rest of the JavaPlenty crew, and whoops, look at the time, oh well, make the next one a double. She knew Wayne had nothing else to look forward to, no one else to think about, no one but her, but he didn't understand what a burden that was. She couldn't live up to that. No one could.

The blender rumbles and grinds, drowning out something that Spencer's trying to say, and the sound makes Jo think of cracking teeth. Finally, Spencer sets the two salt-rimmed glasses on the table. He moves a chair so he can have her talking to his good side. "Do you think he's dangerous?" he asks.

She makes an effort to sound confident. "Not really," she says. "It's just Wayne."

She can't remember why she and Spencer went into Missy Crenshaw's old bedroom in the first place, or how long they've been in Missy's bed together.

"Pictures," Jo says. There used to be pictures on the wall, photos of her and Missy together as kids, at an apple orchard, at a soccer game, on their eighth-grade double date with the Fagelson twins. All gone, replaced by Missy's diplomas, three of them, smartly mounted and framed. By moving her head, Jo can make the moon reflect off the glass of each of them in turn.

"What did you say?"

"Nothing," she says.

She hears a series of plastic clicks. Spencer, setting the alarm. Responsible.

"Give me another," she says.

"Another what?"

"Pill."

"No," he says. "I don't want you to die on me."

"I can handle it," she says.

"You've had enough."

She crawls under the covers and goes to work on him. When she's done, Spencer, red-faced and sheepish, drops two pills into her hand. She takes one and feeds him the other, then closes her eyes and rests her head on his chest, feels his fingers trace the back of her neck. "Happy," she says. "Happy." She says this word again and again. She doesn't know if she means that she is happy, or was, or will be—if it is a statement, a lament, or a hope—but the sound of the word comforts her, lulls her as she falls away.

At seven-fifteen Jo is jolted awake by the clock radio, tuned to a jazz station. Loud. A squealing, sick-cat saxophone. Spencer doesn't stir. For a moment, Jo is worried, but she feels breath when she puts her finger under his nose. He's not dead, just wasted and sleeping with his good ear down.

As soon as she sits up, she feels ice picks behind her eyes and a burn in her stomach. She makes her way to the bathroom and pops four aspirin. In the shower, she tries to shake the heavy fog in her head, running through the checklist of inspection procedures, but she keeps missing steps, easy ones. She can feel herself start to sweat—stinky, cold flop sweat—even as she's drying herself off. She almost decides to blow off the test, just bail on everything, crawl back into bed, hide, but she takes another look into the medicine cabinet and sees a prescription bottle labeled MARY CRENSHAW—KLONOPIN—AS NEEDED FOR ANXIETY. She shakes a few into her hand. They're small, so she swallows two. After she dresses, she puts three more tablets in the pocket of her cutoffs, just in case.

She walks softly into the laundry room, where Shane is sleeping on a fluffy tartan dog bed, and she sits down next to him, watches him breathe, in and out, in and out. His ears twitch when she scratches his head. "Shane," she says quietly. "Wake up, Shane." He opens his dark eyes halfway, looks at her dreamily. "You want to tell me good luck, baby?" she says. Shane sneezes and falls back asleep.

In the kitchen she makes coffee and pours it into a travel mug. The unrinsed blender sits on the counter in a dried margarita puddle. Broken glass in the sink, pizza scraps on the table, sticky dog tracks across the floor. The phone rings but she just takes a deep breath and walks out the front door into the sun and the dew and the mist of the tick-tick-ticking sprinklers she left on all night. The lawn gleams and there are puddles all along the blacktop. Water, water, water.

She climbs into her car, the blue Fiesta she's been driving since high school. She'll have to back out of the U-shaped driveway because Spencer parked his Beetle facing her car, with only a foot or so of space separating them. There's resistance when she tries to shift into reverse, so she forces it. More resistance, and she hears a grinding noise, then a metallic whine. Still not in gear. She tries again: up off the clutch, then down, shift, grind, whine. Again. Again, until she pulls back on the stick shift so hard, she feels a twinge in her shoulder. She curses the car. No fourth gear, no reverse, but it better get her to Gilroy. Now.

She shifts into first and tries to steer around his car. When the bumpers meet she gives it a little more gas, trying to nudge it out of the way. Fortunately Spencer left it out of gear, so it slowly rolls backward, and a few feet later Jo is free. In her rearview mirror she watches the Beetle ease forward again, settling comfortably back where it had been. She is so focused on the gentle motion of Spencer's car, though, that she's slow to realize she has gone off the driveway and is leaving a deep muddy track in the Crenshaws' sculpted lawn. *Fuck me*, she thinks. Can't worry about it now, though. Got to drive.

When she gets to the freeway, she turns on her hazard lights because the Fiesta can only do forty these days. The transmission slips whenever she tries to accelerate hard. Somewhere south of San Jose, in one of those moments before the gears catch, with nervous heat running up her spine and that goddamned sweat dripping down her sides, she dry-swallows another one of Mrs. Crenshaw's pills and prays to no one in particular: Please, just let me get there. I need this.

The Sunbeam receptionist sits behind an old wooden desk that looks like it was scavenged from a school. Around the edges of the blotter, Jo can see memorials of crushes hacked into the wood: KD + CS. WT AND AB FOREVER.

"I'm here to take the test," Jo says. "Bud's expecting me."

"Oh," the receptionist says, looking up. "You're back." She calls Bud on the intercom, then looks at Jo and says, "Have a seat. There's coffee if you want it."

Jo fills a paper cup with coffee, black, and sits in a green vinyl chair pocked with cigarette burns. She picks up a newsmagazine from a box on the floor and tries to read an article, but her vision blurs around the edges and she finds herself locking onto one or two words at a time, not absorbing them but not able to move on. She leafs through, looking at the pictures, and stops on a two-page spread in tropical colors. On the left is a toucan sitting in a tree, its beak open so that it seems to be smiling; on the right is a Happy Couple in bright bathing suits frolicking on a deserted beach. In neon red letters across the bottom it says, *Lose yourself in Belize*. Which, honestly, sounds like a pretty good idea. But as she stares at the man and woman in the magazine she starts to feel that there's something important she has forgotten to do, something else she's fucked up. She can't figure out what it is, but that thought is there, bubbling around in the tar pit of her brain. What?

There's a touch on her shoulder and she jumps, dumping her coffee into the box of magazines. She looks up and sees a lanky man with a red goatee and a baseball cap that says YOU PISS ME OFF in block letters. He smells like Right Guard and cigarettes.

"I'm Jim," he says. "Bud's busy, so I'm going to give you the test."

"Sorry about the coffee," she says. Her tongue feels wrong. Swollen.

"Brenda will clean it up."

"Clean it up yourself, Jim," Brenda says from behind the desk.

Jim looks at Jo. He has greedy eyes, she thinks. "You ready?" he asks, and she nods.

He leads her out the back door, onto the paved lot they use for the driving course. As they walk toward the tractor-trailer, he says to her, "We don't get many girls wanting to drive. Not many good-looking ones, anyway."

She says nothing.

"Be nice to have a pretty face around here," he goes on. "Brenda looks like a horse. You got a boyfriend?" He moves closer to her, their arms almost rubbing, his smoke-and-deodorant cloud closing in on her.

She knows how to play this game, she learned a long time ago, but she's tired and a little nauseous now and she can't quite focus her eyes, and, you know what, she's really, really sick of big, stupid men who have to have everything their way. Fuck that and fuck them. "Yeah, I have a boyfriend," she says. "He just got out of jail. Assault with a deadly weapon."

Jim whistles through his teeth, looks around to see if anyone's watching, leans in closer. "You're tough," he says. "I like that. Gotta be tough for this job."

"Good," she says, and she keeps walking.

"Bud said you've taken the test before."

"Yeah."

"Twice."

"Yeah."

They stop in front of the rig. It looks impossibly long and

unwieldy. She understands in theory how you're supposed to control the thing when you're backing it up, but she can't get her brain to make the right decisions when she's up there. Not without time to think, breathe, talk herself through it at her own pace. "A pretty girl like you could get certified in about five minutes," Jim says. He nods up at the cab, huge and red and painted with a tomato haloed by the sun.

She could do it—just say yes, get him off, get the job, and run. Let's face it, she's not at her best right now, all floaty and exhausted and numb—really, she's so out of it that she'd hardly even notice he was there—and to fail again is to fail for good, and then what? She doesn't *want* to do anything else. The thoughts spin and buzz around until she realizes she *expects* herself to say yes to him, and that's when the calm blooms inside her head and drapes warmth all over her, and she decides she can beat this test, she can drive that goddamn rig as well as anyone, she could take the thing in reverse down Lombard Street if she wanted to. "Cut the shit, Jim," she says. "Let's just do the test."

"Have it your way," he says, pulling away, his eyes narrowing. He takes off his cap, smooths his thinning, greasy hair. "Start with the inspection. Go."

Deep breath. She knows the drill, knows it cold. Check the hoses, check the oil, check the coolant. Check the belts and the clutch, the signals and the horn. Driveshaft, air brakes, tires and rims. There's a rhythm to it, a groove, feel the patterns and forget your nerves. Shock absorbers, slack adjusters, torque arms, mounts. Mounting bolts, locking jaws, kingpin, and so on. It's a breeze. She climbs into the cab and the engine growls all around her and she feels more powerful, more in control, than she can ever remember.

"All right," Jim says from the passenger seat. "Now back out of here and follow the yellow lines through the cones. And I want you to pretend that every single one of those cones is a member of my family."

It's reverse time but that's cool, she still has the rhythm, still has the groove, and when she grips the shift she hears that Feat song in her head: *If you give me weed, whites, and wine, and you show me a sign, I'll be willin' to be movin'. I'm willing*, she thinks, *I'm willing and I'm moving.* She drops it into reverse and starts back, smoothly, smoothly, no problem. She checks her mirrors, she's drifting a little, no problem, turn into the drift, get the trailer righted, turn back, no problem. She's on a roll, she's rolling, she can do this in her sleep, and a month from now she'll be waking up in her rig just off Highway 58 in Tehachapi with Lowell George singing to her as she watches the sun rise over the fields of windmills.

"Congratulations," Jim says. "You just flattened my fucking grandmother."

She winds her way up the Los Altos hills, the Fiesta's engine slipping almost every time she hits the gas. Sometimes, instead of backing off so that the gears can catch, she stomps the pedal harder, making the engine scream. She wants to hear the noise.

The pint bottle of Jack that she bought in Gilroy is in the

passenger seat, half-empty. All she wants to do is get back to the pool, to Shane and his tennis ball, to the floating chair, where she'll be able to sit alone and drink and enjoy the warmth of the sun and the fruits of the Crenshaws' medicine cabinet. She'll call Wayne and promise something vague, buy herself some time.

Jo turns into the driveway. Spencer's car is gone, but now there are two others: in the open garage, the Crenshaws' convertible; in the driveway, Wayne's pristine white '72 Comet. Before her foot touches the brake she remembers that the house is a mess, that the Crenshaws, who have always trusted her, always given her a place to stay, have come home to dead plants, a pool full of beer cans, tire tracks across the lawn. And now Wayne is there. He could be sitting in the living room, sobbing. He could be holding them hostage with a kitchen knife. Hard to know with him anymore. One thing she does know: they're waiting for her.

She also knows that the gas pedal, the true patron saint of lost causes, is the one thing that'll get her out of this, but she feels drawn to the house—feet on the driveway, on the flagstone path, on the front steps—feels like she's marching toward something she's meant to confront. The only question rolling through her mind as she stares blearily at the wood grain of the door is whether she should ring the bell or just walk right in.

The four of them are sitting around the table by the pool. Mrs. Crenshaw is sipping iced coffee and Kahlua from the astronaut mug—*That's mine!* Jo has the urge to tell her—and gazing off at the summer-brown hills in the distance. Jo and Mr. Crenshaw have vodka gimlets that the older man insisted on mixing. Wayne is holding a bottle of mineral water loosely by the neck. Birds are chirping. Shane is racing around in the yard, chasing squirrels, snapping at bugs like nothing at all is amiss.

"I'm a reasonable man," Mr. Crenshaw says. "I don't expect the house to be perfect if we come home early. But this?" He raises his palm up. He could be referring to the entire universe. "This is too much. It raises serious questions." He rattles the ice in the glass to free the last few drops of his drink. He pours himself another from the cocktail shaker, which is sweating.

Jo nods. She glances quickly at Wayne. His head looks too large for his frame now that he has no hair. Four red-spotted bandages decorate his scalp, covering the nicks. He sits tall in his seat, composed, looking waxen in the bright sun. "It looks like there was a party here last night," Wayne says, in a flat, uninflected voice she hardly recognizes.

"It does, Wayne," Mrs. Crenshaw says.

"A regular Cinco de Mayo," Mr. Crenshaw says.

This feels wrong to her, like it's happening on a soundstage, everything and everyone too quiet, too detached. Confusing and creepy. Or is she just too wasted to understand everyone's angle?

"It's rude to bring strangers into other people's homes," Wayne says, tapping his glass on the table—gently, but it makes her nervous anyway. He's never had a good sense of his own strength. She wonders if he found Spencer here. If he hurt him. But those aren't the kinds of things you just ask out of the blue.

"I'm sensing a pattern of irresponsible behavior," Mr. Crenshaw says.

Wayne turns to the other man. "Me, too," he agrees. "Jo isn't focusing on her responsibilities these days at all."

Wayne is up to something, she thinks. Or he's on new and weirder meds. Maybe both. Even the Crenshaws seem strange, precariously calm. "I'm sorry," Jo says. "I let some things get away from me."

"Would you like to talk about it, Jo?" Mrs. Crenshaw asks.

"We could help, if you'd let us," Mr. Crenshaw says.

"I took a workshop on enneatypes," Mrs. Crenshaw offers. "You're definitely a Six." She puts down the mug and drops her hand, limp and sweaty, on Jo's bare arm. "I'm a Three," she adds.

"Can someone tell me what's going on?" Jo says quietly.

"Your friend Wayne has been very worried about you," Mr. Crenshaw says. "And, from the sound of it, for good reason. It sounds like you might need some help. Guidance. Therapy. Something."

Jo doesn't know what Wayne told them, but it had to have been a lie. And they're trusting him over her? She's not the one who ended up in the fucking emergency room getting her stomach pumped. But she feels too tired and sunken to mount a defense. She stands up on shaky legs. "This is too weird," she says. "I'm leaving."

"See?" Mrs. Crenshaw says. "That's classic Six."

"Suit yourself, Jo," Mr. Crenshaw says. "But if that's your attitude, we have to sever ties. We have to let you go."

"What?" Jo asks. "Let me go where?" She steals a glance at Wayne. She thinks she sees a ghost of a smile appearing at one corner of his mouth.

"You're burning bridges here, Jo," Wayne says.

"We're not saying you're a bad person," Mrs. Crenshaw says.

"No," Mr. Crenshaw says, swirling his drink. "But you don't seem willing to give us the respect we think we deserve."

"That's not healthy for us," Mrs. Crenshaw says.

"We've done a lot for you," Mr. Crenshaw says.

"We've known you a long time."

"Well, we *thought* we knew you."

"Relationships are important, Jo," Wayne says. "You don't just go around burning bridges."

"Exactly, Wayne," Mr. Crenshaw says. He drains his glass, spits an ice cube into the bushes. "We've said our piece," he says. "I'm sorry it has to end this way. I'm guessing now that you two have things to talk about. Which we'd prefer you did elsewhere." He pulls out his checkbook, clicks his pen, and fills out a check while humming tunelessly to himself. He thumps a period after his signature, then tears the check out and slides it across the table to Jo. "Happy trails," he says.

Mrs. Crenshaw watches Jo closely as she gathers up her belongings, then stands in the foyer and holds the front door open for her. Wayne is in the driveway, leaning on the Comet and smoking a cigarette. *Can you please walk out there with me?* she wants to ask. *I can't trust him right now.* But the front door closes behind her, and she knows that the Crenshaws will be just as happy without her, a Happy Couple with a house and a dog and a pool and numbered personalities and a daughter who'll soon be able to write any prescription they want.

Wayne flicks his butt into the grass and stares at her. Jo, her face burning, specks of light dancing in her field of vision, says, "Are you trying to scare me? If you are, can we get it over with?"

"Don't be silly," he says. "I love you." He pats his chest, his legs, as if to say, *Look, no weapons.*

Shane prances up to them and drops a tennis ball at Wayne's feet. Wayne winds up and kicks it into a dense patch of pachysandra. The dog runs after it and paws gently through the green, unconcerned as ever.

"I'm hitting the road next week," she tells him. "You know, driving. Hauling tomatoes." The lie comes easily. She tries not to look surprised that he buys it.

"I want you to do some thinking while you're out there," he says, nodding slowly. "While you're out there alone."

She looks into Wayne's eyes, which are almost all pupil, only a razor-thin ring of blue wreathing the black, and she knows she is staring into the eyes of a dead man. If he's not dead yet, he will be soon. "I don't need to think," she says. "I've made up my mind." She climbs into the driver's seat of the Fiesta.

"You'll be back," he says through the open window, leaning close to her.

A drop of sweat falls from his naked head, and suddenly she feels sorry for him. "Please don't get your hopes up," she says. "I couldn't live with that." She turns the key and the engine coughs to life.

"I'll be here," Wayne says, smiling, rocking back on his heels.

Only then does Jo notice she has parked right behind Wayne's car, too close, the bumpers almost kissing. She leans her head on the steering wheel. "You have to move your car," she says without looking up. "I can't back out."

Three days later, Jo gets the Fiesta back from the shop and drives out to San Gregorio Beach for the afternoon, where she sits alone watching people and dogs and gulls and fishing boats. When the fog settles in, she drives the twisting roads back toward Spencer's apartment. Before dinner, they share beers and Percodans on the cramped cement deck overlooking the complex's pool. They don't talk much.

The salmon ends up a little burned and the mashed potatoes are out of a box, but that's all right—Jo doubts she'll be able to taste much, since the pills have made her mouth numb. Spencer opens a window and tries to wave the smoke out of the apartment, then drops himself into the other chair at the table. He brushes bits of food off the stolen JavaPlenty apron he's wearing. "So what happens now?" he asks her.

"The Fiesta's fixed," she says. "It's time to get on the road."

"Why Belize?"

"It sounds like a happy place. Like *feliz*. Happy."

"Can you really get all the way down there? There are roads?"

"I'm pretty sure."

He adjusts his glasses and studies her face, and for the first time in a long, long time, she can't tell what he's seeing in her. The smoke alarm goes off, but Spencer waves a dish-towel under it and it falls silent again. "Do you want company?" he asks.

"I don't think so, no," she says. She stares at the dinner he has cooked for them. "Thanks, though. Really."

"If you need money—"

"I'm good, Spencer. Really. I've got what I need."

Long after midnight, under the galaxy of glow-in-the-dark decals on Spencer's bedroom ceiling, she realizes she does want company. Just not his. Or Wayne's, or anyone else's she knows. She turns onto her side and watches him sleep, snoring lightly, with his good ear on the pillow. She'll be able to leave without waking him.

It's three a.m. and the sprinklers are still on. Their steady beating washes away the clink of the flowerpot as Jo removes the key from under it. The side door opens noise-lessly. Inside, she punches a keypad (the code, in phone letters, spells out SHANE) and a winking red light turns cool green. In one hand she has a stick of beef jerky, in the other, a small piece of duct tape to stop the jingle of his tags. She walks toe-to-heel toward the laundry room, her rubber soles quiet on the hardwood. The dog is in his bed, curled up like a fawn. "Hey, baby," she whispers, petting him softly. "Hey, baby. Hey, Shane."

The rest of the plan? They'll drive. As fast as they can. Like two astronauts trying to reach escape velocity.